Undressing the Devil

'You shouldn't excite me', Gianni growled. 'You can't push me without taking the consequences, whatever they are.'

Angelina moved her body closer. His resolve was clearly melting. She excited him beyond all reason. He reached for her, took her in his arms and kissed her. Her body was so thin. She was so different to Petra, whose soft roundness of form quivered in submission every time he touched her. He could almost feel the will beneath Angelina's skin, strong as iron, hardening in triumph. He was the only man who had ever broken her. She was irresistible to him.

Undressing the Devil

Angel Strand

BLACK LACE

Black Lace books contain sexual fantasies.
In real life, always practise safe sex.

This edition published in 2005 by
Black Lace
Thames Wharf Studios
Rainville Road
London W6 9HA

Originally published in 1996 as *The Big Class.*

Printed and bound by Mackays of Chatham PLC

ISBN 0 352 33938 1

Chapter One

His lips were barely dry from his mother's milk and here he was sucking at her little breast like one of the baby pigs in the farm further down the valley. Cia remembered the day she had inadvertently come upon the farmer's wife killing a pig, her hands in a bucket full of blood. She chased the thought from her mind and stretched back lazily, feeling something that, uniquely in the soft bed they had made in the humming meadow, was a little prickly. It was only a sharp piece of grass. Above her head the Italian sun shone down on them. It was late spring and perfectly warm.

'Let me try once more. Please, Cia!' Plomer L. Fitchew the Third raised his blond head from her breast. He had ejaculated prematurely on the first attempt, leaving her body disappointed.

Cia smiled indulgently at him. 'Of course,' she breathed.

The gratitude in his eyes was charming. She had known he would not be the perfect lover. Only the day was perfect. Only Italy, the sun and the meadow were, just now, perfect. And his soft skin next to her own was perfect.

'Will it be long?' she asked, lazily. Already, the

warmth of the sun was drying the little drops of sperm on her pale belly.

'No!' he said. 'Look!'

She looked down at his outsize young penis springing up again, hard and desirous and wondered if it would one day produce a Plomer L. Fitchew the Fourth. Not with me, she thought! They had brought contraception and it was in the putting on of it that the excitement had been too much for him. Dear boy! He was only twenty.

Cia herself was only 27, but making her own way in the world had made her so much more mature than this boy that she could bask in the generosity a woman can feel towards a pretty young thing with a giant penis just aching for experience. How very large it was, she thought, too large for a little boy. He would grow into it, perhaps, or feel lumbered with it, eventually. She had seen it bulge in his loose trousers, sometimes even when his mother was in the room.

As he stroked her belly tenderly, she raised one leg. It was almost as pleasurable to look at herself as to look at him. Hers was a fine body, a young woman's sun-drenched body, full of life waiting to be lived. The contrast between the dark hair on her sex, spreading across her thighs and her pale skin, was succulent in the clarity of the Italian light. She knew she didn't have wonderful breasts. They were small. It was a problem. But they were tender, sensitive bits of her.

She rested back in the sun. Her face was not quite as pale as the rest of her. She had one or two freckles sprinkled across a delicately small nose. When her eyes closed, her long dark lashes swept her cheekbones. Open, her irises were now blue. But they changed, depending on what they were looking at and what was reflected. Her hair was dark, wavy, shoulder length and unpinned.

She reached for Plomer's hand. 'Here,' she said, and she put his fingers shyly into the folds of her vulva and showed him how to unwrap her clitoris.

He immediately attacked her with nervous fingers,

hitting her clitoris right on the tip and causing strange pain to shoot like lightning into her belly.

'Owww!' she yelled, laughing. 'Not like that. You have to do it gently, like this, otherwise it hurts.'

He blushed. The pinkness of his embarrassment spread from his fine Nordic-American chin to the roots of the thick blond hair on his forehead. The tender pinkness spread downwards too, on to his collarbone.

How odd, thought Cia. It told her something. Despite being outwardly full of the confidence that wealth and a powerful family brought, he blushed all over his body.

She reached for him, kissing away his embarrassment, kissing everywhere that it showed. She wished she could kiss away his inner shame. She kissed him until he rolled over, falling like a collapsed angel to the ground. Then she sat up and looked at him as he lay on the tartan blanket, among the green grass, with a tenderness that she really felt. She kissed his little nipples, kissed his warm stomach and, as his fine penis rose and rose, she kissed its taut skin.

'Now, Cia. Now!' he begged. He was holding his raised head, with one hand, looking at her lips on his cock, the way her breasts fell towards him, and the round spectacular curve of her buttocks against the grasses.

'Put on the safe, please,' said Cia. She watched him. His thighs were parted. The pale hair on them was wiry and tough like the hair on his head. But its blondness seemed feminine to her somehow. His youth and slender beauty excited her because in all other respects he was so male. He was a sportsman. He rolled the rubber over the engorged tip of his penis.

She spread her soft thighs and climbed on top of him. She lowered herself slowly and wickedly on to him. Her sex at last tasted his, and she swallowed the length of him.

'Oh God!' he groaned dangerously.

'Don't you dare come again quickly!' The tone of her

voice seemed to bring him round. He looked startled. Perhaps he was thinking about his reputation. Once was tolerable. Twice would be indulgent and he clearly knew it.

'Concentrate,' she said, both to him and as a reminder to herself.

Oh, what a little concentration could do! He drank in the sight of her, his head turned a little to the side, as she moved on top of him. Every pore of her skin seemed to hold a fascination for him. She felt like a queen at that moment, powerful in the most delicious kind of way. Off with his head, she thought! Off with his beautiful head. She knew her orgasm would be easy and that it was going to be soon, and she didn't give a tinker's cuss if his was near or far away in the distant future. She would have her own. She would have it now. Now.

Now it was beyond her control. The agony of its distance gave way to the ecstasy of its onslaught.

As it subsided she basked in the little shocks that her woman's flesh was heir to. Yes. Yes. She was done and to hell with him.

But presently, he turned her body with a mastery that took her satiated flesh by surprise. He rolled until she was underneath him, and with a new confidence he fucked her into the ground. The maleness of him at that moment, piercing through her softness and taking what he wanted, aroused her again, even in her contentment. It opened her and then it dropped her, gasping, as he came before her second cycle could complete itself.

She lay in the sunshine with his weight on top of her. Her thoughts took a new turn. For one glorious moment the feeling that there was potential between them invaded her senses. For one glorious moment – how long was it? – she was utterly at his mercy. And then what was left of her mind reasserted itself and the feeling was gone. I live for such moments of undiluted surrender, she thought.

* * *

It must have been more than an hour later that they rose, fully dressed again, from their nest in the meadow and began slowly to walk back up the hill towards the villa. Cia felt, rather than thought about, the complications now that she had become his lover.

Before it had happened they had agreed that this would be their secret; that his mother should never know. Implicit in this pact was the certainty, for both of them, that their sex would be temporary. It might be mingled with their friendship – with a kind of love – that had grown between them during the months she had worked as companion to his mother.

Before sex, a brief, beautiful, lustful interlude had seemed perfectly plausible. But at the moment of surrender he had whispered that he loved her at least a dozen times. Perhaps there was no such thing as an uncomplicated love affair.

'Will it happen again?' he asked suddenly. He lifted his eyes from the ground and looked at her.

His words cut into her daydreamy tenderness. She had assumed it would happen again. He hadn't! What did that mean? It crossed her mind to say 'No.' Perhaps it could be as simple as that to cut the newly formed bond.

'I expect so,' she said softly and she looked at him out of the corner of her eye.

'Signora?' The guttural, male voice called into the darkness of the big, luxurious bedroom inside the villa. A voluminous mass in the four-poster bed grunted and turned under the covers.

'Signora!' pleaded the servant.

A pale, plump face rose in the darkness, just above the horizon of the coverlet, and yelled, 'Get out of my goddamn room. Leave me alone!' then collapsed back again into the gloom.

'Dianna! Signora! It is Niccolo! Your own Niccolo. It is important, Dianna. *Suo figlio*. Your son. It is trouble.'

Niccolo the servant, who was a small man, hoisted his ill-fitting brown trousers up by their thick, brown belt.

'What the hell is it?' groaned Mrs Plomer L. Fitchew the second, rising again. 'I'm so depressed. I'm so depressed. Don't make it worse!'

'Angry is better feeling, my darling Signora Dianna,' whispered Niccolo, and he crept right into the room and sat on the high, ancient bed.

Dianna Fitchew sat up. Her face was a picture of woe. She had been sweating. Her flimsy, hand-stitched nightgown was stuck to her plump shoulders and clung damply to her fat, pendulous breasts. Her hair was a mess.

'Oh, my Dianna. You are so beautiful this morning. The flowers have gone into hiding as you sitting up.'

'Cut the crap, Niccolo. What do you want?' she said.

'Only to be close . . .' He shuffled up the bed and took one of her damp breasts in his small, brown hand. He massaged the summit of its mountainous flesh.

Dianna smiled as the sensation aroused her and she undid the creased ribbons at her neck with a girlish coyness that brightened her dishevelled appearance.

Niccolo crooned over the pale, plump skin of his mistress.

'What did you say about Plomer Three?' she asked absentmindedly as she stroked her servant's head.

He was in no hurry to leave the roseate nipple that was the size of a chrysanthemum, but eventually he tore himself away and put it back in its nightgown. Then he sat up.'He is with your Cia,' he said. 'Doing the humpy.'

'Whaaaat!?' shrieked Dianna, quivering.

'I have spied them.' said Niccolo. 'Together in the south meadow, making sex. Come quickly. Come to the window and you can spied them coming back.'

'Niccolo, if this is some stupid ruse to get me out of my bed when you know I do not want to be got out of the goddamn bed, I really will murder you.'

'Oh, never in my life!' shrieked Niccolo, and he

prostrated himself on the bed with extraordinary flair and dramatic effect.

'Hand me my wrap,' said Dianna.

She scratched her head vigorously as she got out of bed. Niccolo ceremoniously led her over to the window and drew the curtains back. Tall, elegant glass doors opened on to a scene of breathtaking beauty. The spring-green of the hills surrounding Florence stretched far away into the distance. Down below, the city itself, with its dome shimmering in the early afternoon sun, went about its business noiselessly from this, the most perfect of distances.

But it was not the city that drew the gaze of the fat, lonely woman. It was Cia, flushed with the climb and the power of her feelings, emerging from the south meadow with Plomer Three, a man at last.

Dianna could tell just by looking at her son that what Niccolo had told her was true. She wished her servant had kept his mouth shut and allowed her the luxury of putting it to the back of her mind along with the rest of Cia's awkward behaviour.

'Leave me, Niccolo,' she said.

Niccolo disappeared soundlessly.

Damn it, thought Dianna. It was the last straw. Could this have been part of the plan from the very beginning? Was Cia just a gold-digger underneath it all? Dianna found it hard to believe Cia was that cold-blooded.

In fact, Dianna suspected it was Plomer Three who had initiated the affair. His father had the same taste in the titless, long-legged type of girl. This time last year she had discovered that Plomer Two had been having an affair with his secretary for over two years. It had broken Dianna's heart.

She had screwed him to the wall. Nothing less than a year in Europe would stop her from divorcing him, she had told him. And of course he couldn't divorce her. He was governor of the state. He was going for the presidential nomination in '35.

She had thought that the glittering connections she had in Britain and Europe would be some solace. But while she was undoubtedly one of the vainest creatures walking the planet, there was a very small part of Dianna which, although hidden much of the time, sought something more serious than fashionable travelling life. She was homesick sometimes. But for what? She didn't know what.

She had met Cia in Cowes, at the regatta. Plomer Three was besotted by boats of all kinds and, despite the wind and water, Dianna had had the time of her life in Cowes with all those royals. To Dianna, there was nothing like a fleet of European princes in naval uniform, with all the little gold doodahs on them; nothing in this world.

Cia had been introduced to her by the socialite, Nora Wycke, who had committed suicide not long afterwards, poor woman. Cia was a childhood friend of Mr Wycke, Nora's husband, and his sister, Edna. Dianna had been captivated the minute she met her. Cia fulfilled all her Mrs Gaskell-induced fantasies of the distressed English gentlewoman! Dianna had offered her the job of companion on her trip to Italy as soon as it had been polite to do so.

Little did she know! Cia's real purpose in travelling to Florence with her had become apparent the instant they arrived. She had gone to confront Count Cadenti di Ravanello with the fact that he was her father. Dianna had been dumbstruck! She forbade her completely to do it. Cia took no notice and did it anyway. She had not only got herself thrown out of the count's *palazzo* but also been barred from the vicinity by the Fascist police.

The worst of it was that the Ravanello family's offence was considered an offence by all the best in Florentine nobility. The doors of the best houses closed silently, not only in Cia's face, but in Dianna's. If it hadn't been winter and the South of France hadn't been teeming with people who knew her husband, Dianna would have left Florence in one direction and sent Cia in the other.

As it was, they were stuck together for the winter. Besides, Dianna believed Cia's story. Dianna could sense a skeleton in a cupboard a mile away and from the little contact she'd had with the Ravanello family, she had gathered a very strong impression of one.

But that wasn't the only mess Cia had got herself into. There was also the business of the dressmaker.

Dianna searched for an apt description of the girl now crossing the patio below her. She was all over the place, like a boat without a rudder. Dianna had loved her. She was charming, intelligent, passionate and original. But now Dianna was fed up. She had come to Florence to study art, for the love of Christ! How was she supposed to do that if she did not have access to the salons? Social exclusion was too high a price already. She wasn't going to offer up her only child as a sacrifice as well.

The young couple down below waved to her. The cheek!

'No,' said Dianna to herself, 'this is the end of the road, honey.'

Chapter Two

Cia climbed the ornate stairs dreamily and opened the door of her room. It was a big room, as were all the rooms in the fabulous old villa. There was a queensize bed with a soft, white counterpane, and one wall was lined with hand-built wardrobes. The shutters were pulled to against the strong sunlight, and the room was dim and shadowy. Cia kicked off her leather pumps. The cool ceramic tiles under her bare feet felt good. She climbed on to the bed and lay on her back. Her skin was moist from the exertion of the walk back to the house.

Her whole body felt hot and deeply touched. As she lay still in the sultry room, she felt the sweetness of wonderful danger fill her. She knew she could lose her head.

She sat up and unclothed herself, tossing her dress into the hand basin. It would wash. She took off her silk knickers and threw them after the dress. Then she sat on the edge of the white bed and gave herself a talking to.

He's too young, she told herself. It just happened because we were thrown together in this place and I needed passion. . .

Cia came from a long line of sexually active women, almost a matriarchy. From Great Grandmama, Lady

Finnemore, down. The only one who had hankered after respectability was her own mother, Penelope, and so when she had married Mr Render, Cia had been sent off to live with Grandma. Either the house or the marriage was too small to accommodate a boisterous eight year old.

Cia thanked her lucky stars for it later, although it hurt at the time. Grandma's influence had given her the courage and the confidence to follow her own passions.

There was a difference though, between Grandma and Cia. Grandma didn't have any doubts about love. Cia did. In love, she lost sight of something very deep in her own soul – she lost sight of herself.

Life with Plomer Fitchew the Third was an altogether bizarre future prospect. Cia was too familiar with the Fitchew family to want to become completely enmeshed in its spells and its prejudices. Plomer was a good chap. He was bright as a button and full of spirit. Even at twenty he had a growing reputation in powerboat racing. He had the risk-taking, clever spirit in sport that drove his father in politics and love. Cia was a risk-taker too, in her own way, she knew. They were too similar and too much apart in years for her to even think about a future. But here she was, thinking about it all the same. It was time to stop.

She stood up and opened one of the wardrobe doors. She ran her fingertips over the abundance of dresses inside, like a child runs her hand along the railings. There was barely a rustle though as the gorgeous materials and myriad patterns swayed. Cia opened the next set of doors along. This compartment too was filled with dresses and gowns, some of them reaching to the floor. There were silks and cottons, there was organza and crepe, there was sarsenet, charmeuse, mousseline and linen. There were plain colours and patterned ones; there were woven designs and printed ones.

Cia still clung to the conviction that she had struck up a partnership with Signora Cammello, the dressmaker.

She still remembered the conversation at the beginning, when she had shyly shown Signora Cammello her designs and he had agreed to make them up.

Cia had done a lot of drawings, alone, to stave off the despair after the fiasco with the Count di Ravanello. That man knew he was her father, as sure as her mother, grandma and she herself knew it. It had been his daughter Angelina who had orchestrated the embarrassing scene and the gossip afterwards.

Dianna had encouraged her to draw and Cia not only gave expression to the talent she had doodled with since she was a child but she had made it concrete with Signora Cammello. Then Signora Cammello had turned up at the villa, angrily waving an enormous, unpaid account and Cia had realised her Italian hadn't been up to dealing with sharks.

Dianna, thank God, had found it amusing. She had paid the bill instantly. Unfortunately she amused herself by needling Cia constantly about it. What she said was true, though. When Cia's passions were up, they crushed sense out of her.

Plomer, who had been moping around the villa feeling landlocked, took an interest suddenly as the dynamics between his mother and Cia took on an edge. He found Signor Volpe, a tailor who was willing to strike up a partnership, and helped Cia negotiate properly. Cia had tried to pay Dianna back for her generosity by designing some stunning clothes for her. Cia's conscience was salved but the whole affair brought her and Plomer closer together and Dianna remained fractious and depressed, always a little apart.

Cia took a white linen shirt dress out of the wardrobe. The linen was so fine you could almost see through it. The skirt had two pleats in the front and a thin, stiffened belt with a golden buckle. The buttons were like sugared almonds.

There was no need to dress again yet. Dianna never demanded her attention before siesta was over. Cia hung the dress on the stand by the shutters and went back to lie on the bed. She watched the linen stirring in the breeze that skittered across the hills.

Dianna heaved and puffed and hissed herself into a corset with two-way stretch side panels. Some things had to be done in a corset.

She was in her forties and she was fat – there was no getting away from the truth. She had always been buxom, even as a fifteen year old. She was wearing a corset before many of her friends were out of the tree-climbing stage. But she was no longer buxom. She was fat. Her fat breasts squeezed themselves over the top of the all-in-one. Her cleavage was a deep, dark gully. The flesh on her back rolled softly over the corset's hand-decorated iron strength. It was as smooth as a child's. Her figure, clasped inside its tubular prison, was a figure that a schoolboy might draw on his blotter: a real woman-shape, an ideal. Her thighs, starting from the tops of her legs where the corset ended its regime, were tantalisingly dimpled. It made you wonder if her bum was also dimpled. Or was it round and smooth and the biggest bum you were ever likely to see in your life: the archetypal bum? If Dianna had been a Renaissance lady, she would have been prized beyond the wildest dreams of any woman.

But men seemed to have gone mad since the war, in her opinion. All they wanted were titless wonders. The more like a boy you looked, the more chance you had of stealing somebody else's husband. What was it Cia had said? God, she had even talked to the little strumpet about it. It was something very perceptive, as usual: men, Cia had said, went for the fashionable type of woman to bolster their standing with other men, not because they really found a type attractive, whatever it might be in a particular age.

Dianna combed out her heavy blonde hair and its permanent wave fell into place. What a pity to have to rid oneself of such an intelligent companion, she thought, as she stuck in her hairpins. There would only be Niccolo left to divert her from motherhood. Sometimes she thought she might swallow him between her thighs and never see him again.

She zipped herself into an aqua-marine day gown that draped over her breasts like a wave flowing over the rocks on a Mediterranean shore.

The knocking on the door of her room entered Cia's consciousness through half-dreams and remembrances of Plomer's love-making. In the dim sultriness of the room, the white linen dress hung still now. The light breeze had dropped. The slats in the shutter let in tiny slivers of silvery light. The sun outside was so strong it seemed to penetrate the soft wood itself. Eventually, the knocking became more insistent and Cia roused herself from her siesta and went to the door.

She was surprised to see Dianna all dressed up and it crossed her mind that the poor old girl might have gone wholly mad. Her lips were so red they looked like a wound in her face and her rouge was not completely rubbed in.

Dianna fixed Cia with an eye, which added to her strange appearance. The finer details of the distress on her face didn't quite register on Cia's sleepy mind and when Dianna burst into tears, Cia thought it was the old wound that her husband had inflicted on her. She sleepily poured some *aqua minerale* from the covered Majolica jug on the table and handed it to her employer gently.

Dianna raised her hand and dashed the glass away. It skidded along the floor.

'Why have you betrayed me over and over again, Cia, after all I've done for you? Oh, my poor darling boy!'

Cia's heart sank and she was suddenly fully awake, all in the same instant. Surely he hadn't run straight to his mother and told her?

'You will have to go this time, Cia. It's just too much.'

Cia sat down with a bump on the edge of the rumpled bed. It never occurred to her to deny it.

'Isn't it a good idea for him to have his first affair with someone you can trust?' she ventured.

'Trust! Oh, the nerve! How can you be so insensitive?'

Cia didn't understand her. 'It had to happen some time or another,' she said.

'Not under my very nose! You're no different to any other gold-digging little piece! You've taken advantage of my family for the last time.'

Cia didn't know what to say. She was angry and hurt and acutely aware that she was only wearing her underwear.

'Fancy corrupting an innocent boy!' yelled Dianna.

'Oh, Dianna,' said Cia, finding her voice, 'it wasn't corruption. Better me than one of the big-eyed boys on the street.'

'Oh, you pig! You pig!' cried Dianna, and she lifted her hand and struck Cia's face. 'Get out of this house immediately!' she screamed.

Cia stood where she was, hurting with rage as Dianna flounced from the room. Cia couldn't believe it! What was she going to do? She had no money and nowhere to go except home. But how the hell was she going to make the journey? And how was she going to leave Italy and all its beauty and go back to her crumbling old house on the Isle of Wight, and not die? She slumped on the bed and cried her eyes out.

When the tears were spent she was angry again and she was damn well sure she was not going to plod off meekly into poverty. She washed her face and marched down to the elegant reception room, where Dianna was waiting for a tisane to be brought to her.

'If you are going to throw me out, you have to compensate me!' she shouted. 'You know I have no money to get back to England.'

'You have to be joking!' said Dianna. 'Not when I've

spent a goddamn fortune indulging you, I don't. Sell some of your wardrobe, dear.'

Cia burst into tears.

Dianna wavered. 'You'll have your ticket home,' she said. 'Now get lost.'

Cia turned and left. Outside in the cavernous lobby, Plomer was standing still as a tree.

'We were found out,' said Cia.

'My mother?' asked Plomer.

'Aren't you lucky,' snapped Cia, 'to have a mother who will defend you against the evils of women like me?'

'Oh, Cia!' he said, still stuck to the floor.

She left him there and went back up to her room. What a mess. What a rotten, bloody mess. She opened the shutters. Damn! The view was spectacular. Damn! It was no longer hers. It never had been.

The afternoon wore on slowly and Cia stayed in her room, in disgrace, trying to organise in her mind what her next steps would be. As twilight began to draw in, Plomer knocked on her door and handed her a ticket to England. Cia barely looked at him. She was concentrating hard on the way the light seemed to change the tulips in the window box to velvet.

'I bought you a trunk,' he said.

That did it. The tears spilled over.

He looked acutely embarrassed.

'Come with me,' said Cia, wiping her eyes with a small, embroidered handkerchief. He didn't answer. 'Come with me,' she repeated. 'Let's travel. We don't need much money. We can work. Let's go...' But even as she said it, it felt ridiculous.

'I can't leave her,' he said. 'She's devastated. Why do you think I spend so much time here? I'd much rather be at Lake Garda. Since we found out about my father's betrayal it has been a battle to keep her sane. It's up to me. She has no-one but me. I'm her man. The only man she can rely on.'

Cia wasn't surprised by his true heart. He meant what he said, she could see that. The responsibility lay heavy on him but he was facing it. She remembered her dear grandma's illness and the necessity of nursing her until she died. She hadn't shied away either.

'You are a good boy,' she said, and held her hands out to him. 'Come here and kiss me, one last time.'

But he wasn't going to settle for a kiss and Cia didn't want him to once his body was in her arms. He undid two of the sugared almonds that held her dress together. . .

They never did get their clothes fully off. Cia's dress rasped at her armpits as he fell with her on to the soft bed. He kissed her breasts tenderly and ran his hands over her belly. He massaged her clitoris as she had taught him. His expression was full of wonder, as if he was stroking some magical animal to life. But there was a shadow of something else in his face; something like pain. Cia loved the way he looked at her body like that, all wracked with pain and desire and wonder. Why pain, she wondered?

She would remember his face like that. He would have many loves, she didn't doubt that. Would those women see that too? How would his emotions have etched themselves into his features by the time he was a man of 35? Somewhere, perhaps, in his face, would be the lines first begun in the pain of wanting her here in this room. She didn't want to say goodbye. A great, sad sob broke from her. He took her body in his arms and pulled her so close that she felt like a child.

She kissed him. His lips were wet. He was her daddy now, her man, taking care of her. He parted her legs. She found his sex and she pulled it into her own. Take me, she thought, take me somewhere so I don't have to think about where I really am going next. She felt so pliant, so sad, that she might dissolve. He reached into her passion and drew an orgasm from her.

* * *

Later that evening, at about ten, the trunk arrived. It was handmade, with a blue satin lining and secure metal clasps, like a huge treasure chest. She carefully packed as many of her clothes into it as she could. She was still packing in the wee small hours, while the *cavalletti* chirruped in the grass outside. When she had finished, the stillness in the house was total. It felt dead. She curled up in the love-scented bed and tried to sleep. Her eyes burned with unwanted wakefulness and when she finally did sleep, she dreamed of fires raging and purple flowers closing against a bruised sky. She woke again as the lavender light of morning crept across the silent hills.

The driver took her canvas travelling bag with a kind smile and held out his leathery, brown, short-fingered hand to help her into the cart. Plomer had ordered the cart for her, instead of a motor taxi, because he knew she liked Carlo, the old man who drove it. He had taught them both most of the Italian swear words they knew.

As Carlo climbed on to the front seat and picked up the reins, Cia had a moment to turn around. Plomer stood next to his mother at the top of the steps up to the front door. The pair of them were dwarfed by two overgrown cypresses, too near to the house.

Dianna appeared to be crying but Cia wasn't sure. Perhaps she was feigning it. Cia had no illusions about Dianna. There was a side to the older woman that was pure sham. Cia loved her anyway, for all her faults. One day, she thought, she'll regret this.

Plomer looked strained. He had pressed a cluster of dollar bills into her hand a few minutes earlier and Cia had tucked them into the soft leather pouch that hung from her shoulder on a thin strap.

'Aya!' cried Carlo to the horse. The animal pulled away and the cart began creaking over the dry earth of the track.

Cia was ready to go now. She turned forward. The

meadows drifted by on either side and the cart slowly made its way down the valley towards the city.

After the utter peace of the villa, the noise at *Santa Maria Novella* was an assault on her senses. The great steel trains clanked and screeched. On one wall was a huge *Nazionale Industrie Turistiche* poster: a thrusting silver and red train rushing like a phallus at full steam over the words *Nella Rivoluzione Facista.* The place smelt of coffee and diesel oil. There were black shirts in evidence; those of the railway officials.

Cia followed Carlo and the porter to the baggage office where she paid for her trunk to be carried all the way home to England. Carlo found her a forward-facing seat and, as she settled, a sense of adventure stole over her. Anything could happen! The train jolted and wheezed and Carlo waved his last goodbye.

Arrivederci, Cia mouthed.

Chapter Three

Back at the villa the usual sleepiness of the morning routine was cast off. Dianna was dressed in red by eleven and on the telephone by ten past. By teatime, which her British acquaintances kept religiously, Dianna had company, and by six she had her heart's desires: an invitation to see the great Carlo Galetti sing on the 29th and an engagement to go with Louisa Penhaligon to the life-drawing class at the Uffizi.

In the Palazzo Fiancata, home of the Cadenti di Ravanello family, the contessa took a telephone call just after siesta. She nearly burst a gut keeping the news to herself. To her chagrin, the count and Angelina were otherwise engaged. The count was, as usual for this time of the day, closeted with the Fascist *podesta,* the mayor. There was grave business on. They were planning the slaughter of the *squadristi* in the annual historical game of football, early in May. The *squadristi* represented the dedicated end of the fascist movement whereas the count and his peers were merely tolerant of whatever political movement did not disrupt their continued status and wealth. The game was between the footmen of the commune and the nobility, and they dressed in sixteenth-century knickers.

Angelina, the daughter, and Cia's half-sister, had left strict orders that she was not to be disturbed. So the contessa drummed the elegant fingers of her left hand on the table where the treaty was signed to bring Florence into the unified state of Italy. As she drummed, the diamonds in her ring sent rainbows skittering among the cherubs on the pale ceiling of her state room.

Angelina's apartments were in the east wing of the *palazzo*. She sat in the drawing room examining her newly arrived guests. The room was furnished completely in white. The doors, the walls, the floor, the chairs, the clock on the mantelpiece and the statuettes – they were all of the purest white. In a recess there was a huge white bowl full of water in which only the heads of pure white roses floated, scenting the room. Until February of this year, the room had been quite normally multi-coloured. But then Angelina had had a whim for white and when Angelina had a whim she made sure somebody else put it into action. It was a statement, her white, against her father's black shirt.

Her hair was bleached, as were her eyebrows. She looked like a Hollywood actress. She was not beautiful but very striking, with her mother's Roman nose and grey eyes that smouldered. She wore ivory Japanese silk trousers that hung loosely, and her blouse was so sheer that her skin was visible underneath. The blouse was decorated at the breasts with white birds that just about hid her powdered nipples. Even her lips were lightened. They were luscious red in their natural state but now they were the palest pink imaginable.

Her guests were a man and a woman. The man, Gianni, was dark and typically southern in appearance. He was young and overly muscular in the body and limbs. He was dressed in a dark blue suit and he looked uncomfortable, as if he would much rather be naked, or at least in a vest, sweating.

The young woman, who had been hovering behind the sheltering bulk of Gianni and peering at Angelina with big eyes, came out of hiding and walked briskly to the big white couch that Angelina was waving her long nails at. Petra moved neatly. Everything about her dress was neat, in fact, as if she had carefully taken herself out of a box for the afternoon. She wore black polished pumps and carried a small black handbag. Both were cheap and matched her black and orange print dress, a hundred of which could be found in Florence's street markets. The overall effect though, because she was a bouncy and pretty little girl of barely eighteen, was sweet rather than tawdry. A wealthy man might have fallen in love with her and dressed her, and she would have been queen of Florence. She had eyes that slanted and high, wide cheekbones. She had a straight nose and a full mouth. Her luxuriant curly black hair was pinned neatly behind her ears with two silvery clips. She had full breasts and hips and she wore a corset that kept everything from moving but the fabric of her skirt stretched itself across a rounded belly.

Angelina knew that Gianni hadn't had Petra's virginity, that he was saving it for their wedding night. Until this very minute, Angelina had wished him well. Gianni had been her own lover for a long time, on and off. Sex with Gianni was rude and rough on both sides. They did it everywhere, like cats in alleyways. They did it under her father's window in the courtyard at night. They did it in his mother's back kitchen and one of them always came away with torn skin. Angelina kept her nails long purely for the pleasure of scratching him. It was a guilty pleasure but she liked to wound him. He was upset the first time but afterwards he laughed. He liked to think that this noblewoman turned into a hellcat at the touch of him. He pinned her down sometimes. He tied her arms behind her, to stop her lashing out. He got a great deal of pleasure out of that. She did, too – she loved the pleasure of intense frustration that found its release in his invasion. But she had become more and more his own creature, no longer her own.

He had convinced her that his marriage should not disturb her because she offered something completely different to the child-bearing, home-making potential of Petra. But faced with the sweet, neatly packaged and bursting virgin, Angelina was consumed with the desire to destroy her.

Gianni remained standing while Angelina rang for the servant. The three of them sat in silence until he arrived. It amused Angelina to see dark circles of perspiration appear on Petra's dress under the arms. So, she was nervous. Good. She ought to be.

Gianni stepped out on to the balcony. Then he turned and walked back in again, silently.

Angelina ordered drinks from the servant and when he had gone, she smiled at Gianni and then at Petra without speaking. Petra was clearly too intimidated to begin a conversation. It looked to Angelina as if she wanted to say something but was searching for words and couldn't find them. Angelina didn't help her. She kept the silence. Only the steps of the servant, walking to the cellar across the courtyard, broke it.

Gianni went to sit down next to Petra.

'Oh no. Gianni, don't sit there,' said Angelina. 'She looks so pretty there, all alone in the middle of the couch. Don't spoil it. Sit over there, in that chair.'

For once he did as he was told. Petra looked nervously at him. He gave her a reassuring smile. The three of them sat in silence, waiting for the drinks.

The re-entry of the servant made Petra jump, Angelina noted. The servant placed a chilled bottle of white, unlabelled wine on the low table in the centre of the room and prepared to pour it.

'Leave it,' barked Angelina.

When he had gone she let the bottle sit there a moment or two in the silence. Eventually she said, 'Gianni, you ought to pour us a drink. Petra, you want a drink, don't you?'

Petra shook her head and opened her mouth but no words came out.

Angelina looked at Gianni. He had a smug little smile on his face. Hypocrite, thought Angelina. He likes the fact that his little virgin wife-to-be doesn't drink. A flitter of images of the drunken sex they had had together went through her mind. Some of the things she did for him when she was drunk made her cringe afterwards. She pretended she was his slave and worshipped his cock. She'd draped it in purple cloth and lit a candle in an elaborate ritual that had almost driven him into a frenzy. He liked to curse the Madonna as he ejaculated.

'I like to drink,' she said. 'A woman loosens up when she drinks. She finds out about herself and so does her lover. Pour me a drink, Gianni.'

Gianni poured her a drink and gave it to her.

She drank it down in one and wiped her mouth with the back of her hand. 'Give me another,' she said. The alcohol hit her brain and her legs parted.

She saw Gianni's gaze run up her legs to the seam at her crotch. She smiled at him again and slowly leaned forward so that her breasts fell. Her nipples almost peeped out of the top of her blouse. She did it as she put her glass down on the table. It could, conceivably, have been an accidental exposure, but it wasn't.

Petra clearly didn't miss the trick either. She looked startled. Angelina arched her back as she sat up so that the little grey ring of the whole of one powdered nipple was exposed.

Petra couldn't take her eyes off Angelina's breasts, not for a second. Her sweet face spoke volumes. She was out of her depth but she was enthralled. The scent of her drifted round the room in the charged atmosphere.

Gianni too was looking at Angelina's breasts. He wouldn't be able to put a stop to anything she might do, she'd bet. Angelina was so excited she could feel her knickers becoming damp. She had him. She looked at his crotch and she saw the familiar swell beginning, unmistakably. She knew he was hot and sweaty too.

'Perhaps I will have a little wine,' squeaked Petra.

It surprised Angelina to hear her speak. She found herself getting up and serving the girl. As she gave her the glass she bent down. She couldn't help but notice how Petra still couldn't take her eyes off her breasts. Angelina bent over more than was necessary and she knew the girl had seen everything. Her breasts felt bare; they felt gazed at. Angelina kept her eyes looking straight at Petra's beautiful brown ones. When Petra took the glass Angelina allowed her own hand to stay on the glass a moment too long, so that their fingertips touched. She looked deliberately at Petra's full breasts. A thrill of pleasure slipped through her when she saw the girl's nipples hardening under the thin fabric of her dress.

Well, well, thought Angelina. Perhaps this girl could just as easy become a lesbian as a wife.

Still there was no talk between them, and they sat in the humming room above the city, drinking wine in silence. Angelina reflected how the educated classes would have, at least, covered themselves with small talk. But she liked it this way. It was more brutal. Eventually, as she saw the little Petra's face beginning to glow with the wine, she said, 'Gianni, go and pluck some flowers from the courtyard for Petra, please. I want to show her some clothes.'

He got up hesitantly but he went. As soon as the door was closed behind him, Angelina said to Petra, 'Follow me,' and she took her hand and led her along to her bedroom.

It was a huge room with a beautiful cream brocade counterpane on the big bed. It was sumptuously decorated. On the dressing table were acres of expensive bottles and boxes, the articles of war. Petra's eyes goggled at the richness of her surroundings.

Angelina opened the wardrobe, revealing dozens of

beautiful dresses. But instead of taking out any of the gowns, she reached up to the top shelf and took down a large Moroccan-bound book. She took it to the bed and sat down with it. 'Join me,' she said, smiling.

Petra perched her ample bottom on the edge of the bed, not too close.

Angelina opened the book. Inside were photographs. Angelina flicked through quickly. 'I want to educate you,' she said. 'I know you are a virgin and Gianni likes you that way and he wants to marry you intact. But there is a way that a woman can get sexual pleasure and still retain her suitability for marriage.'

Petra was peering at the pictures flashing by as Angelina turned the pages. There was a lot of flesh on the pages. Suddenly Angelina stopped turning. 'Look,' she said.

Petra gasped.

The picture showed two women kissing each other passionately. One had the other's naked breast in her hand, its nipple squeezed and pouting. Both the women were naked apart from stockings and garters and the second woman had her hand on her friend's sex, her finger sliding in between fleshy thighs.

Slowly Angelina raised her eyes from the photograph and looked at Petra's face. The little girl's mouth was open and her lips were moist. Angelina waited for her to raise her eyes to hers. She smiled at her and very slowly but surely arched her back, pushing her breasts forward. Petra gazed lustfully. She gazed and she gazed. She was transfixed. She wriggled her arse on the bed.

Angelina sighed. The stupid bitch was too gormless to touch what was offered. She closed the book. 'I'm not sure I have anything that will fit you,' she said. 'I'd like to give you something but your breasts are so much bigger than my small little things and my legs are longer.' Angelina stroked her own legs and lifted up her silky dress, way up over her long thighs, so that the lace on her knickers was on display. She lifted it right up, revealing both thighs and her knickers to the other girl on the bed. 'Look what long thighs I have,' she said.

Petra was looking straight at Angelina's pussy, hidden behind its layer of silk.'My thighs are fat,' she mumbled.

'They don't look it under your dress.' said Angelina. 'You look lovely; voluptuous.'

'Gianni says I'm on the fat side,' said Petra.

Angelina was frustrated. It must be because the girl had absolutely no sexual experience. Anyone who had half an inkling would have taken the hint by now and either touched her or revealed something of herself, surely!

'I think Gianni doesn't know when he's well off,' said Angelina. 'Show me your thighs. I bet they aren't fat.'

Petra stood up and pulled up her dress in a business-like manner. She had shapely, pale thighs, a little chubby and covered with a soft layer of fine hair. The skin looked soft as heaven. 'I don't like this,' she said, pinching the soft inner flesh where the chubbiness was most lumpy.

'But it's lovely,' said Angelina, and she held out her hand to touch. She felt Petra's body quiver as she stroked the soft skin on her inner thigh.

'Well,' said Petra, and she dropped her skirt resolutely on Angelina's hand.

'Ohh!' groaned Angelina. 'I was enjoying that!'

Petra moved away. 'Gianni will be back,' she said.

'Don't worry about him,' said Angelina softly. 'He won't be back for a little while. Come, let me see the rest of you. You are so pretty. Wait! I know just what will suit you.' She spun round and opened another wardrobe door. She searched through and pulled out a pale blue kaftan robe. 'Here,' she said. 'You can have this for your trousseau.'

Petra eyes lit up and she reached out her hand to touch the offered garment.

Angelina pulled it back. 'Only if you try it on.'

Petra hesitated. But then, with her beautiful mouth

set in a line, she reached for the button at the neck of her dress.

Angelina said, 'Let me,' and she began unbuttoning.

Underneath, Petra wore a very plain cotton cami-knicker that barely revealed anything. Angelina gave her the kimono and she slipped it on. It suited her, although it would have to be shortened.

She took it off again and Angelina, unable to control herself any longer, touched her shoulder.

Petra moved away again. 'Gianni really will be back soon. I'll come back and visit you another time when he isn't with me,' she said.

'When?' slavered Angelina.

'Next week?'

'So long?'

'It isn't long,' said Petra gently. 'I'll come and show you the material for my wedding dress.'

Petra seemed to have no idea of the effect her words might have on Angelina, who kept any sign of what she was really thinking under an inscrutable mask. 'I would love to see it,' she said. 'I know you are going to look lovely.' She stepped forward and put her hand gently on Petra's shoulder again. She let it drop down her arm and slid her hand across to the girl's full breast and down to her waist. 'You really are lovely.'

'You are too, Angelina,' said Petra, and she too reached out and traced the outline of the other woman's figure.

'Oh, this is too much. Kiss me, Petra,' said Angelina, pulling Petra close.

Petra seemed to yield and Angelina took her in her arms and their lips met in a kiss. Angelina slipped the thin strap off Petra's shoulder and peeled the cotton away from the girl's breast. She stroked it urgently. She stopped kissing her mouth and pressed her lips to the soft white flesh of the partially exposed breast.

Petra moaned softly. 'I will come back,' she said.

Angelina took no notice and reached for the other thin strap and pulled it down too. This time the whole of the top of the camiknicker rolled gently away from Petra's breasts and left them exposed. They were beautiful and pale, while the nipples were dark. Angelina fell on them like a hungry child.

Suddenly, Petra pushed her away. 'I will come back. I'm terrified. If Gianni catches me he won't marry me.' She sobbed as she spoke the last word.

Angelina gently protested. 'Fuck Gianni,' she said. 'Fuck him. I want you.'

Petra capitulated. Her body softened. She buckled almost. It was easy for Angelina to throw her on to the bed and cover her mouth in a kiss. Angelina's hands moved all over Petra's body like flames. She burned up the virgin and delved for her cunt. Angelina's hand was drenched in Petra. She straddled her, pressing her own sex to its mirror image. It was fast. The two women strained and heaved against each other in a dual frenzy until their orgasms came. Angelina held on to Petra's hair as the last of the shocks passed.

Petra kissed her gently and got up, straightening her underwear and looking for her clothes. 'We must get dressed. Gianni will be back.' She stumbled and breathed deeply.

'When will you come again?' asked Angelina.

'Thursday? It's my day off,' whispered Petra.

'Good,' said Angelina.

'I must find Gianni,' said Petra. 'I must.'

'Send him to me in my library before you go. I'll get dressed.' Petra looked at her suspiciously. 'Don't fret. I just want a word with him. Nothing that concerns you, my sweet,' she said.

Petra hurried away.

Instead of dressing Angelina went naked into the library by the side door. She lay on the couch and opened her legs, displaying herself to the door.

Gianni entered and she merely smiled at him. He was by her side immediately. He stood over her and she could see his hardness.

'I've just given your little girl an orgasm. I've sucked her tits too,' she said. 'I bet that's more than you've done.'

'Bitch,' said Gianni. 'I knew it.'

Angelina cackled heartily.

Gianni unbuckled his belt and quickly opened his fly. His cock emerged and he commanded her to suck it. She took it between her lips and wet its head with her mouth. The paleness of her lips was giving way to the natural blood-red underneath. He wasn't long at her mouth. He pulled away and her lips made a popping sound. He knelt over her and shoved it mercilessly between her legs into the ripeness of her vagina. Angelina was so tormented with excitement she came a second time and yelled at the top of her voice with the power of it.

He stood up, towering over her. 'That's the last you'll ever get of me, bitch,' he said. 'And if you ever go near Petra again I'll have you killed.'

Angelina laughed. 'That's what you say now,' she sneered. 'But you'll be back. You won't be able to stay away from this for long,' she said, and she shoved her vulva upward.

He turned on his heel and left.

Angelina giggled to herself and lay for a while in daydreams of fucking both of them together. She wanted to ruin their little marriage. What did they matter to her? They were just little people really. She was wealthy; she could play with them for a while and then she could drop them. She was still smiling to herself when she sat up. It was as she stood and started for her bathroom that fear began to seep into her soul.

She tried to keep it at bay with a little tune, humming to herself quietly as she turned on the golden faucets and watched the steam rise from the big, oval tub. But her fear would not go away. Her thoughts tumbled one over the other, rushing at her like the water, mercilessly. He *can* kill me. He can.

Once, Gianni had introduced her to a member of the *squadristi,* a special friend of his. The man was terrifying. He had cold, blue, almost luminous eyes that showed you nothing of the man who owned them. After he had left them in the shade by the market that day, Gianni had told her that that particular *squadrisiti* had killed probably the most men during the Fascist union-breaking on the railways. If the price was right he would kill for anybody.

Angelina got into the tub. She felt shaky. But then it occurred to her that the *squadristi* did only work for money. Gianni didn't have the kind of money it took. Angelina laughed out loud with a kind of snort. As quick as a flash though, the laughter ceased. None of it mattered if she had lost Gianni. She loved him desperately. If Angelina could have cried, she would have done. But she had never been able to, even as a child. Her teeth began to chatter, even in the warm bath.

There were four people at dinner: Angelina herself, the count, the contessa and the *podesta.* As she sat down, Angelina noticed the reflection of her own face in the slender, silver salt cellar, elongated out of all proportion.

'Dianna Fitchew has sacked that girl,' said her mother. 'Signor Lumaca's wife telephoned me this afternoon. She's giving a luncheon for poor Dianna and wondered if we would go.' The contessa's vacuous mind hadn't made itself up on the question of how to deal with this invitation. She waited for either her daughter or her husband to lead the way.

The count didn't seem to be listening. He went on talking to the *podesta* about the team they were putting together.

'I hear she was sacked for stealing,' said Angelina. It was as if someone else had said it. Perhaps the reflection in the salt cellar was talking, she thought.

The contessa looked at her in surprise. 'You've heard already?'

'Oh yes, she was caught with her hands dirty. Dianna Fitchew has been losing a lot of money. I don't think it was just stealing. I think it was fraud,' said Angelina, and she took the last mouthful of her chilled soup.

'Well,' said the contessa. 'We are vindicated. I had the nasty feeling that some people thought our behaviour towards her was unjust. Ha! If we gave alms to all the waifs who claimed to be one of the count's wild oats grown to fruition, then we would be bankrupt.' She looked at her husband with a smug little smile.

He *was* listening. He had the skill of listening to two people at once, always had. He looked at his wife and then his daughter. Sometimes he really detested them.

Chapter Four

A silver, streamlined train sped through farmland, alongside olive groves, past villages with red-roofed houses and tall church towers with sleeping bells.

Cia was travelling first class, in padded leather luxury. But she was bored. She felt empty. Waves of loss hit her and mixed with thoughts of home, of the turquoise sea of Cowes, of her house. There was no-one else in her compartment. She had been for a walk down the corridors of the train twice already. Soon she would be able to go again. It must be nearly lunchtime. It must, surely. She got up and stretched.

She didn't pass anyone at all as she walked down the corridor, swaying to the motion and clatter of the train. She passed through the rubber concertina into second class and closed the door behind her. The noise of the train was more insistent in here. The lampshades covering the unlit globes on the moving walls were plain white.

The curtains of the first compartment were drawn but one curtain had come loose from its moorings and left a triangular peep-hole. The first thing Cia saw was the countryside rushing by through the outside window. Then she saw the couple on the bare, red bench inside.

She looked away immediately. The third thing she saw was her own reflection on the glass as the train sped along the outskirts of a forest of tall trees.

She moved back towards the coupling. Her breath came heavily, and she could feel the nakedness of the slender, handsome man's genitals, as if her mind had hands. What on earth were they thinking of? Here in the train? Lucky, lucky people.

She knew she shouldn't look again but it was irresistible. Before her very eyes, the man cupped the breast of the woman with a movement so appreciative, it seemed as if his hand was in love.

Cia peered round the rich wooden window frame, making sure she kept out of their line of vision. The glass of the windows reflected her image a hundred times back and forth.

The woman's face was slack with pure enjoyment. Her painted lips parted in a serene smile as her eyes closed contentedly. Her hand caressed his sex; her fingers were embroidered with his hair. Cia suddenly had the urge to run in and slap the bitch!

As she gulped air, trying to calm herself, she remembered something. Just before her mother had sent her off to Cowes, she had watched the newly married couple on the couch together; untouchable, untouched, prim and proper. How could this couple remind her of that? There was something about that woman that reminded her of Penelope, though: perhaps the smugness.

The only communication she had had from her mother since Grandma's funeral was a series of letters warning her of the dangers of approaching thirty unmarried.

Suddenly a hand reached across the window to hitch up the curtain. Cia flattened herself against the chugging wall. The curtain fell. The hand hitched it up again. It fell. Cia waited a minute or two. Then she peeked again.

How would the man feel if he knew there was another woman watching him? Perhaps he would come out and ask her to join them. The man lifted the woman's skirt and his hand delved into her underwear, exposing the raw skin and hair of her sex. Cia turned away.

She debated with herself whether to go back for lunch. Then her irrational self drew her back to the window. He had his prick out. It was an average sort of item, neither big nor small. Beautifully shaped though, and straight. She watched until he pushed the woman down on the bench to fuck her, and then she turned away, green with jealousy.

She walked back into first class and stopped by an open window. It had all taken place in a few minutes but she felt as if she had been away for hours. Her feelings were raging. She shouldered open the door of the lavatory and came face to face with herself in the gilt-edged mirror. She pulled down her knickers and sat on the wooden seat with a bump. She stayed there, swaying and bare arsed, then took a cigarette from the crumpled packet in her pouch. She held it between her lips as she dried herself and pulled up her knickers. The smoke stung her eyes as she rinsed her hands. She looked again at her reflection; at the face with the white stick drooping from its lips.

Loneliness. The one word explained her anger and her need. She was lonely as hell. She felt poisonous. Tears came to her eyes and overflowed. Who knew or cared that she was on this train? What would become of her?

Perhaps, she thought, her mother was right. She ought to have married. There had been one or two likely men but she had seen what marriage did to her contemporaries. She didn't want to be anyone's prisoner or social secretary. She wanted to be an equal; a lover.

Sex, she believed, was the most important thing to bind a man and woman. So she had had sex with her lovers to find out if they might do. None of them had done so far. Some of them didn't even think a woman had the right to try the goods before she bought them. A lot of them, in fact, thought that way. It really was amazing how daft a lot of people were. But they had organised their daftness into a moral system and she was on the outside looking in. And she was nearly thirty.

'Things are going to change,' she said to herself resolutely.

She washed and dried her face and went out into the corridor as a middle-aged portly man approached along the corridor, looking for the toilet.

Cia looked at him and thought she could fuck him, whoever he was, right there up against the door. Perhaps someone else would see *them* and they would fuck and the whole train would fuck all the way to Milan, like dominoes.

He smiled at her and was clearly about to say something when a Blackshirt pushed through the door right at the end of the carriage. The man scurried into the toilet. The Blackshirt stared at Cia as she walked back to her compartment. Just as she reached the door, he strode towards her. He asked her for her ticket.

She took it out of her pouch. It was creased. He frowned and told her to keep it flat. Then he punched it and gave it back to her. Cia mentally stuck her tongue out at the officious little twerp. She shut the door of her compartment behind her and headed off in search of food.

The waiter led her to a table in the dining car. It was impossible, in small heels, not to sway her hips. She tried to walk straight but failed. It wasn't unusual for her to be looked at by men. She was young and lovely. But there was something more to her now than physical accident; something every woman has, no matter what age. Her sex felt huge, as if underneath her linen dress it was ready to drop itself on to any prick in the room.

She thanked the waiter and took the menu card absentmindedly. Her sex was hot and scented. She could wander the train until Milan, like a tigress in a cage, looking for meat.

Luckily, though, the service was fast. Along came lunch and she was calmed by the munching of spaghetti.

* * *

The train pulled into Milan in the twilight. The brakes screamed as steel met steel and clung.

Cia took down her travelling bag and waited for the final halt. She felt as if the train had dragged her body slowly over every inch of track. She had dozed fitfully and dreamed about a boy from school who always used to flirt with her. He was married now, with about four children, and he no longer flirted but nodded respectfully in the high street. In the dream he had asked her to come and watch him and his wife fucking. She had been right there on the bed with them, so close to the goosepimply flesh on his buttocks that she could touch. . . and as she did it she woke up.

Then, in a daze, she had gone searching for coffee and had ended up back at the compartment of the copulating couple. They had disappeared.

She wondered if they had ever really existed. She hadn't heard the train pull into a station.

There was a crush on the platform. Bodies pressed against hers as people swarmed. She gripped her bag tightly and wondered what part of people she was touching. Backs mostly, and sides. Bodies. Bodies. Bodies.

There was a lot of excited talk. Two words kept coming up: *'Il duce, il duce.'* Cia remembered a headline she had glimpsed on the next table in the dining car. Mussolini was speaking from the balcony of La Scala that evening.

Perhaps he'll sing his speech, she thought. He might as well. She had heard him often on the crackling radio at the villa, barking through the still Florentine night. She had seen how people were stirred by his rhetoric. Even Dianna had sex dreams about *il duce*. Imagine! Fat pig. Cia's soul revolted against the military nationalism of the Fascist hoo-ha. Why should anyone dominate the world at all? Hitler's election as Chancellor of Germany this year had stepped up the madness.

In the swarm of people moving along the platform

there was an excitement that was almost irresistible: something greater than all of them.

According to the timetable that she got with her ticket, Cia had two and a half hours before her connection on the Simplon Express to London.

She decided she would go and listen to the barking *duce*, just so she would be able to say she was there.

She was unaware that anyone had been watching her, so it was a surprise when a man offered to carry her bag. He seemed nice. She gave him her travelling bag. It wasn't really heavy but she had a long way to go. Why not? He was tall and slender and had a nice smile, but was a bit intellectual-looking for her taste. He had a high forehead and wore glasses.

In her bag were two dresses: one was a sleeved black jersey, cut on the cross with a slit in the back seam from waist to neck. It could be worn in the day but would provide a little glamour for the evening tomorrow, when she would be in London, should she need it. She hadn't decided yet whether to take a room in London for the night. She had just enough money to do so, but it would be an expense that she might regret. She had no money to go back to. If she was careful, the money Plomer had given her would last until she had figured out how to make more.

The second dress was made of a fine, blue wool that resisted creasing. She also had a woollen jacket that her grandmother had knitted, a silk wrap, some soft velvet travelling slippers with Chinese women embroidered on them, some stockings and garters, a plain lawn cami-knicker and a beautifully hand-figured brassiere and knickers in transparent triple-weave silk, just in case.

'How far are you going?' the man asked.

'To London,' Cia replied.

'So far!' he said. 'I thought I might be able to offer to drop you somewhere but you are leaving Milan. I am devastated.'

He amused her. 'Do you live in Milan?' she asked.

'Yes,' he said. 'Well, just outside Milan. I have a villa there and a factory. I build cars.'

Cia's clitoris jumped; she swore she could feel it. Cars. Sex. Ask me to dinner, she thought. Please do.

But he didn't. He left her with a porter at the barrier and said, '*Ciao!*'

Cia sighed. It didn't happen like that in films.

The concourse of the brand new central station in Milan was like a Hollywood set dreamed up for a film about ancient Rome. Monumental columns towered overhead and great marble ogres stared from the walls. She looked around for the departures board. She didn't trust timetables, even efficient, Fascist ones. But this was Italy and the trains ran on time because the Fascists had broken the striking railwaymen and sacked most of them.

She decided she would find a cheap restaurant to have a long leisurely dinner in and then she would go and stand on the edges of the rally, just to observe human nature at its current fever pitch.

Suddenly, a bolt hit her solar plexus, as if one of the stone gods overhead had pointed his finger at her. Over by the stairs to the exit she saw a man she recognised.

Surely not! But it was. It was Rudy Wicked. Cia giggled to herself. His name wasn't really Rudy Wicked. It was Rudolph Wycke. But Rudy Wicked was what she and the other girls who went to the local school in Cowes used to call him and there was a rhyme that went on to sing something about knickers, which she couldn't remember. He was gorgeous, like a film star (only without make-up), and ten years older than her. He had married a woman so beautiful, so elegant and so unbalanced that she had killed herself.

It *was* him! The woman with him was Edna, his sister. Cia's heart leapt. Edna was a terrific woman. Cia loved her.

She had known they were in Europe because Mrs Penhaligon, Dianna's gossipy friend, had come across them in Cannes. Travelling would be just the sort of thing Edna would insist he did at such a time – to take his mind off Nora's suicide.

Cia hurried as much as she could through the swarm but another train had come in. By the time she reached the top of the stairs Rudy and Edna were nowhere to be seen. She hurried down the marble stairway, but outside there were only taxis pulling away and no sign of them.

She couldn't imagine either of them being remotely interested in Fascism. Edna was a Fabian and Rudy was a gentle spirit who built beautiful boats. He had been in the British navy for a short while but that was because his father had been. He was out as soon as his father had died. Besides, they were Jewish and although Italian Fascism was no more anti-Semitic than European culture in general, Hitler's Jewish conspiracy rubbish was quite likely to spread.

Rudy and Edna could be travelling on the same train as her, with the same wait. If that was the case, it would make some sense of what fate had thrown at her.

She prolonged the meal as long as she could but she was restless. She asked the restaurateur's wife if she might leave her travelling bag with her while she went to the rally. The woman was happy to keep it in the back room. Her husband positively beamed; thinking, perhaps, that the *duce* was inspiring to the beautiful Englishwoman.

Outside in the soft Italian night, some of the shops were still open, cashing in on the excitement.The piazza in front of La Scala was virtually full of bodies in the dark, standing quite still. There were many courting couples with their arms around each other, and at first Cia found this reassuringly normal. But perhaps an unthinking allegiance to Fascism was just as dangerous for the world as the zealous kind. For so many people this was just somewhere to be at a certain time; somewhere to hide from the chaperone and unwittingly swell the Fascist ranks.

Cia found a pillar to lean on and suddenly thought about Nora, Rudy's beautiful wife, fluttering around him after he had won an eights race back in Cowes. It was strange to think of Nora being dead, but perhaps not that strange. Cia had always seen something dead in her eyes. There had been rumours that she was having an affair with Stephen Kent. The man was a social-climbing user. Cia was at a loss to understand why any woman would prefer him to Rudy.

She was brought back to the present as a great roar went up from the crowd in the darkness. She stood on tiptoe to see Mussolini stride on to the balcony and stand a full minute, hands on hips, fixing the rabble below with his eye until they were still. Eventually, the whole square became still and silent. The tension was palpable. When would he begin speaking? You almost begged him to begin and release you. And finally, when he did, he had you in his power.

Would he be like that in bed? Would he have his minions do the foreplay duty in black underwear, while he waited in the wings to come and penetrate you at zero hour?

Cia noticed a young man at the edge of the crowd, standing in the glow of a streetlight. He was looking at her. Something about him made her feel as if she didn't want his attention. She looked away.

At the end of the speech, the crowd erupted in thunderous applause and Cia saw the young man heading towards her. She braced herself to give him the brush off. But he was on a collision course. A knife gleamed in the darkness and she felt her money pouch disappear.

'*Mia borsa!* My bag! Stop that man!' she screamed, running. Startled faces turned her way. Several men pushed through the crowd and gave chase. For a few moments there was hope. Surely the thief couldn't get away in such a crowd? But then the same men were coming back to her, shaking their heads and telling her he had disappeared.

All the money Plomer had given her was in that purse. For a moment, she thought her passport and ticket were in there too. But then she remembered she had put them flat in her travelling bag, and that was back at the restaurant.

She saw two *carabinieri* heading towards her and her heart sank. They would only make things worse. She started to walk away. Her one thought was to get back to the restaurant and get her ticket and passport. Somehow she would manage without money... But the people around her were talking all at once and the *carabinieri* were upon her.

She raised her voice above the din, almost shouting. 'My train is leaving for England. I don't care about the money. My travelling bag is with a restaurant around the corner. I can get it and go on my way. Just let me go on my way.'

The policeman puffed up like a bird. Who was this Englishwoman shouting her plans at him in Italian in his own beloved country when his *duce* was going to restore him an empire?

Cia could sense her mistake as she made it. There was no point in asserting herself with this fool. She changed her tack, forcing a sweet smile on her face so that he softened a bit. But the crowd of men who had given chase after the thief also wanted to speak. It was chaos.

When she finally got back to the station with her travelling bag, Cia had missed the Simplon Express. She slumped on to a bench. She had missed Rudy, Edna, a tolerable journey home... The situation required clear thinking but she was in no state to think. She stared blankly into the concourse.

After a few moments a middle-aged man approached her bench and sat down. He was well dressed and balding; a fatherly figure. Cia ignored him. The departures board, which she could just about see from where she was sitting, was sparse. There was a train going to

Lausanne in an hour. The only other two trains were for suburban Milan. She decided to go to Lausanne and wire Plomer. She could pick up the Express tomorrow and have money sent further down the line. She refused to think about how she would be able to pay for a telegram, or her stay in Lausanne, or where she would sleep. Somehow those things would fall into place.

'May I get you a cup of coffee?' the man next to her asked. 'I am going to the buffet.'

When he returned with two coffees, he asked her where she was going. Before she knew it, the whole story rushed out like water from a pipe. He listened without saying a word. Cia began to find it strange that the conversation was all one-sided.

'And you?' she asked. 'Where are you going?'

'Oh, nowhere,' he said.

'What brings you here, to the station?' she asked.

'I like to be where people are travelling,' he said, his voice lowering. 'I find it exciting.'

Cia smiled. It seemed reasonable. 'What do you do during the day?' she asked. She wondered if he was lonely all day.

'Oh never mind that,' he said. 'Let's not talk about me. Let's talk about you. I find you very exciting.'

An alarm bell went off in Cia's brain. She smiled with all the sweetness she could muster. 'Well, I must be going. Thank you for the coffee,' she said.

'You have nowhere to go!' he cried. 'Why don't you come with me, to a hotel. I'll pay for the room... I'll make it worth your while.'

She got up and walked away so quickly she was almost running. She crossed the wide open space of the concourse, listening all the while for heavy footsteps behind her.

Eventually, when she had put what felt like enough distance between herself and the monstrous man, she turned around and looked back at the bench where he had been sitting. He had gone.

She stood in the sepulchral gloom next to one of the great columns at the top of the stairs. If anyone had wanted to find her they need only look. She wasn't hidden. But she felt sheltered by the shadows. She breathed deeply and scanned the edges of the concourse for the predator.

After a while she remembered she had a small bottle of grappa in her travelling bag. She drank some of the firey liquid furtively, not wanting to be taken for a drunk. As the alcohol hit her tired mind, her thoughts took a new turn. What if she had said yes? He wasn't all that threatening really. He wasn't going to kill her. He hadn't come after her. What if she had gone back to a hotel room with him? Imagined scenes in some cheap hotel flittered through her mind in the gloom. Her doing it to him with her clothes on, just hoiking her camiknickers to the side. He would have taken out her breasts hungrily and she would have loved to wiggle them in front of him like a saucy picture-girl. She could even have done it in the hour before the Lausanne train went. No need to stay with him all night. Just a quick fuck and then away, with some spending money.

She felt aroused, as much by the thought of taking money for sex as anything else. 'I'll make it worth your while.' She remembered his words. Now that would be something different: a memory to take home . . .

But this was no time to dally with erotic thoughts. She must be on guard. She snapped herself out of it. Men are amazing, she thought. Imagine being able to go up to someone and proposition them like that. A woman could never do it. There was no acceptable way to say: I am dying for sex and I want you.

The station clock jumped forward a minute and she waited.

Chapter Five

The mail train to Lausanne ambled its way through the dark foothills of the Alps. Cia had been on the train for hours. It had stopped at every small station in the border country. She was cold and shaky. For all she knew she might be the only passenger. There must be a driver, she thought, although it seemed almost possible, in this hour before dawn, that the Fascists might have done away with train drivers. Perhaps it was just her and a mechanical robot. She felt like crying. But she wasn't going to let herself cry. She sniffed a bit, blew her nose, wiped her eyes, and when she looked up again, dawn had begun to stomp, with reassuring practicality, across the mountainous landscape. More and more lights came on in the windows of houses alongside the track as the train rumbled past.

It presently pulled to a halt at another tiny station with clean white fencing. A deep velvet, most unrobotic, male voice announced that there would be a thirty-minute stop for a change of driver and breakfast. Passengers were asked to have their documents ready for border control. Cia looked at the name of the station. She recognised it as the very last in Italy and she almost cried with relief. She was so glad to be leaving.

Outside, the air was soft and surprisingly warm, given the fact that there was still snow on the peaks. There was a lighted cafe on the road just beyond the platform and in the silence the sounds of china clinking within carried to where she was standing. Beyond the station was the border with its black-shirted guards, pacing up and down. Beyond that was the dark mouth of a tunnel.

There was no-one else on the platform. She had been right. She was the only person on the train. But her fears were gone. She felt lightheaded. Despite knowing she had no money for breakfast, she was irresistibly drawn to the cafe. As she got closer she could hear the murmur of voices and slowly but surely, she became aware of a delicious smell of hot chocolate. She almost cried out. The thing she wanted most in the world at this moment was a bowl of hot, creamy, life-giving chocolate.

There was a thud as two feet hit the platform at a jump behind her, and she turned around to see who it was. She suddenly felt burningly self-conscious. The driver was tall and sandy haired, with a wide mouth and brown eyes that some instinct told her she must avoid at all costs.

She turned back to the steamy windows of the cafe. There were little holes where the bodies inside had brushed against the glass. Through them she could see the plumes of steam curling from the bowls of creamy brown chocolate.

'Why are you standing outside?'

Cia turned towards the voice and met the eyes. Oh dear. She couldn't conceive of lying. 'I haven't got any money,' she said, in Italian.

He looked at her squarely, for a moment. 'I'll treat you,' he said.

She hesitated. She couldn't stop her eyes straying to his shoulders, his arms, his chest, even his crotch. He was huge and strong and manly. He was a vision of loveliness. He really was. The immediate thought of sex in those arms was almost better than hot chocolate.

Behind him, the train and the mountain suddenly came into focus, and she had the strangest feeling that if she accepted his offer her life would take an entirely different path than it had followed so far. God, she was tired and hungry.

'Come on,' he said, and he walked around her to the cafe door. He was just as impressive from the back.

She followed him. The workmen inside looked around at her slowly, like cows do in a field, and went back to the serious business of breakfast. Some of them knew Giordano, as the train driver was called, and they said hello. Cia felt safe and warm. There was nothing threatening at all about the workmen; just the opposite in fact. They were strength personified. Nothing could harm her here.

Giordano, on the other hand, standing in front of her at the counter, threatened her in the sweetest possible way. She dreaded speaking to him. She was frightened she might tell him she wanted to fuck him. She looked at his broad back, his long legs and his exquisite derrière, and her knees literally wobbled. What was it, she thought, about a particular arrangement of bone and muscle that could turn you to jelly? And then she realised she must be suffering from sleep deprivation.

She followed him and the two bowls of chocolate he carried to the table in the far corner of the room. It was the cosiest, warmest, most intimate of corners. Cia sank on the bench seat happily.

'So,' he said, 'what are you doing on the mail train?'

Cia presented herself as a traveller who had fallen foul of villains. At the mention of the Fascist rally he studied her so hard she felt she had to elaborate.

'I wasn't there because I like Mussolini.'

'What are your politics?' he asked her quietly.

'I don't get excited about politics as a rule,' she replied.

'You're a fool if you think you can be apolitical in today's world,' he said. His brown eyes scorned her.'But then you are a woman, so you have something of an excuse.'

His hands were beautiful very big and strong. The sort of hands you could imagine holding a gun or your breasts.

'What has being a woman got to do with it?' she asked.

'Well, you aren't really encouraged to think about the wider world outside the domestic environment. So I think you have an excuse for not understanding the importance of politics. But once you realise that politics is going to affect your whole life, then you are a fool if you ignore it,' he said.

'Is this the price of my chocolate, then?' she asked. 'A lecture?'

He shrugged but he didn't say anything.

'Are you a communist?' she asked.

'If I were,' he said, *sottovoce*, 'I couldn't answer that question, could I?'

As he spoke, he leaned across the table. He was so close she could see that his skin was very clear. His teeth were beautiful too.

There was something really exciting about coming across a communist survivor by chance. The Fascists had sent most of them to jail without proper trials.

'It's not fair,' she said petulantly. 'You are a complete stranger to me and I've told you about myself but you won't even tell me one thing.'

'You are no stranger,' he said.

His words cut straight through the thin veil that comprised her defences. Under the table her thighs parted involuntarily. God, his eyes were so dark and shiny they seemed to reflect your own self back at you.

The cafe door opened with a clatter. Two Blackshirts strutted in.

'Do you have a passport?' asked Giordano.

She nodded and, to her surprise, he hailed them as if they were friends.

Her heart beat faster as she handed over her passport

to the Fascist. But she felt absolutely safe in Giordano's hands, as if he had become her friend in a matter of minutes and she was protected by a quiet strength and intelligence.

The Blackshirt handed her passport back and wished her a safe journey.

She suddenly felt too warm and she slipped Grandma's knitted cardigan from her shoulders. Her linen dress was sleeveless. The bodice swept across her breast and buttoned high at the neck. She picked up the steaming bowl of chocolate again and drank. When she looked up Giordano was studying her arms.

'Tell me about your home,' he said, pushing away his empty chocolate bowl. 'Tell me everything.' He rested his chin on one brown hand and studied her face.

She found herself wanting to.

'I have my own house on the Isle of Wight,' she began. 'But to be honest, it's a weight round my neck. It was beautiful when my grandma was young and I'd like it to be beautiful again. But she never had any money and I haven't any either, so it's in a bad state of repair. It's called Finnemore, like me. My great grandmother's husband built it as a kind of birdcage for her to go quietly mad in and die so he could spend the rest of her inheritance up in London.'

'She didn't go mad and die,' said Giordano, smiling.

'She didn't. She fell in love and had my grandmother, illegitimately. She started a long line of bastards, in fact, of which I am the latest.'

Giordano grinned. 'Are you going to follow the family tradition?'

'There's no money to bring it up on,' she said dismissively.

'What will you do when you get home?' he asked.

'Get a job,' she said gloomily. 'Something like housekeeping.' She didn't want to talk about it. 'Look, I'm no saint. I hate working.'

'You're not a saint?' he asked playfully.

'No,' she said. It came out sexily, despite trying to dampen it a bit.

'What are you?' he asked, leaning forward.

'Just a human being,' she said, rather cleverly, she thought.

'Might you be a sinner?' he asked.

Underneath her skin, under her navel, a quiver began and travelled down over the mound of her belly to her sex. How pleasant, she thought, not to have an erection to cope with.

'How do you plan to feed yourself on the journey back to England?' he asked, breaking the spell.

'I'll manage,' she said in a small voice. She didn't want to move. She didn't want the spell broken.

'You're very vulnerable,' he warned. 'Without money – '

'I've already found that out,' she sighed.

He looked as if he was going to ask how but then clearly thought better of it. She had the urge to tell him that she was aroused by the thought of having sex for money. Something stopped her. Common sense.

'Do you have a standard ticket to England?' he asked, leaning back in his chair.

'Yes' she replied, wondering why he was asking.

'Come home with me,' he said. 'I'll pay you to keep house for me for a while. I need to finish some work without interruption and it would be a great help not to have to do the household chores.'

And sleeping together? she wondered. Perhaps she would get whoredom with housekeeping duties. Why, it would be just like being someone's wife. The idea of being his woman made her womb churn. If it didn't work, she could pick up any train.

'Do you live in Italy or Switzerland?' she asked.

'Just in Switzerland,' he said. 'Beyond the next mountain.'

The sound of the train whistle blasted into the warm,

steamy room and there was a scraping of chairs as the workmen got up.

'I won't commit myself to a long stay but . . . but I will come,' she said softly.

The smile he gave her made her feel she'd done the right thing.

Outside a whole new day had begun; a perfect day with blue sky and sunshine. The day and the decision almost took her breath away.

Giordano closed the cafe door behind them and waved to the new driver. He took hold of her hand and helped her back on to the train.

'He'll drop us off,' he said.

The train pulled past the border and into the tunnel. As the darkness enclosed them, his voice became rich and desirous. Cia could feel it vibrating in her belly as he spoke. She knew she would be at the mercy of that voice before long. His warm, hard thigh was next to hers. A dim light, fixed into the dripping wet, black wall of the tunnel, loomed over their heads and briefly illuminated the contours of his face.

'I'm glad you are coming to stay with me,' he said. 'I want to find out much more about you, human being. The minute I saw you I thought – I want to kiss that woman. I haven't felt like that for a long time.'

The train burst out of the tunnel and Cia swallowed loudly.

The train drew to a halt on a stretch of track before the next tunnel. She took the hand he offered to help her down. Just the touch of his fingertips made her sex glow.

Few people she knew would understand why she had taken a risk like this with a complete stranger. It was absolutely barmy. Still, she thought, what's the point in living if you don't take risks?

It was a twenty minute walk up a path that sloped gently around the mountain they had just travelled through. It was as close as it could be to the border.

'I wonder about your name. It sounds Italian or Spanish,' he said.

'Wonder away,' she returned.

'Tell me about yourself, woman. Don't play the coquette,' he said sharply.

Surprised at his change in tone, Cia said, 'It's Italian.'

'But you are English?' he asked.

'Yes,' she said. 'My father was Italian. But I was brought up by my English grandmother in England.' She looked at him. The mountain was behind him again. He was a bit mountainous himself. Rock-like. He strode along at a good pace and she had a job keeping up with him.

'So, have you been to visit your relations?' he asked her.

'I suppose you could say that,' she said. 'Except they didn't want me there and the visit was very short. I was thrown out.'

'I suppose you can't pick who you're related to. I'll pay you forty Swiss francs a week. Is that a fair rate?'

'I don't know,' said Cia. 'It doesn't sound like much.' It was equivalent to about fifteen shillings.

'You'll get fed,' he said. 'It's really all I can afford. I have to send my wife and son a good part of my earnings.'

The word 'wife' stung Cia like a giant wasp and she stopped in her tracks, face to face with her own bloody foolishness.

'They're in France,' he continued, stopping too. He looked at her sideways.

What was his game then? Cia was so angry that he hadn't told her before they left the train, she could have slapped him. She was also scared. He'd trapped her. God knows what else he was capable of!

'What's the English expression?' he asked. 'Penny for your thoughts?'

You wouldn't want to know, you bastard, she thought.

'You wish I'd told you about a wife before we left the station, don't you?' he said.

'Yes.'

'You wouldn't have come.'

She looked at him, realising that he wanted her so badly he was prepared to go to desperate lengths. It was flattering.

'I wouldn't,' she said, and carried on walking. Why should she let him off lightly?

His house was a solitary chalet at the foot of the mountain. It looked welcoming enough. She liked the blue door. But the real beauty of it became apparent as they climbed the slope that led to the door. The lake beyond spread out in front of them; glass-smooth and pine-fringed.

He opened the door and led her into a cavernous ground floor, in the midst of which was a boat having its hull cleaned.

'I moved the boat in when my wife and son moved out,' he said.

'I could help you with that.' She had forgotten to be angry with him.

He gave her that smile again.

Bastard, she thought. Why did he have such a nice smile?

There was a kitchen at the far end of the ground floor, screened off. He opened shutters on to the lake beyond. The last of the morning mist was drifting away from its surface into the trees and mountains on the far shore.

She had an unfathomable feeling of happiness. She wanted to sleep with him and see life through his eyes. That was the truth. She watched him open the door of a stove. There were a few embers still glowing in it, and he filled it with wood from a stack by its side.

'You can have a bath. Come upstairs.'

Hot water pipes shone brassy gold and weaved like snakes from the wall to the free-standing bath.

'I put it in,' he said proudly.

Cia couldn't think of anything she would rather do than take a bath right at that moment. He turned on the faucets and hot, steaming water gushed out into the gleaming white enamel.

They left the bath to run. His study was piled with papers and books. In the midst of all the piles was a desk, clear except for a typewriter. She followed him behind another set of screens. There was a big bed and a smaller one next to each other. He opened the bedroom shutters and the fantastic view of the lake appeared again. But this time Cia's eye was drawn to the soft toy on the child's bed.

'I'll make some coffee,' he said, and he turned and went downstairs.

Cia peeled off her clothes in the bathroom as the steam drifted around and went sailing out of the window. It was glorious to be naked, knowing he was downstairs.

She stepped into the warm water and took up the soap and washed her body and her hair.

Could she become a mistress? It would be temporary; on the way to wherever life sent her next. Yes, she could. Should she sleep with another woman's husband though? No, she shouldn't.

Would she though? She felt detached, as if fate, not she, must decide. She knew she had it in her to be a bad, bad woman. Didn't all women?

She stepped out of the bath a little while later, on to the bare boards, and wrapped herself in the towel that hung over a straight-backed chair. There was a book on the chair. She picked it up. It was a volume by Karl Marx. Nothing could have been less likely reading material for her but she noticed a couple of lines inside underlined with a pencil. She struggled with the German. It wasn't her strongest language by any means.

Philosophers have only interpreted the world in various ways; the point is to change it.

Mmm, she thought, a man of action.

She opened her travelling bag. Inside, the silk wrap was crushed to nothing. She pulled it out and it sprang into shape, the way silk does. Where will I sleep? she wondered. In the child's bed? It would be good to decide to do that, even if the decision was wrested away from her. She put her bag at the bottom of it.

Out on the lake a single rowing boat with one fisherman in it was floating faraway. Suddenly she saw Giordano stand up in the water, close to the shore where the pines leant over the lake. She waited, almost holding her breath, for him to wade out. The ache in her to see him naked was so strong it cut through everything.

But she was disappointed. He dived again and swam to a spot behind the trees that was out of her sight, then emerged after what seemed like an age, wearing trousers.

Cia slipped her feet into the slits of her velvet travel slippers and descended the stairs.

'Come and have some eggs,' he called.

It was dim in the kitchen. The brightness was all beyond the window.

'Pretty slippers,' he commented.

She didn't reply. All men, she mused, like Chinese women. All men think women can make an art out of slavery.

He placed a plate of scrambled eggs on the big table and took the loaf of golden bread off the stove where it had been keeping warm. He sliced tomatoes cleanly with a sharp knife and dribbled olive oil over them. Their redness made her ravenous.

Cia plunged into the plate of eggs. He sat down with his back to the window. She couldn't help looking at his mouth as he chewed his food. It was such a lovely, sensual mouth.

After eating, when they were drinking coffee, he spoke. 'You look lovely, human being, all fresh from the bath.'

'I saw you in the lake,' she said. You looked lovely too, she thought. She could feel her sex opening; wanting him.

He took a sip of his coffee. 'Will I get my wish? Will I kiss you?'

She summoned all her willpower. 'I'm not sure I ought to kiss a married man.'

'You haven't heard the whole story yet,' he said, leaning forward in his chair.

'I'm not sure I want to.' She got up and put the dirty dishes in the sink.

He turned round to look at her. She could feel the caress of his admiration as his eyes lingered. He looked so hungry for her. It was a delicious look. She felt her knees giving way.

He stood up, trapping her by the sink.

'I wouldn't have asked you to come here if I wasn't free to do so. My relationship with my wife is over. We have separated,' he said.

Oh really, thought Cia. What she thought showed plainly on her face. Her dark eyebrows went up into the lines of cynicism on her forehead.

'You don't believe me!' he exclaimed. He sounded amazed. 'Ha!' he snorted, and he slung his coffee cup on the draining board. 'I've got work to do.' He got to the other side of the table and stopped. 'If you walk around the lake shore to the village you'll be able to get some meat for our dinner. There's dried pasta in the cupboard.' He took some coins out of his pocket and put them down on the table. 'Here's some money. Turn right outside the house and follow the path around the lake. You'll find it. Go soon.'

With that he went upstairs. Almost immediately, Cia heard the typewriter start clicking. Round one to me, she thought. She could barely breathe.

But she hadn't bargained on how long she would have to wait for round two. When the kitchen was clean, she took the money and started out for the village. Although it was a tiny village she discovered a telegraph agency in the bar. The barkeeper allowed her to send a telegram on a promise of payment after she told him where she was staying. She wrote to Plomer, asking for money, just in case.

When she got back, Giordano was hard at work.

'Can I go to sleep for a while?' she asked him. She felt a bit stupid asking, but as he didn't even hear her, her embarrassment was short-lived. She lay down on the child's bed and listened to the typewriter.

She woke up much later and looked at the time. It was seven. She was hungry. She dressed and asked him if he wanted dinner soon. Once again he didn't seem to hear her. She decided to make it anyway.

She cooked a very basic dinner of pasta with garlic and olive oil, followed by a thin steak and a salad.

This time, when she called to him he yelled, 'Coming!'

If I ever do get married, she thought, I must remember that smells work better than words.

'That was delicious,' said Giordano, when he had finished eating. He drank a glass of wine as he watched her picking up the plates and putting them in the sink.

She could feel him again. This time she didn't confront him. She longed for him to reach out and demand, in some way, that they make love. She wouldn't be able to put up any resistance this time.

'The future is female, I think,' he said.

She turned to look at him. He was frowning with concentration. 'What do you mean?' she asked.

'Women will run things in the end when communism wins out. There will be women in power for the first time. It won't happen if Fascism wins the fight. Fascism is anti-female.'

'Does there have to be a winner?' she asked. 'Can't Fascism and communism live side by side?'

'Fascism is a vile extremity of capitalism. Communism and capitalism are mutually exclusive.'

'That's what we were taught at school,' said Cia. 'Grandma thought so too.'

'I thought you had no interest in politics,' he argued.

'I don't,' she replied, taking a cigarette out of her packet.

'But you're not entirely ignorant of them,' he said.

She lit the cigarette and blew smoke in a plume towards the ceiling. Then she fixed him with a look of pure contempt.

Girodano stood up. For a moment he held her in suspense. One move on his part and she would be his in a whirl of clothes. She could almost hear them ripping.

'Back to work,' he said ruefully, and he left her.

While Cia cleaned up, she planned the food for the next day. She wandered around and looked at the boat. She went out of the back door and down to the lake. The sun was low in the cloudless sky – soon it would set. She wished he were by her side right now. She walked along the lake shore a little way but the pines barred her path, their trunks close together and forbidding. So she made her way back to the house and up the stairs.

He was reading some typed pages.

'Would you like some more wine?' she asked.

No answer.

Cia poured herself one and poured him one anyway. He said thank you, at least, when she put it on the desk beside him. On the way downstairs she took the volume of Marx from the bathroom. She struggled with it for what seemed like hours under the low lightbulb in the kitchen. When she gave up and went to bed he was still working.

The next day she got an advance on her wages and went down to the village and paid the bartender his fee for the telegram. She got food and went back to the house. Giordano worked all day, breaking only for lunch. He virtually ignored her. She gave up on the thesis and German and hunted for an Italian or an English book.

Finally she came across Ernest Hemingway and promptly went to sleep.

She awoke with a stiff neck and went for a walk by the lake. Under the clear blue water there were fish swimming around. She searched for a fishing rod and found one by the boat. But the stringing up of the thing was so fiddly she got impatient and threw it down in disgust. By the time Giordano appeared for the dinner she had cooked, she was so fed up that she planned on leaving as soon as either her money came through or he paid her – whichever was the sooner. To hell with him. She would go mad with boredom if she stayed any longer.

He sat down and looked at her and smiled his lovely smile. 'I've broken the back of it,' he said. 'Would you like to go visiting this evening?'

Chapter Six

Giordano put some typed sheets and a torch for their return journey into a canvas bag. They took the track almost to the village but veered off to the left before they got there and climbed a steep path up and back down again towards an arm of the lake. They reached a big stone house surrounded by a high wall. Giordano put his hand through the tall iron gate and unlatched it. Inside the grounds was a dense, dark, unkempt forest of pines. The fallen trees made strange shapes in the undergrowth.

A tall, plump man of about 35 opened the old door. He seemed delighted to see both of them. He had kind eyes, with lots of laughter wrinkles around them.

'It's been a bit morbid here, just myself and Auburn – and she's very gloomy,' he said, as he stepped back into the big hallway.

It was cheerful inside: brightly lit and painted. Tellino, Giordano's friend, led them to the back of the house to a huge kitchen crammed full of utensils and general living paraphernalia. Sunlight still dappled the walls and danced on the big old table in the centre of it. The windows were open and there was the lake, in a different aspect, beyond a roughly cut lawn and a sunken garden grown wild.

The three of them sat around the table and Tellino opened a bottle of dark, red wine that tasted delicious. 'Have you brought me the latest?' he asked Giordano.

'Yes.' Giordano took the papers he was carrying out of the canvas bag.

Cia looked around. Her gaze alighted on a red velvet pouch on the floor under the table, looking as if it had fallen. She thought about it for a long while before she picked it up. Inside she felt two round things that made a little clicking sound as they bounced together. There was a strange feel to them, as if they were weighted and the weights made them jolt and move of their own accord.

Tellino looked up, noticed what she was holding, and grinned like a naughty little boy. 'Take them out,' he said. 'Oh do. I made them.'

Cia did as she was told, albeit hesitantly. She was suspicious. She held up the two porcelain balls by the string that held them together. They clicked.

'What do you think?' asked Tellino earnestly, looking from Giordano to Cia and back again.

'What are they?' the two of them asked simultaneously.

'They are a toy. A woman's toy. She inserts them into her vagina and they give her the most exquisite pleasure when she walks.'

Cia blushed to the roots of her hair and dropped the balls on the table.

'They're not a new invention,' continued Tellino. 'They're an ancient Chinese idea. I made them up after one of the girls told me about them. Oh dear. Are you upset? Good God, you're not a virgin are you, dear?' Giordano seemed amused. Cia glared at him. 'Oh Giordano,' continued Tellino, 'she's shocked. You mean to say you didn't tell her about this place before you brought her here? He didn't, did he, dear? He has a mean streak, you know.'

'No!' protested Giordano. 'I don't. I didn't even –'

'Oh shut up, you oaf,' said Tellino. He was looking at Cia quizzically. 'This is my fleshpot. We entertain. We give sex parties. We have a big party coming up from Milan next week. But I draw the line at virgins. If you are a virgin you can't have a job. I say, lose your bloody hymen elsewhere. My girls are all experts.' He paused. His voice went up an octave. 'Giordano, who is this woman? Why are we having this conversation? Giordano?'

'I met Cia on the train,' said Giordano, matter of factly. 'She had been robbed and she had no money, so I gave her a job as my housekeeper. I brought her up to visit you because she was bored but I suppose she might be interested in earning some more money . . .'

'Do you want a job?' asked Tellino, filling their glasses again.

'What kind of job?' asked Cia nonchalantly.

'Well, it's whoring dear, of course. Although we could use you as a waitress next week, if you have qualms. But it often turns into the same thing. These people have voracious appetites, dear, so you'd have to be prepared. It's good money. We've all made good money.

'I think I might have a buyer for the house now, Giordano. I'm saving very hard. The twins have gone already, to New York.' Tellino paused. The ticking of an old-fashioned clock clicked through the kitchen. 'In this party from Milan,' he continued, 'there's one man who has expressed interest in someone like me. I'm tempted by the money, but I don't want to do it, really. I want to go to America and live with a woman in a pioneer homestead. I want to be macho, a cowboy. I love horses.'

It was Giordano who burst out laughing. 'Cia, your face is a picture,' he spluttered.

She supposed it was. The thought of a cowboy in the

wild west was so far removed from this ebullient, plump, almost feminine man who sat opposite her.

Tellino was offended. 'Giordano, she doesn't know anything. She makes me feel freakish when she looks at me like that.'

'Tellino has spent a lot of his life being studied like a freak,' said Giordano.

'I'm sorry,' said Cia. 'I didn't mean any offence.'

'No, I don't suppose you did,' said Tellino. His voice had grown much more serious.

'Why?' she asked softly, wanting to know but not daring to say. She looked him in the eye.

'Do you really want to know? Well, that's something,' he said.

'I think you should tell as many people who ask,' said Giordano, and he got up. 'I'm going to take Auburn a glass of wine.'

'I was mutilated in the name of God,' began Tellino, when Giordano had gone. 'By a group of obscenely powerful clergy who still believe that women should not be allowed to sing in church. I am a castrato.

'They are still doing it. No-one stops them. Italy still has people so poor that they sell their children into that kind of slavery. It's illegal and most people are disgusted by the idea. But I know it still happens.

'I was six years old – the younger the boy, the higher his voice, you understand, and the higher the note, the more it is prized.

'I was drugged with opium and submerged in a very hot bath until I was insensible. The ducts that lead to my testicles were severed so that eventually my testicles shrivelled and disappeared. I'm not a eunuch. I still have a penis.

'Under the covers of history there have always been castrati. Casanova loved castrati. He wrote how majestic and voluptuous we are. He also said that holy Rome makes men into pederasts while denying the effects of the illusion which it strives to create. A moot point, I think.

'I ran away, eventually, after years of disciplined training. I just ran. I was fifteen and I was sick of being used by my tutor. I sang in Bologna for a while but I started drinking. In the end, I prostituted myself and I lived on the streets. Then the man who owned this house found me and I was saved. He was homosexual too but he was an exceptional human being. For the first time in my life I learned what it was to love someone, to make love rather than to take abuse. He took me over, completely, in the most gentle of ways. He spent a fortune on my psychoanalysis. It wasn't only me he helped either. I was his love but he collected abused people and helped them get their lives back. He was a true philanthropist.

'When he died, he left me this house. There were quite a few of us living here then and there was enough money to live on for a little while but it dwindled away and we had to do something. So we turned the place into a house of sex. There are plenty of rich people who will pay for something they think is exclusive. That's why they become rich, so they can indulge tastes that the great mass of people outlaw.

'We made a pact though, that we would never again allow ourselves or anyone else we worked with to be abused. No exploitation! That was our rule. Very communist!'

He stood up and stretched. Then he beckoned Cia to the door that led into the garden.

'See the pool, there?' he said.

She could see a pond, with tall rushes growing by its banks. In the middle, on an island, were naked statues. They were too distant to see in detail.

He walked out of the house and Cia followed.

'Imagine,' he continued, 'up to forty or fifty naked bodies fucking the breath out of each other in the mud on the shore; imagine them running through the forest, doing it up against trees like nymphs and satyrs.

'We had a party of men and women once, who just hired the place, like a hotel, without any requests for sexual services. They really were fascinating, most unusual. The usual is a group of men who hire girls, and sometimes boys. They mostly want to all fuck the same woman. Heaven knows why! I think it creates a bond between them. Germans and Swiss do that rather a lot. Italians tend to be a little more sophisticated.

'The mixed group were Italian. They seemed at first to be having a conventional picnic, just like any group of friends. I suppose they were in their thirties and forties, quite young, all married couples. They ate the picnic fully dressed and drank a lot of wine. Then one of the men undid the buttons of his wife's blouse. He didn't fondle her breasts. He just undid the buttons. I remember it was a pale green blouse. As soon as she moved, her breasts were exposed and everyone stared at her. I really didn't know if it was planned or if it shocked the other people in the party. She lay down on the grass and her blouse fell open. Then the woman next to her took her blouse right off. Then another one did it and then one woman took off everything.

'The men were still clothed while the women lay around like wonderful Venuses, absolutely beautiful in their nakedness.

'I thought they might be naturists but then a man, not her husband, began caressing the breasts of the woman with the green blouse. His wife was watching him and she was trembling, whether with anger or arousal I couldn't tell at this point, but then she reached for the swell in her husband's trousers and started caressing him. After a minute or two he began to caress the other woman's legs, sliding his hands up her skirt. He bared the tops of her stockings and pulled down her knickers and took out his sex. Everyone watched as he fucked her.

'When they had finished she told everyone she wanted another man and she spread her legs and played with her sex invitingly. One of the other men left his wife and fucked her too.

'She seemed as if she was in a state of dazed happiness. But she wanted another and another. The woman who had encouraged her husband in the beginning turned on him and started pummelling him with her fists and screaming. I was terrified.

'I was hiding behind a tree some way from where they were and I feared they might end up killing each other. I'd almost made up my mind to step in on some pretext when another man prized the tormented wife away and took her apart from the others to fuck her passionately.

'It went on like that, with the gradual inclusion of everyone in the web of sex and emotion. I admired the way they did it. There were such extremes of emotion being explored but they seemed to triumph as a group in the end. It went on all day and half the night. We just fed them! The next morning they upped and left in their cars like ordinary bourgeois couples. They seemed very friendly with each other.

'Of course, we get a good deal of ritualised behaviour too. I sometimes think it might be better transformed by good psychoanalysis. But, it paid the expenses. Imagine, Cia, being able to do exactly what you want with someone who is entirely at your disposal!'

Cia was aroused. The stories of latterday nymphs and satyrs in the overgrown woods brought out a lust she had always felt when she was close to woods. The smell of the soft earth underfoot and here, in the last of the sunlight where they stood, the overgrown grasses, wet with evening dew licking her legs, were powerful aphrodisiacs. But she prayed he wouldn't ask her what exactly she would do with a sex slave of her very own. She wouldn't know what to say. The sex she wanted at present was with Giordano. Oh yes, she could see him, naked on the pine needles by the lake. She could see, in her mind's eye, him fucking her on the sweet-smelling earth, but she didn't want to tell Tellino.

He seemed content to let her imagine and not say. After a few moments, he said, 'We've reached the end now. All you see before you is about to disappear, like Atlantis; like Europe come to that. Europe is becoming a dangerous place for people like me. Giordano is a hero. He risks his life disseminating anti-Fascist information. I'm not made of that kind of mettle. I think America is the place for me.'

When they got back Giordano was sitting with an old woman with violent red hair who was eating soup. She sneered at Cia. Cia didn't think it was personal – the woman looked extremely unhappy.

'He can't wait to get rid of me,' she growled. She was looking at Tellino but her remarks were plainly about him, not to him.

'When will I be rid of you then?' asked Tellino, as if it was a tiresome detail.

'As soon as Herr Hansmeyer comes for me,' said Auburn.

'But he's not coming, Auburn dear. Why don't you face it? He's got you out of Germany and out of danger. His conscience is clear. He has no intention of keeping any promises he might have made. . .'

'You've said all this before!' cried Auburn.

And then, to Cia's horror, the woman burst into loud, heartfelt tears.

'That's better,' said Tellino smugly.

'Why do you do this to me in front of a complete stranger?' screamed Auburn.

'I didn't do anything!' squealed Tellino.

She's right though, thought Cia. The scene was very uncomfortable; freakish in some way. 'Perhaps it would be better if I wasn't here. Shall I go and look around the house?'

It sounded pathetic. But Auburn shot her a grateful glance.

'I'll show you,' said Giordano.

'Take her to the ladies room,' said Tellino, and he sparkled with mischief.

As Giordano closed the door behind them, the sound of raised, angry voices exploded within.

'What's the matter with that woman?' Cia asked.

They crossed the hallway to a door with gold lettering on it.

Giordano turned the handle and went in. Following him, Cia caught sight of a little china plaque on the door in the shape of a woman. She thought at first that it was an ordinary ladies powder room sign. But on a second look she realised it wasn't. The figure had her little porcelain skirt raised up high – showing a perfectly moulded miniature vagina.

'She narrowly escaped execution in Germany,' said Giordano. 'She's a herbalist – a witch, if you like. She performed an abortion for this Hansmeyer's wife. One of the things Hitler has done in his first few months of power has been the outlawing of abortion. But he hasn't just outlawed it. He has been executing abortionists.'

The room was quite dark because the curtains were drawn but there was a strange fire burning in the grate. It looked artificial. Giordano padded across the room and switched on the standard lamp next to the fireplace.

'There's pure evil abroad in Germany,' he said. 'Over 56,000 people designated unfit have been sterilised.'

'What kind of unfit people?' asked Cia.

'Handicapped people,' said Giordano. 'The mentally ill, the people they see as freaks . . .'

'Tellino's people,' said Cia quietly.

Giordano nodded.

One heard things differently, she thought, from a distance. In Italy, the measures Hitler took to build a strong nation were considered rational, even laudable. The details were missing though, weren't they? The story was warped. Leaving out the grubby little facts of murder and abuse, you got quite a pretty picture of a wholesome country. She suddenly felt like crying.

'Look at this,' said Giordano. He beckoned her over. His left hand was touching the carving on the lamp stand. It was smooth ebony. 'Touch it.'

Cia touched it. She stroked it, her finger following the carving of two slender bodies entwined. As her eye travelled up she saw how the carving changed and the stem of the lamp became bulbous like onions, except. . .

Cia looked closer. She ran her hand upward until she felt exactly what it was. She looked up into the gleam of the lamp. It was magnificent. A curving ebony phallus bathed in electric light, so lifelike it made her mouth water. The switch to turn it on and off was a ruby ring on a smooth white bakelite hand, which clasped the exquisite, ebony tip.

Giordano was watching her hand. He reached out for her waist.

She moved back.

It was enough to stop him being physical. 'Let me?' he pleaded.

'You belong to someone else.' She said it quietly. She was still holding the ebony prick in her hand.

'I don't belong to anyone,' he replied. 'I really don't. It's such a waste for us not to . . . We shall always feel sad if we don't. I know it. I can't explain why.' He stopped talking and touched her face, stroking her chin. 'One day the Fascists will lock me away. I want to be able to remember you naked. You are so beautiful.'

The intensity of his touch travelled through her whole body. Even though his fingers were only on her chin, they reached into her womb and churned it. Her sex opened and her senses filled with the sight of his sweet brown eyes. Take me, she thought. Do it roughly. Don't ask. Take me by force so that I have no responsibility. Don't let me choose because I have chosen not to. If you kissed me now against my will, I would be released from a moral dilemma.

His hand dropped to her collar as if he was going to pull her to him or rip her bodice. She was breathing hard. Her breasts were heaving. She knew it but she couldn't stop. She stayed stock still, not meeting his eyes. She knew that all she had to do was lift her chin and he would take it as a sign of acquiescence and kiss her. She pressed the ruby and switched off the phallic light.

'I can't have you, can I, Cia?' he said, in the gloom. 'You won't bend.' She put the light on again and looked at him. 'Is it a moral dilemma for you? Does it come down to good or bad?' he asked.

'Yes,' said Cia, feeling unsure of herself. Why shouldn't it come down to good or bad, she wondered?

'What a nice, simple view of life. Is God going to cast you into hell if you break the sanctity of marriage?'

'Not exactly,' replied Cia huffily. 'But if I do this to your wife, I think fate will pay me back one day.'

'You need have no worries about hurting my wife,' he said. He paused for a moment, turning his back on her. When he spoke again he leaned on the mantelpiece. 'My wife has a lover. She went to France with my son, to be with him. She had been unhappy for some time. I thought I was everything to her, but I was mistaken. She wanted to have an affair. So she has gone to have one.' The bitterness of his tone was frightening. But a door opened in Cia's breast. Yes. She could have him. Yes.

'Does the truth make a difference?' he asked.

'Of course it does,' she said, smiling at him gently.

'How?'

'Well, you are free.'

'I don't want sympathy.'

'Why not?'

'Can't you imagine why not? A man doesn't want a woman on the basis of her sympathy.'

'Sympathy isn't the only thing I feel for you.'

'Hmmm.' He was still keeping his distance.

Cia was damned if she was going to say anything

more. His pride was obviously hurt but she had her own.

'I ought to see if Tellino has finished the proofreading,' he said, and left the room.

A few minutes later Cia tripped over the rug by the fireplace and it was only then that she realised she had been pacing the room.

She knelt down to pull the curled, silky fur of the rug straight again. It was an animal. Alive, it had been a polar bear and had lumbered through Arctic wastes but now its yellowed fur and the skin on its underbelly were frozen in time. Its black eyes stared motionless from its highjacked head. Its teeth were bared in a final snarl.

Cia picked up one of its flat haunches and was about to turn it when she saw its great polar prick. It was stuffed to perfection and it bounced, rampant. It was quite beautiful. She was curious to see how it was stitched to the hide and she grasped it in order to have a look. No stitching was evident.

She turned the whole rug over. The neck stretched back, the whiter fur of its throat stretching back in deathly agony and ecstasy. Had anyone fucked it, she wondered? A woman? One of the ladies using the ladies room? How had she done it? With a lover by her side, watching her and encouraging her?

The orange, even flames in the fireplace licked at the deep black chimney inside. The inner edge of the fire surround was lighter and reddish. Up above the chimney there was a hood sculpted in plaster; a red cape-like moulding almost like a pair of –

With a start, she suddenly realised that she was looking at a huge pair of labia. The outer rim was painted brown and the plaster was moulded to look like curls. She slid back on the floor and looked at the whole thing. It was true. The fire burned at the heart of a detailed, plaster vagina.

The room suddenly took on a new dimension. She looked around it, searching for other sexual objects.

The couch was covered in harlequin diamond shapes. She touched the fabric. Each diamond was hand-stitched to its neighbour with fine, silk stitching.

There was a book lying open on a table. She picked it up and looked at the title: *The Sexual Ritual of Prehistory*. She read the open page:

> *... and the craven idol most common in this supremely phallic civilisation stood tall within the circle, towering and rampant in stone and they came to that place at nightfall and performed seminal libations of repeated masturbation and communal sodomy.*
>
> *The high priest concluded the ceremony by passing on the fluid of life to a young neophyte ...*

She put the book down, not daring to read further. As her fingertips brushed the harlequin fabric of the couch, they encountered an orgy of textures – smooth satin, brittle brocade, rough chambric, cretonne and sweet, soft velvet. There seemed to be an order to the pattern but every time she thought she could see it, she was tricked by a slight difference in one of the comparisons.

Nestling at the other end of the couch was a pair of red satin cushions. Where the body of one met the other along a dark red line of intimacy, a tiny, stuffed, prick stabbed a tiny, stump-work vagina. The cushions were fucking each other!

She looked closer. They were! She sprawled across the couch and took one in each hand and pulled them apart a little, then a little more and a little more. The tiny prick popped out. On its tip was a cluster of tiny, tiny sequins, like frozen, fluid gems. The vagina in the other cushion was stitched into a slit in the seam. It was small but perfectly formed, its red labia open in anticipation of sex. She gently put the two together again and replaced them.

As she put her hand on the arm of the couch to straighten up, one of the harlequin panels gave way and something sprang up under her, wedging itself between her thighs. Cia lifted her skirt. Another prick! Yellow satin this time. She opened her legs a little and it sprang up. God! It looked like she had a prick!

She giggled. She had never really liked stuffed toys, but this was irresistible!

She wriggled a bit to get it into a nicer position, close to her clitoris. Her vagina was veiled by the silk of her best underwear. She closed her thighs and dropped her skirt. It was hilarious – there was a tent in her lap! – but it aroused her, much to her perplexity. She glanced at the door. Freud says we're all supposed to want one of these, she thought. Maybe he's right. To have one, just for a day, and to see what it felt like to get an erection, was an idea that held a fascination for her. I wouldn't want the rest of manhood though, she thought. I like being a woman.

The door clicked, interrupting her thoughts. She reached hurriedly for the secret harlequin as Tellino walked in, carrying a bottle of champagne.

'Caught you!' he said, grinning and pointing at her crotch. 'Do you like it? We had a lady novelist here once a few years ago. She called that couch "The Liberator".'

Cia pressed the harlequin panel and the prick retracted slowly, brushing against her sex and driving her wild.

'You blush so easily, it's quite charming,' Tellino said. 'Do you like my room? I did most of it myself, except the cushions. They were the bearded lady's. They taught her to do stump-work at charity school. I don't expect the nuns dreamed what she was going to do with it!' Cia laughed. 'That's better. Let's have some champagne,' he said. 'For some reason I feel like drinking champagne all night.'

Chapter Seven

Sometime later Cia and Giordano staggered out into the dark night air. Tellino stood in the doorway, swaying, and watched them to the gate where Giordano waved the torch to signal goodbye.

For a while they didn't speak. Up above, the stars were so close they seemed like a sparkling blanket. The moon was waxing and low in the sky. Below their feet the earth of the track was soft and dark.

The village lights became visible down below as they rounded the mountain. There were only one or two lights. It was very late.

With her gaze on the village, Cia missed her footing and almost fell. Giordano caught her. There was no real danger but he fussed over her as if there were. He took her hand and didn't let go.

Cia felt so happy with her hand resting in his, she thought she might feel happier than she ever had before. The strength of her feelings for him was as mysterious as the night. Why? She had no idea.

When they were almost home, Giordano said, 'Let's go down by the lake.'

He didn't wait for her to say yes. He led her through the edge of the forest to the lake shore. The water lapped on the small strip of beach. He let go of her hand and stared out into the darkness of the water. Somewhere, the wild call of a bird sounded through the night. Giordano hardly seemed aware that he had company.

Cia had the luxury of being able to look at him without being seen. What did she mean to him?

Suddenly, he turned. 'It's late,' he said. 'Let's go in.'

His face was close enough to touch. She was mesmerised by his lips, and her own parted involuntarily.

Her parted lips were too much for him. He looked so vulnerable in that second before their lips met. She responded hungrily; she wanted him so much. They kissed for a long, long time. She touched his hair and then his shoulders for the first time. She felt his hands on her back and she nestled in his arms as he held her tight. There was such an energy about him, she thought she would levitate. Every inch of her wanted him, and she knew his body was hungry for her. It was taut, stretched to the limits of control. She felt she had to tell him that she wanted him. He wanted to hear it, didn't he?

But when she opened her mouth, he put a finger on her lips and stopped her. He led her inside the house to the foot of the stairs.

'Go to bed, Cia,' he said.

It was very difficult not to argue, but some absurd propriety told her to accept his will this time. As she was walking up the stairs, her whole body wanted to turn around and run to him, take him by the hand, lead him up to bed and undress him. But she couldn't. She wouldn't.

Sleep eluded her. She lay naked under the covers in the small bed and listened. Eventually, she heard a chair creak. He was in the kitchen. The chair had creaked, that was all. Would she hear his footsteps on the stair? She willed it. She waited but he didn't come.

The moon was just enough to read the white clockface by. When she had been in bed an hour she was still so aroused she could no more sleep than fly to that moon.

She found herself suddenly thinking about her grandma as she looked at the waning moon. She remembered the summer in Cowes. Sometimes they went down to the gazebo and sat in the dark, with the moon, and chatted.

What shall I do, grandma? she said to the air. 'Grandma, what shall I do? Shall I go downstairs?'

'Of course. What are you waiting for?'

It wasn't exactly a voice that said it. It was more like a spirit removing some prejudice and clearing the way for herself to say it.

She got up quickly, slipped on her robe and Chinese slippers, and combed her hair. It shone glossily dark against her pale skin.

Giordano was not in the study. She went downstairs. He was not in the boat room. She took a deep breath and went into the kitchen – but he was not there either. The back door was open.

Outside there was a chill in the air. She stood at the edge of the yellow pool of light from the kitchen lamp. She could see nothing close. Far away, a slice of light that must have been on the other side of the lake disappeared into blackness. The last of the world had gone to bed.

'Giordano?' she called softly. In reply she heard a splashing sound and a voice. She stepped out into the darkness towards it. 'Giordano?'

'I'm here,' he shouted.

Her eyes got used to the darkness very quickly and she saw his head. The rest of him was underwater.

'I couldn't sleep,' she said, feeling she had to offer some excuse for being outside.

'What's the matter?' he called.

She opened her mouth to tell a lie; something a little girl might say when she is frightened of the bogeyman. But nothing came out. The truth was she was lustful.

Her sex was swollen and her breasts felt ready to burst from her clothes. Her sex dripped on to her thighs. She was a fuckable, fuck-wanting, grown-up woman.

She kicked off her Chinese slippers. She peeled the robe back off her shoulders and let it fall. She stood on the shoreline in the moonlight like some goddess released from a tree. The air on her naked body felt delicious. She exulted in her nakedness.

She waded into the cold, dark water. It shocked her skin and took her breath. She waded until the water was breast-high and then she swam, swift and strong, towards him.

It wasn't deep. Giordano was standing on the bottom. She clung to him like a gentle octopus and wrapped herself around him. She pressed her sex against him and kissed his wet face. She circled him, kissing everything. Finally, his lips – red and open and wet – met hers.

He wrestled with the octopus and tamed her enough to wade out of the water with her white body attached to his, sucking him sweetly. On shore, the water ran down their naked bodies and dripped around their feet. He put her down on her back on a bed of pine needles, and took his towel and rubbed her skin to take away the chill. The friction sent pain mingling with desire through her.

Then he took her breast in his mouth, and whatever was left of her self-control fled under the soft assault of his lips while his hands held her ribs in their strong embrace. She could feel his sex lose its chill, then harden and grow hot next to her body as he kissed her damp belly. The touch of his soft lips acted like the gentlest of levers, somehow prizing her legs apart. His fingers reached inside her opening cunt and searched. She moved on his hand, pushing her clitoris into the softness of his wrist where his pulse beat. The honey inside her poured all over him.

In the hiatus between his hand melting away and his sex penetrating her, Cia heard an animal rustle in the forest somewhere and the tiny waves on the lake lapping at the dark shore.

When he entered her, she enclosed him like a glove and wriggled unconsciously to eat his pelvic bone with her clitoris. There was no escape; only surrender to the pressure and pleasure of his body.

She gasped as she began to come. His groans filled her ears and she felt him come as she came and came and came.

When she awoke she was in the big bed, with the light of dawn on her face. Giordano was looking at her intently, studying every contour. His sex was hard against her hip. She rolled against him. She raised herself, climbed on top of him, and dropped on to the erection like a siren riding a wave. She fucked him hard, gripping his torso and grinding on to him. She was completely uninhibited, and she pushed wildly into his belly, her thrusts puncturing his calm. His head jerked back and she triumphed. She rode him. She dismissed everything from her awakening mind but the feel of him in the dawn.

Orgasm was not instant. She settled in a slow rhythm, like a song without words, knowing something of power. She squeezed the muscles of her vagina. It wasn't easy, but she put all her concentration into it. Slowly her reward emerged, beginning deep in her womb, then becoming a spasm.

Now it was unstoppable. He grasped her hands and held tight until the inevitable took them over and flooded every cell of their bodies. As they came they were gourmands at each other's mouth.

Her emotions were pierced so thoroughly, Cia began to cry, and she hid from Giordano in his neck. But he felt her tears and kissed them away, then held her head to his chest and enclosed her safely.

When it seemed right to get up, he took her down to the lake and washed her all over – every little part of her. She shivered. Her teeth chattered. And then her stomach gave a great unladylike rumble. So they prepared their breakfast together and everything tasted fantastic.

'I must finish my work today,' said Giordano, placing his drained coffee cup on the table.

His words felt like a knife cutting into Cia's cocoon. She kissed him goodbye and stood up until he had gone upstairs. Then she went outside to retrieve her wrap and slippers, and took them upstairs, passing him in his study on her way to the bedroom. This time he reached out a hand and drew her to him for the softest kiss. It was hard to part.

The day was interminable. Cia went to the village and bought some fish for their dinner. She walked determinedly past the bar, deciding she didn't care to know if she had money enough to leave. She rushed back to the house just to be near Giordano, and she listened to the clicking of the typewriter upstairs. Every key seemed to beat on her body somewhere. Her sex, her heart and her abdomen all came in for the gentlest of beatings and she imagined all kinds of wonderful things. He was a marvellous lover. Marriage was good for making men better lovers. This one also had the pull of being a dedicated man; a hero perhaps. Tellino thought so. All day long, scenes of the hero of the Italian communist movement, his head on her breast and his soul groaning helplessly as he came inside her, lent a magic to the chores.

She marinated the fish. She rinsed out her best underwear and hung the wisps of silk out on his washing line between two trees. She picked wild, exquisitely coloured flowers and arranged them in a vase in the kitchen. They looked beautiful. Everything looked beautiful. She felt beautiful. In the afternoon she slept, lulled into dreams by the clicking typewriter.

She was awoken by him calling her name.

'Get that, Cia, will you?' he called.

Mingling with the typing sounds was a light knocking on the back door. She crept, sleepily, to the edge of the big bed and looked down, sticking her head right out of the open window. Auburn was standing there, carrying a parcel and a suitcase.

'I'll be down in a minute,' called Cia.

Auburn nodded.

Cia ran down, wrapped in her robe.

'I've brought you a present,' said Auburn. 'And I've come to say goodbye.'

Cia took the parcel Auburn handed to her. 'What is it? Shall I open it or is it for Giordano?' she asked.

'It's for you,' she said. 'Open it when you are bored.'

Cia placed the mysterious parcel on the table. 'He's working,' she said, 'but I'm sure he can break off just for one minute to say goodbye. Where are you going?'

'To Holland first. Then America perhaps.'

Cia ran upstairs and fetched Giordano. She felt a twang of ridiculous jealousy as she watched him hug the tiny woman.

A few moments later, Giordano was back at work, and Cia was watching Auburn take the route down to the train tracks. Then she took the scissors out of the kitchen drawer. Well, she was a little bored.

Inside was a length of printed red silk. There were geese and grasses on it. On closer examination, Cia saw that the scenes were all different, and in between each there was a yard of plain red. The first scene was a lone goose sitting in the branches of a tree. The next depicted three geese on the shore of a lake, and on the next a whole flock were floating on the lake. On the next they were flying across it. Each scene unfurled as she handled it. On the last, the goose was gone.

There was more than enough for a dress, a coat, or an evening pyjama. She began to think about it. To cut it would take some nerve – there was something very powerful about the images. She wished she could know more about it. On impulse, she ran out of the house and down the path to the point where she could see the train tracks. But there was no sign of Auburn.

When Giordano finished work, he helped her with the cooking and they ate a lazy dinner. Afterwards they sat together against a tree and he held her waist in a gesture of unselfconscious ownership.

'What are your obsessions, Cia?' he asked.

She wanted to say 'you' but she dare not. It didn't sound right.

'Think about it,' he said.

She took a long while to think. Too long.

'Come on. There's something wild about you, Cia. You could have grand obsessions.'

She thought she might tell him about designing clothes. What was that, if not an obsession? All that money she had spent in Florence! You were obsessed, surely, if you were that uncontrolled. But she decided against it. She was still a little in awe of his seriousness. What was something as trivial as designing clothes to someone like him?

He was doodling on her knee with a finger, bored with waiting for her to answer. He pushed up the fabric of her dress, first up one thigh, then the other. His touch was like the breath of a bird. Her thighs parted involuntarily.

He kissed her legs. 'Let's go inside,' he said.

He led her upstairs to the big bed and pulled her down on to it, still clothed. He kissed her passionately, then pushed up her dress and bit playfully at her clothed sex, teasing a release of powerful feelings from her. He chewed at her for a long time, taking her to the realm of sex, where anything was possible. His tongue reached in her knicker leg and licked at her. He pulled apart the press-studs and dipped his tongue deep into the folds of her cunt, easing her clitoris out. With the tip of his tongue he flicked rhythmically.

She opened her eyes and watched his head with a love

in her heart that might rip her open if she let it. Why did he affect her so deeply? Was this love? Could it be? Is this how it happened? With the wrong man? He was someone else's. He was supposed to be a temporary ... all the reasons why not skittered through her mind. But they were powerless with this man. She had never felt so deeply before.

She stretched back and heard the rip of one tiny stitch at her armpit. Her head fell over the side of the bed. She pushed her sex into his face. His tongue entered, right inside, then he encircled her with a gentle arm, bringing her back on to the bed so he could kiss her mouth. She tasted the cool saltiness of her own sex on his lips, and she pushed her sex on to his hand, seeking his wrist again. She found it. She knew she was going to come on his hand – her whole day had been waiting for this moment. Now the moment was here and she could not stop herself. She pushed; she opened. She swallowed his fingers in her sex. She rammed his arm. She gripped his bicep between her two hands and held it.

For one blind moment, his arm was a disembodied instrument of pleasure, its sole function to give her orgasms. She took her bliss.

He lay still, his hand inside her. After a moment, he stroked her head with the other and she sat up, emptying herself of him.

She curled her legs under her and looked at him. His sex was stiff and straight as an arrow, jutting from his hair. His abdomen was flat and muscular, and at his waist there was a slight curve where it was beginning to thicken. The muscle definition on his torso was delectable, accentuated in the last of the evening light that gently fell through the open shutters. The small amount of hair on his chest was wet with sweat. He raised his abused arm and put it under his head. Something about the way he did that aroused her so much that she ached.

She felt vulnerable under his scrutiny. She fixed her eyes on the bodice of her crumpled dress.

He raised her chin. His eyes looked gentle and she had the feeling he understood her. She kissed him full on the lips.

In the back of her mind she knew that she could refuse him, make him wait. She had had her pleasure. What did it matter if he had his or not? She could be a petulant, spoilt cat if she so chose. But she chose to please him instead. She enclosed his stiff sex in her hand like a rudder, and she steered him into deep water.

Beyond his writhing body, she could see that the lake, the trees and the mountains in the distance were all still and calm. All was peace. But here his passion was exploding. He reached for her and feebly tried to undo the buttons of her damp dress. He couldn't do it. He was too much overcome. She pulled the dress over her head for him, then she sat naked and watched his face change to an expression of pure joy. He lunged at her nipples and bit, sending a deep throb of desire right through her.

He kissed her belly, licking the sweat. 'Are you ready again?' he murmured.

She thought it was sweet that he asked. She heard his words as if from a distance. She smiled, assenting.

He took her body in his firm grasp and used it with determined and extreme passion. He drove all thought from her mind.

She opened her legs more and more as he fucked her. She felt as though she was opening them as wide as the window, as the lake, as the darkening sky. She felt the passion beating through his skin, filling her. Everything that she was – all her beauty, her womanhood, all of her – was with him there at that moment, fucking. Orgasm overtook her like nightfall.

The next day Giordano had to go off and drive trains. Cia felt desperate, as if she had been grafted on to him and was now being ripped off. She prepared his breakfast like a *hausfrau* in a Nazi fantasy, complete with an apron she found in a kitchen drawer. He kissed her passionately with lips tasting of coffee and hurried away. She watched him until he was out of sight. He would be gone a full 24 hours – this was the shift required of him.

With his disappearance she suddenly became self-conscious. What was she doing here? She walked back into the house, past the boat to the kitchen. She automatically went to wash up. But there was no need to wash up. He was gone – damn the dishes. What was the point? What was the point of anything if she was without the constant nearness of him, the smell of him, the sound of his voice? What the hell was she going to do until he returned? The prospect was so bleak, she went back to sleep.

She awoke refreshed, with a sense of purpose regained. Not only did she wash up but she cleaned the kitchen because it was his kitchen, their kitchen, their life. She was possessed of a certainty that she wanted to be absolutely his in everything she did.

When she finished, she took the carbon copy of his communist news-sheet and went to sit down by the lake to read it. She adored every word: the list of Fascist lies, the truths about Germany. She felt so proud that he was hers – today, here, now. There was no need for anything else, she told herself. No need for her to do anything but be his.

But it was different when night fell. The dark corners in the house disturbed her. She needed something else to occupy her mind. And then she remembered the silk. It was lying in its package on a paint-splattered chair in the boat room. It felt heavenly as she touched it. She suddenly wanted to feel this silk over her whole body. A great sense of excitement made her heart beat faster as she climbed the stairs. She took off her linen dress and her camiknickers. She took the red silk out and brushed it against her face. She draped it about her white body and let it fall, red, over her thighs. Her hair on her sex made a little bulge, rustling against the silkiness. She draped the fabric up, around her neck. Geese flew between her breasts. It was fabulous on her skin. She lay down with it covering her. It was enough to just lie and feel.

As she lay, inspiration came. In her mind she saw ways to cut and use the silk, ways to respect it while making it hers. She imagined in such detail that she knew she had to draw.

She got up, found a box of scrap paper beside Giordano's desk and took a whole pile out. She drew for hours at his desk. She skipped dinner. It was one o'clock when she had to stop because her muscles were stiff. She fell into bed and slept.

When she heard him arrive home the following lunchtime Cia felt a wave of self-conscious excitement.

'Where are you?' he called.

'Upstairs,' she replied, and she gathered her drawings together.

He smelled of work. His clothes felt rough under her hands as he hugged and kissed her passionately. Eventually he held her at arm's length and saw her drawings on the desk.

'What have you been doing?' he asked. His brown eyes were alight with curiosity. She showed him. 'These drawings look lovely to me,' he said. 'You have a talent, don't you?'

'Maybe,' she mumbled.

'Don't be so self-effacing. You must develop this work. You must believe in yourself.'

She loved him for saying that. 'You're not just being kind?' she asked.

'No.' He shook his head. 'Why would I bother to do that?'

She believed him – he wouldn't patronise her. She was overjoyed that he didn't think her obsession trivial.

She watched him as he turned on the water for a bath. As he started undressing, she ran to him.

'Let me do that,' she said.

He laughed a little nervously. But he let his arms fall to his sides and acquiesced.

She peeled his work clothes away from his body. Each opening revealed the delight of him. At his collar her fingers shook as she undid each button. She calmed herself and resisted the urge to kiss him. She felt strange, as if by this act of service and self-control she gained power. He lifted his hand to undo his cuffs but she stopped him firmly and did it herself. When his torso was bare she undid his trousers and slipped them to the floor. She knelt before him and took them off. She reached up his legs to pull down his underwear and he took hold of her arms and lifted her up.

'What are you doing to me, Cia?' he growled.

'I want to serve you,' she whispered. She was trembling. She could feel his hard sex against her belly.

'I don't want you to,' he said. 'I don't want to be served. No-one should serve.'

'You want something,' Cia responded, pressing her belly on to his arousal.

'I want a bath,' he said. Cia recoiled. 'And then I want you.' He lifted her chin and gave her a peck on the lips. Then he climbed into the bath.

She wanted to watch his body become clean; watch him soap up and stroke away the tiredness. But a great desire to respect his privacy overtook her lust and without a word she slipped away.

She went into the bedroom and unbuttoned her dress. It rustled around her thighs as it fell. She took off her best underwear and picked up the red silk. It felt heavenly in her hands. As she wrapped herself up, the geese flew around her body.

She began at her ankles, winding herself a skirt. She wound it tightly, wanting its constraint. Round and round her waist she wound it, then up between her breasts, leaving them bare. She wound it round her neck. She draped it over her head and round her shoulders.

She held the surplus over her arm. She felt like a handmaiden or a slave. She straightened her back and took tiny steps towards the bathroom. A train flowed from her arm. She stepped around the screen. Silently she looked at him.

He was under the water, rinsing his hair. He emerged through a wall of water and stared at her, blinking away the water. 'Madonna!' he cried softly.

He jumped out of the bath and went for her. The water on his skin soaked through the silk and on to her skin as he held her and kissed her. His sex was hard against the fabric. The silk fell away from her head and tightened at her neck as his embrace pulled it. She gasped for air and he unwound it.

'Are you mad, Cia? Are you going to make me mad?'

She raised her face to him. Her neck stung. He kissed her flesh. He stood back from her and unwrapped her. Bit by bit her body was exposed. On her white flesh there were red weals where the silk had imprisoned her.

'Look at you!' he exclaimed.

She looked down at her body and touched the redness between her breasts. Then she looked at him; a long slow look. She was thinking, I am yours, wholly yours, do anything you wish to me. I have wounded myself for you. Devour me.

She didn't dare speak.

He took her hand and led her to the big bed. She scooped the red silk off the floor and trailed it behind her. When she lay down on the bed she draped it across her waist, cutting herself in two. His fingers played with it as he touched her skin and she felt once more that there was a silent understanding between them. He knew that she was his devotee and that he had incredible power over her. What would he do with it? Danger made her tremble.

He wrapped the silk across her breasts and bit her nipples with only his lips, leaving mouth shapes on the fabric. She relinquished her mind to the exquisite pleasure of being bitten. His lips toyed with her wrapped breasts for a long time and when he stopped the fabric floated on them.

Their kisses lasted an age. She took the fabric and dropped its folds across his body. She wound the end over his back, his arse and between his buttocks, and then she pulled it between his legs so that it pulled his balls. He growled as he too was lost to pleasure.

She quickly wound the silk across his hips, covering his cock, then across his chest, and arms, immobilising him. He lay back, his eyes closed and his face contorted.

She could see a patch of darkness seep on to the silk where the tip of his trapped cock creamed. She touched it. She pressed hard. He thrust his hips upward and opened his eyes. He went to grab for her, but his arms were constrained and he fell back and watched her, his brown eyes full of thunder.

She put her hand up into the skirt that the fabric had made around his hips and teased his inner thigh and his sex. She manipulated him for a long time.

He struggled to shake the fabric loose enough so that he could get out of it and then he took her roughly by the shoulders and pulled her his way. His lips on hers were hard and demanding.

'Turn over,' he breathed.

She lay flat on her belly on the soft bed, with her arse feeling huge and beautiful, waiting to cushion his fuck and get it all inside her. She opened her legs a little and the air breathed on her sex. She turned her head to look at him. She decided to play coquette and damn him. She raised her arse and wiggled it a little, like a tail.

He slipped his hand under her waist and pulled her up like a doll so she was on all fours. She felt his legs between her knees, then felt his body pressing at her arse and his fingers on her clitoris.

She gasped as an orgasm began even then. He spread her sex wide and penetrated her. She hung on him like a fruit on a bough and he thrust. As her own orgasm overtook her, shook her and detached her, she felt him come.

He held her tightly afterwards and told her she was beautiful. She kept quiet. She kissed him. He squeezed her so tight she could hardly breathe and then he stroked her hair and she lay still. Gradually his hand grew still and she listened to him breathing. She loved every breath he took.

Chapter Eight

That evening, Cia noticed the silk had a small stain on the panel where all the geese congregated on the water. The discovery brought tears to her eyes.

'Can't it be washed?' asked a bemused Giordano. He was cooking the meal. He looked good at the stove.

Cia felt a bit daft. She took it upstairs and washed it in the bath, gently moving the material through the water. The geese seemed to come alive. The stain washed away. She took it, dripping, downstairs and outside. Giordano watched her as she pegged it to the line. The breeze lifted it and sent it wriggling into the air. Giordano approached her from behind and hugged her waist tight.

Then he burst into a chorus of 'Bandiera Rossa'. They fell about, laughing joyfully in their love and the dizziness of its inspiration.

Cia spent three weeks with him in absolute bliss. When he was there she was perfectly content just to be close to him. In the evenings she helped him clean the boat, and they floated it one day when he took half a day off from the typewriter. They rowed it out to the middle of the lake and fished until a red and orange sunset, streaked with wisps of cloud, sent them home.

When she was alone she worked on her drawings. He

bought her some huge pieces of drawing paper – so she could really expand, he said – and she worked away, perfecting her ideas. She couldn't bring herself to cut the silk though. She needed to try her ideas out on some fabric that didn't matter. Giordano bought her some and she set to work. She was glad she hadn't cut the silk – she wasn't the world's best cutter or sewer. Her designs were impractical and the result was a mess.

Giordano was a good friend. He drove away her misgivings about her talents with a constant, gentle insistence, and she learned to value her mistakes.

Towards the end of the three weeks Cia realised that she had hardly been outside the cosy little world she had made herself around him. She thought of going to a city – to Lausanne perhaps – and looking in the shops. But that evening, when he arrived home, she forgot the stirrings of the day when he made love to her.

Their sex took her to heights and depths of love that perfectly fulfilled her. A new sense of herself began to build in her. It was because of who he was, she thought, because he was so different, so grown up in some indefinable way, that she had changed. Her doting love could have become a clinging with a lesser man. Living with him, his dedication, his industriousness and his ability to let it all go in her arms, taught her to discipline herself. She copied him unconsciously.

The night it was all ripped apart they had made love with abandonment and passion and fallen asleep still dewy from the exertion. When Cia heard the crash she thought it must be morning, but her eyes opened on a darkness full of the sound of heavy, running feet. Then someone turned on the light.

There were two of them, in black shirts. One of them raised the butt of his pistol and smashed the glass in the bookcase with an obscene gesture of hatred. The other one pointed his pistol at Giordano.

'Get up,' he spat.

Giordano slowly sat up next to her. '*Figlio di putana,*' he shouted. Son of a whore.

Cia raised herself too, bringing the bed sheet up to her throat with hands that shook wildly.

The Blackshirt pulled back the safety catch on his gun.

'Get dressed,' he said angrily.

Giordano got out of bed and picked up his clothes.

When he was dressed they pushed him into the study. All Cia could think about was getting her clothes on fast. They were shouting at Giordano to put his 'communist shit' into boxes. Cia put her clothes on but she didn't know what to do next. Could she climb out of the window? Could she find his gun and somehow get it to him? She knew he had one somewhere. She had seen it. But she was too terrified to move.

One of the men returned to the room and stared at her, called her a whore and told her to put her shoes on. She couldn't remember where her shoes were. She moved about the bedroom hopelessly looking for them and she trod on the broken glass. The pain brought tears to her eyes.

'I don't know where they are,' she blabbered.

The Blackshirt raised his hand and hit her hard across the cheek. She cried out in pain.

Then a shot resounded through the house. The Blackshirt turned towards the sound and Giordano's second shot went right through his body. He fell. His blood seeped among the splinters of glass. Cia was shaking badly.

'Get your stuff together; everything that you had in that bag on the train. Leave no trace of yourself . . . your drawings. Get it all together, quickly. Now!' Giordano ordered.

As she packed everything, she heard him putting papers in a bag himself. She hurried but her hands shook and slowed her down, or seemed to. Her clothes were crumpled and bulky. She panicked because it seemed impossible that it would all go in. Her drawings folded small but they were bulky. She stuffed the red silk in as much as she could. It was still trailing when Giordano reappeared.

'Ready?' he asked.

She nodded.

He handed her a small pearl-handled pistol and a box of bullets. 'Keep this with you always,' he said.

They left the house quietly. He took her hand and they ran to the edge of the forest. Cia's cut foot was very painful but she tried to ignore it and kept up with him.

After a few minutes they reached their boat.

'Get in,' Giordano shouted.

'What about you?' Cia suddenly dreaded being parted from him.

'Don't worry, I'm coming,' he said.

He pushed the boat out. The darkness was complete around them – there was no wind or moon. Still, heavy cloud hung over the mountains.

Giordano rowed silently and strongly far out into the middle of the lake, and then he stopped and the boat drifted.

He reached for her hand. She stretched out to give it to him and they both moved to the middle of the boat. The relief of being in his arms was so big she cried.

'I knew it would happen one day. But I didn't know how much I would regret it,' he said softly.

'What's going to happen? What now?'

'I'm going to take you to Tellino's,' he said.

'And then?'

'I'm going to make my way to France.'

Her heart shuddered and sunk like a stone. She felt cold. Was he going to join his wife? She struggled to believe it. She looked at him. He avoided her eyes. She turned away from him.

Giordano took up the oars again and rowed.

'Why can't you go to the Swiss police? They crossed a border. They tried to kill you! I could testify,' cried Cia.

'Sssh!' he hissed. 'That's a nice, naive idea. Every capitalist country in the world is terrified of communism. The Swiss are no different. They wouldn't help me. They'd turn me over as a murderer. I can only change my identity and disappear.'

'To France?' she asked scornfully. 'Why not England?'

He looked shame-faced. She swore he looked shame-faced! It was disgusting to find this out now. She felt she could kill him herself.

'I want to be with my son,' he said.

'Bring your son to England.' She didn't beg. She wouldn't. She just said it. It came out flat and she knew in her heart of hearts that saying it was useless.

They were nearing the shore. She could see the outlines of Tellino's house and the figures in the centre of the pond.

Giordano took the boat up to the dock, then got out and tied up. He crouched down and gave Cia his hand to help her out. She took it. It felt so warm. She loved it so much.

'Oh God, Giordano,' she cried, as she crouched close to him. 'Don't let's part! It doesn't make sense.'

'It has to,' he said. 'It will. Please believe me.' And he left her. He got back into the boat.

She reached down and held on to the gunwale with a grip of iron. He prized her fingers away but she gripped on again. He pushed her away again, just enough to break free. The boat floated away, leaving her sprawling. He picked up the oars and began to row.

Cia watched Giordano leaving her. She couldn't believe it was happening. It wasn't real. It couldn't be. It was some terrible scene in a film – it wasn't her left alone in the darkness. Anger, humiliation and pain shook through her body. She was violently sick on the grass.

A lawyer sat on the big, four-poster bed writing Count di Ravanello's words down carefully in a spidery hand. The contessa stood silently at the window, her face red with crying. The count had suddenly become an old man. He looked waxy, pale and shrunken in the pillows. A second heart attack had felled him two days before and he had been in and out of consciousness ever since.

'I don't know why you want to do this!' cried the contessa suddenly, and she blew her fine nose into a handkerchief. 'Why should you want to upset things now? Don't you realise what trouble this will cause? Angelina will go mad.'

'The girl *is* mad,' croaked the count. 'Leave me alone. Can't you summon the decency to let a dying man have his last wish in peace? Go! Or I'll write you out completely!'

The contessa fled.

'You can't do that,' said the lawyer firmly. 'It will be too easy to contest in law. She's your wife.'

The count swore. 'Read it back to me.'

'The sum of 29 million lire goes to my daughter, Cia Finnemore, of Finnemore House, Cowes etcetera ... They will try and contest this on the basis that it was the product of an unsound mind – '

'Then you must uphold it, Giovanni.' The count placed a hand on the lawyer's arm. 'It is my wish. I leave her this legacy for my own selfish reasons but it will be for the greater good eventually. This bequest gives me hope that some of my money will be used well. She must regard the di Ravanello family with some respect after I die if I have acknowledged her. The world must respect that surely?'

The cause of the count's heart attack may have been the outrage that had exploded over reports from his closest friends about Angelina's behaviour. She had been seen in the lowest dives in the city, making a public spectacle of herself over a common street trader. The count was absolutely furious.

'I liked the little girl that came here that day. I shouldn't have let the contessa and that no good guttersnipe her daughter influence me. There's plenty of money.' He sounded miserable. 'Leave me. I am tired.'

The lawyer closed the door on the old man.

'If you didn't want this then why did you come?' asked Gianni. 'I warned you! But you keep coming back, don't you?'

Angelina raised her hand to claw his face but he was too fast and too strong for her. He held her arm in an iron grip. Her dress was ripped down the front and her breasts and belly were exposed. Her hair was dishevelled and her make-up ran where she had been crying.

'How am I going to get home like this?' she screamed.

'Is that what you want then? To go home? I don't think so.' He smiled but his eyes weren't smiling.

'I don't want anything more of you, that's certain,' she wailed.

'Yes you do, you bitch. You want me to throw you down on that bed over there and fuck you insensible. Then you'll wail like a pig. Because you are a pig. Despite all your money and your breeding you're a pig. That's why nothing you can do will stop this marriage. You're a pig.'

'I'm leaving,' said Angelina, and she started for the door.

Gianni shrugged. He let her go.

She closed the door behind her and stormed down the corridor. A nosy neighbour opened her apartment door a crack and Angelina glared at her. She started down the winding staircase. But her step faltered. She gripped the banister. She couldn't help herself. She had been following him everywhere for the past three weeks, begging for forgiveness, taking whatever he offered as love in the alleyways of the city. She had hardly slept. She spent her nights trying to grind down his resistance. But he wouldn't budge on the wedding. It was set for tomorrow and she would have to endure it.

She couldn't bear never to see him again! He was right

– she did want him, at any price. She couldn't live without him. Oh, if only he would come out of his apartment now and call her and tell her not to go! But all was silence in the dim stairwell. Down below she could see the brightness of the mid-afternoon street through the half-open front door. It was too bright. She must return to the twilight world of their mad lust for each other.

She knocked quietly on his door. No answer. She knocked again, this time more loudly, and she called his name. He opened the door slowly and looked at her. A smile played around his cruel lips. 'Surprise!' he said sarcastically.

'Let me in, please,' she begged.

'That's better,' he said. 'I like you when you are begging me. That haughty tone in your voice is not pleasant. Say it again. Say, "Please, Gianni!"'

'Don't be cruel.'

'Ha!' he laughed.

'Please, Gianni. I can't bear it if we part. I'll accept you on any terms. I'll do anything you want. Let me in.'

'I don't know why I should,' he said petulantly. 'All you do is scratch me up and ruin my face.'

'Poor boy,' she whispered.

'And you, what are you now, little rich girl, all ripped up and begging like a pig! Begging me! Where are you now, eh?'

'Madonna!' she swore. 'Don't start that again. Your vocabulary is limited.'

He attempted to slam the door in her face but she had put her foot there. The pain shot up through her ankle.

'Owww!' she yelled. 'Owwww!' But even through the pain she could see that he was off guard. She pushed the door with all her weight and sent him backwards into the room.

She shut the door behind her and turned the key. She took the heavy key out of the lock and ran past him to the window. 'Oh look,' she cried. 'There's a drain down there.'

'Give me that key!' he said, starting towards her.

'One more step and I drop it.'

He stopped where he was.

'Now, you fucking low life,' she growled. 'Strip.'

He glowered at her, one of the veins in his neck pulsing. 'What if I don't?'

'Guess,' she said, with a sneer. 'Just guess, brains. Imagine it. You know what imagination is? You do it with your head. Huh? *Capito*? I drop the key and the only way we can get out is by calling the neighbour. Big rumpus! I'm sure when your little Petra gets home to her squalid little parents across the courtyard the whole block will be talking about it and you'll have some explaining to do, even if tomorrow is your wedding day.'

'*Putana*!' he spat.

'Strip,' she ordered. 'Get your clothes off.'

This time he did as he was told. He pulled his vest over his head. His torso was magnificent with the sweat of his anger glistening on it. He unbuttoned his fly, revealing the dark hair on his flat belly.

'Mmmm,' she whispered as he took off his trousers. The bulge in his underwear was so tasty-looking it made her mouth water. He stopped undressing. 'Everything,' she said.

He peeled off his underwear and stood before her, erect and ready. She never tired of him. He was so beautiful. 'Turn around,' she said.

His arse was extremely pretty; so sweet and firm and round. His thighs were big and bulky with muscle.

'Now lay on the bed.' When he was on it, she spoke again. 'Now raise one leg and pose for me, little boy. Do as Mama says.'

'I feel ridiculous,' he said. 'You make me feel stupid, you bitch.'

'Never mind,' she laughed. 'You'll get used to it.'

He lay there, one hand behind his head, his torso stretched and his cock stiff, testifying to his arousal despite his glowering face. His long legs were shapely and inviting.

'Writhe a bit,' she said, 'like you are in agony waiting for me.'

He cursed.

'Go on,' she whispered, waving the key.

Gradually he moved his hips a little. His cock bounced back and forth on his belly. His inhibitions fled as he got used to the idea of her salacious gaze covering him in lust. He held his cock and looked at her. He licked his lips invitingly. He lay back and stretched, pushing his cock her way.

After a few minutes of this she stood up from the window ledge and threw the key over her shoulder. She saw him gasp as he realised what she had done, but as she walked towards him she stripped off her dress and he was too aroused to care.

'Spread you legs,' she said.

She got in between them and went to work with her big wet mouth on his prick. He thrashed underneath her. She took as much of his sex as she could into her mouth, revelling in its wet hardness and the musty smell of his pubic hair. He thrust his hips and she thought she might choke. She pulled away and gasped for air. He grabbed her breasts roughly and squeezed the nipples without mercy, pulling her towards him. His hairy, muscular body rasped on her skin.

He took her breasts in his mouth and sucked them, then he took her by the waist and brought her cunt into his face and sucked and pulled, digging his teeth into her knotted clitoris. The sensation sent agony coursing through her pelvis. It drove her insane.

'Do it!' she screamed. 'Do it to me now!'

He grinned. He pulled her down underneath him and took his cock in his hand and opened the lips of her sex with one swift movement. He looked at it for a long time, watching the way she dripped milky liquid from her swollen labia. And then he squeezed his cock inside her and took revengeful pleasure.

He was so strong and so heavy he crushed the breath out of her. She was ecstatic that she had him there inside. He was hers once more, fucking her and holding her down.

'You're mine,' she whispered. 'Mine.'

'For ever,' he said. 'For ever.'

It was what she wanted to hear. It drove her to wild thrusts with her strong hips. His balls banged against her buttocks. She loved this madness. They were equal here in bed and she loved to let everything go and let it all be pierced through by him. The relentless fucking turned to a dull pain in her pelvis. She liked the pain. She substituted it for orgasm. It was the only place she had control in this desperate love affair. She could deny him nothing except the pleasure of making her come.

He couldn't control himself and that gave her power. As he came she scratched her nails in a long, deep line up his spine. He screamed.

He wanted to do it again half an hour later. This time he wanted her to come, he said, as he always did. She merely smiled.

He dragged her off the bed and held her up against the cool wall. Her vagina was sore but the way he drove her up the wall with a passion excited her. There were stirrings inside her.

'Come on, baby,' he breathed. 'Do it. Come on, do it.' His words only steeled her determination to deny him. 'Petra will come,' he whispered. 'Petra has never had a man. She'll come again and again. That's what I want, baby. I might lose interest in you when I've got my little Petra coming and coming every night.'

She screamed at him, beating him with her fists. The violence increased the stirrings in her and he felt it. A look of triumph spread over his lean face.

He turned her round and threw her over the bed and

fucked her like a dog, killing her with every thrust of his pelvis. He stopped and slapped her buttock, planting a red weal on it. Her clitoris stretched and burned and her willpower weakened.

He slapped her again. Then he covered her with his body and bit hard into her shoulder. His hands struggled underneath her and squeezed her breast until it bruised. Then he fucked her again, hard and rhythmically, holding her hair in one hand and pulling it.

She was in such a state of pain and terror that she lost herself. Her body took over and the shameless spasms of an orgasm finally wracked through her. She pissed the bed, the liquid flowing between her legs and soaking him as he came again.

'You filthy bitch,' Gianni grunted as he realised what her orgasm had caused. He got up.

Angelina sat in her pool of shame.

He washed his cock in the hand basin and then he poured a couple of glasses of red wine from a flagon. He handed her one.

She moved to a dry spot on the bed.

'I like that,' he said. 'I like it when you pee. It's going to cost you a fortune in mattresses though.'

She laughed with relief. 'So I will be your mistress?' she pleaded.

He didn't answer. He got up and took a spare key out of the dresser drawer. She laughed. It all seemed so sweet now; so silly, the hysterics. It was all part of their love-making, even the arguments. It was just part of being his.

'Let's stay together tonight,' she suggested. 'Tonight of all nights.'

'I can't,' he said. 'I'm spending the evening at my brother's.'

Angelina grimaced. 'When will I see you again?' He didn't answer, and she grew more insistent. 'When, Gianni? When?'

He took a deep breath. 'You won't see me again,' he said quietly.

'Stop! Just stop it! Don't talk nonsense! You just said it would cost me a fortune in mattresses. You know you need this.' She grabbed her breast as she spoke.'You can no more stop fucking me than you can stop breathing. You need me.'

She didn't choose her words to make him angry, she just managed to have that effect on him, every time. He hated being dependent on her and she knew it. He was though. He loved the power they generated. It was dangerous. It had a long way to go before it was burned out. She knew it. He knew it.

'Just leave me alone for a little while. I'm getting married, *porca Madonna*! Give me a chance to settle down and. . .' His voice tailed off.

'And what? Get cosy with your orgasmic little virgin? No! No! No!' she screamed, standing up. 'You're kidding yourself if you think you're going to get rid of me. If you don't promise to sneak away from your wedding tomorrow and fuck *me,* I will come and cause hell.'

'I ought to kill you. I ought to. You're evil.' She laughed at him and licked her lips. 'Leave now. I will come to your house sometime during the afternoon. I'll slip away.' His back was turned.

'Good,' she said, then she sat down in the armchair by the window. She picked up the remains of her dress by the arm. 'Now, if you want to get rid of me today you're going to have to go and get my new dress from Fabergé.'

He turned to look at her and she saw the familiar violence in his eyes. He hated fetching and carrying for her.

'Well, it was your idea to rip this!' she said. He put down his glass of wine and pulled on his trousers. 'You'll have to pay them. I was rude last time I was in there.' She took a bundle of notes out of her black leather handbag and gave them to him.

He put them on the dresser next to the key and put on the rest of his clothes in silence.

It was when he saw the money that Gianni realised he could, if he wanted, put into action what had been his dearest wish for some time. He stood in the vestibule at the bottom of the stairs and counted it. There was over 10,000 lire. He hated Angelina for being able to spend that much money on a dress. It wasn't fair. Well, it wouldn't all get spent on a dress this time. First, he would have to see if he could get Fabergé to accept a deposit. He walked out into the afternoon sunshine.

His entrance into the cool interior of the elegant fashion house caused one or two eyebrows to raise. Gianni felt a knot of resentment in his stomach. The rich bitches all looked at him like he was a piece of dirt; until he had them so wild they pissed the bed. He smiled to himself. He had a purpose. He walked casually over to the cold fish of a woman in charge. After some prevarication she astonished him by agreeing to accept 5,000 and let him take the dress. Gianni waited for the parcel to be wrapped. He felt dazed. It was a miracle – a sign that what he was going to do had God's blessing.

Twenty minutes later he knocked on the door of an apartment similar to his own but in an even poorer neighbourhood. It took a good few minutes before the door was opened.

'I need a big favour,' he said to the steely-blue-eyed man who answered.

Chapter Nine

When Angelina arrived home she found a bill from Fabergé addressed to her, sitting in the silver tray in the hall.

The bastard, she thought! He was no doubt buying something for his little virgin with the rest of her money! Hell, she would make him pay for this. She thought about it. She would have to come up with something beautifully sinister and threatening. Something that would give the little bride a fright perhaps. But she didn't want to drive him away completely. It needed to be something that they could laugh about together at the little virgin's expense.

She was halfway up the great marble staircase, absorbed in her thoughts, when she saw her mother standing at the top. The countess's eyes were ringed with shadows.

'He's changed his will,' she said.

'How?' asked Angelina.

'To benefit Cia Finnemore.'

'Well, he's lost his mind. It won't stand.'

'The lawyer seems to think it will.'

It all seemed tiresome. She was sure her mother was wrong. Of course, Daddy's lawyer would be telling him it would stand. 'Well, we'll just have to get a lawyer who doesn't think so, won't we?'

Her stupid mother's face lit up a bit at this common sense. Angelina left her without another word. Was there something in the planets that made her life difficult, she wondered?

Later that night Angelina was sitting up in bed drinking her bedtime hot milk when she heard the door click. She looked at the white handle and saw it turning. She was about to shout at the impertinent servant who dared enter her room without knocking when a man crept round the frame. He was carrying a knife.

She didn't scream. She had no breath to scream. She couldn't make a sound. She recognised him. He was Gianni's friend. The killer.

'What do you want?' she croaked. She instinctively knew what he wanted. She looked wildly around for something heavy. But there was nothing close at hand.

He walked towards her, smiling.

She backed into the headboard. 'Stop! Go away!' she cried. Tears sprang to her eyes. She didn't want to die! She pulled the covers up over her head and shut her eyes.

The killer roared with laughter.

She peeped at him. 'Who sent you?' she asked, somewhat shakily.

The killer climbed on to her bed, among the white frills.

'How much were you paid? I'll double it not to harm me!' she screamed. Hysteria threatened to engulf her.

The man grinned nastily and edged towards her. 'The important question is why,' he said calmly. 'You must get at the important question.'

She kept her eyes on him. 'Why, then?'

'Because you are a hysterical bitch and you will ruin people's lives if you live,' he replied calmly.

Angelina suddenly realilsed where her Fabergé money

had gone. She nearly cracked, irredeemably. Her heart was broken.

'I don't want to die!' she cried. 'I'll be a good girl.'

He laughed again. 'You are funny,' he said. He paused.'Twenty thousand lire will buy you a life.'

Angelina's relief was so profound she felt dizzy. 'Pass me my handbag. I will write you a cheque.'

'I don't take cheques, you silly bitch,' he laughed.

'But the banks are closed!' she wailed. Surely he wouldn't kill her because the banks were closed?

He picked up a white leather belt from her dresser. The buckle was in the shape of a camel and it was encrusted with diamonds. 'I'll take this,' he said.

'That's worth more than twenty thousand lire.'

'But I will have to sell it. The inconvenience – '

'Take it!' she cried. She watched him wrench the buckle from the belt and put it in his pocket.

As the door closed behind him she burst into tears of horror and grief. Oh, the humiliation! After what had happened too! This was what you got if you gave in to a man and let him see you orgasm and make that mess. She buried her head in the pillow and sobbed. She screamed and screamed into the cotton and lace.

Eventually, she calmed down, and a deadness settled in her veins. It was hard to believe that her Gianni had really ordered her death! He had though, hadn't he?

She might as well be dead, she thought, forgetting she had just paid 20,000 lira for her life.

Death came to the Palazzo Fiancata without payment about ten hours later. The count breathed his last breath and the flag was lowered to half mast. It was Saturday and as Petra drove past in her open carriage on the way to the cathedral for her wedding, she saw the flag and felt sorry for Angelina. She was so happy. She was going to marry the man they both loved.

Petra had felt doubts fit to fell a tree after her encounter with Angelina. She had doubts about herself but more importantly she had doubts about Gianni. He had confessed everything to her, desperately. He told her all the ugly details of his obsession with that woman. Petra knew she could save him by marrying him. She loved him. She felt shivery when he kissed her. The past weeks had been a nightmare that could only end in their marriage. Angelina would have to accept it and find another poor man to bewitch. Petra would tear her apart with her bare hands if she came near them once they were married.

At the very moment Petra passed, Angelina was on the telephone to the *polizia,* accusing Gianni of the theft of her diamond belt buckle. When she put the telephone down she smiled weakly. *Va f'an culo* to them. Fuck their wedding. He would be arrested soon. Fuck him. She felt drained. No, she never would fuck him again.

In the police station the duty officer took the case to the chief. He didn't want to act on his own on accusations made by a member of such an important family. The chief telephoned the *podesta* and the two grizzled men met in the piazza, at their favourite cafe. Across the piazza, Petra drew up in her carriage outside the cathedral to the cheers and the uproar of the shoppers and tourists.

The *podesta* confirmed the chief's own suspicions. They would not disrupt the wedding. It was well known that Angelina had caused untold embarrassment to her father and probably killed him with her outrageous behaviour. It was more than likely a trumped up story and if not, well let the man enjoy his wedding night . . .

'Doesn't she look lovely?' sighed Louisa Penhaligon wistfully, shading her eyes to see Petra.

Dianna agreed but she was less concerned with the beauty of the bride than with art. She was as nervous as a kitten. Under her arm, her roll of paper, and in her hand, her pencil case, felt like badges. She was immensely self-conscious, noticing when anyone stole a look at her. Perhaps they thought she was an artist. Imagine! She had dressed for the part in a flowing lilac dress and she had put a scarf around her head. The scarf irritated her, but she knew she looked Bohemian.

They made their way past the wedding crowd and up the steps of the Uffizi, past the hapless art appreciators waiting in line to buy their tickets, straight up to the curator where Louisa announced loudly that they were there for Signor Lumaca. The curator let them in and Dianna could feel gazes of the mere mortals on her back. Aaah! Life was sweet.

Signor Lumaca's large studio was on the mezzanine floor. They turned in the doorway and Dianna stopped and gulped. In the middle of an oval of students making their preparations was a tender young man, stark naked, bathed in natural light.

Dianna followed Louisa and sat at an easel by one of the windows. The model's feet were pointing in her direction, and his legs and his private parts – no longer at all private – hit her not as a refraction of light and an arrangement of rhomboids but as thighs and a cock. The combination of these wobbly bits of flesh and the fact that everyone but her seemed to know what they were doing gave Dianna acute nerves.

'We will begin with a one minute drawing,' said the great man. 'Begin!'

Dianna was still trying to uncurl the cartridge paper at the bottom of her board. It didn't quite reach and the clip wouldn't work. She missed the first drawing completely.

'A two minute one!' cried the master and the divine boy on the mat rolled on to his belly.

Dianna gave up trying to get her paper flat and began. She began, safely, at the model's foot. She got the outline.

'A five minute drawing please!' cried the master and the body on the floor slunk over on to his side, displaying the most exquisite curves of thigh and buttock imaginable.

Oh yes! thought Dianna. This time she began at his head. Five minutes was up before she could get to the beautiful bum, and her frustration was making her sweat. She adjusted her scarf.

Finally, the master announced a thirty-minute drawing and the model turned over, legs akimbo, his cock nestling like a mother swan in repose on the downy bodies of his testes. Dianna's piece of charcoal hit the paper right in the centre of his cascading pubic curls and drew the whole delightful ensemble hugely into being.

It was only when she saw out of the corner of her eye that Signor Lumaca was walking round the class, commenting on his students' work, that she realised all she had on the paper was the biggest cock in the world. Hurriedly, she did what she thought an artist might do. She shed a cavalier line over the page to represent the body, then sketched an arc for the shoulder and at the bottom of the page a foot, which ended up looking like a childish flower.

Signor Lumaca was now with Louisa. She heard him say, 'I see you have brought a friend.'

'Yes,' said Louisa. 'My American friend, Dianna Fitchew.'

She said 'American' in a way that Dianna had become used to. Europeans always said the name of her native country as if it had dollar signs dripping from it.

Signor Lumaca smiled, his teeth glinting, and he walked towards Dianna. He stared at the genitalia on her page and pronounced loudly that she had an exceptional talent. The word genius was hovering behind his teeth just beyond good taste – Dianna could sense it. She was in heaven. Her bosom vibrated. Signor Lumaca caressed it with his eyes.

After the thirty-minute drawing it was time to break and socialise. Dianna was high and dry, not knowing anyone. She watched the great teacher as he approached their table in the cafe. Lumaca was a big man. His clothes were baggy but clean. He wore a cravat, of course. He had a lascivious mouth, unattractive really, she thought. But then she derided herself. How could she be so plebian? His was a greatly talented mouth, wasn't it?

Her whole body thrilled when, catching her eye, he sat right next to her, pulling up a chair specially and sitting with his legs apart, elbow on knee, coffee cup in hand, eyes on a level with her bosom. The coffee break flew blissfully by. He asked her to a party at the art school in the evening. Dianna positively drooled. She rearranged her plans mentally without the slightest tint of conscience.

Out in the sunshine in the square, Louisa surprised and disappointed her by being very sniffy, very English. She was jealous, poor love. Dianna asked her to go to the party with her. Louisa said she was no-one's second-hand Rose and marched off into cocktail hour.

Plomer said he would accompany her. In fact, he insisted he take her out to dinner beforehand.

They ate a glorious meal in the garden of the Hotel Americana, but over coffee an acquaintance told them of the sad death of the Count di Ravanello.

'Did you send money to Cia?' asked Dianna when the man had gone.

'Yes,' he said simply.

'You disobeyed me.'

'Mother,' he retorted firmly, 'we will have to agree to disagree on the subject of Cia. I had no intention of leaving her penniless in Switzerland and that's the end of it.'

'Hmmph. Well, tonight is perfect and I won't let this little lapse spoil it. Let's go to this party and have the time of our lives!' She took his hand.

'Come on, then,' Plomer laughed, smiling fondly back at her. 'My talented mother!'

The art school was a big sixteenth-century building in a narrow street. The windows in the upper storeys glowed with light and tinkled with baroque music in the night. The big wooden gates were manned by two porters in uniform who barred their way. It was a very strange feeling for Dianna. Being a middle-aged respectable woman, she rarely found herself checked thoroughly on the guest list.

'It must be very exclusive,' she said smugly to Plomer as they walked under the wooden-ceilinged entrance arch into the courtyard.

Plomer shrugged.

The first thing Dianna saw was a young woman in a diaphanous yellow ochre cape without any foundation garments on at all. She may as well have been naked, except that she wore a triangle that covered her pubic hair and made her look less human. Her head was covered with a close-fitting cap of yellow leaves, leaving her high forehead bare.

Around her were several young men, some of them dressed in vests, and one with long hair in a ponytail. One particularly intrigued her: a very slender young boy whose pale linen clothes were ripped to shreds so that his thigh peeked from his flapping trousers. His slender arms moved gracefully, bare and creamy pale. His hair was delicately waved and Dianna was sure he was wearing make-up.

But the best was a magnificently red, svelte devil with horns and a bare chest. He had a bulge at his red crotch that Dianna had difficulty taking her eyes off.

Apart from the youngsters there were a sprinkling of older people, all dressed in bright and unconventional clothes. Dianna could have felt awkward in her elegant black cocktail dress with its cape attached, but it was expensive and beautiful and if she wasn't mistaken she was attracting admiring glances. Plomer was really the odd one out, but he did look elegant in his evening dress and Dianna saw the coy looks some of the young women gave him.

'Dianna!' Signor Lumaca had spotted her. He whizzed

over and Dianna glowed. This was it! She felt as if she had truly arrived.

She introduced him to Plomer and there was a flutter of smalltalk between them. To her dismay, Dianna saw Plomer take an instant dislike to poor Signor Lumaca. She could tell by the way he pursed his lips.

At the end of the quadrangle a jazz band played on the grass and a lot of young people were dancing, their bodies bouncing and twirling, their feet nimble.

'Dianna,' said Signor Lumaca, sliding his arm around her waist. 'You must dance with me. Do me the honour!'

Dianna mumbled that she couldn't really. But he insisted, almost dragging her on to the grass in the midst of the youngsters. He was a terrible dancer and she hadn't got a clue how to dance to the modern music. She was used to being carted around the dancefloor by a man, but this was a free for all. She tried to put a brave face on it. Then she saw the red devil moving gracefully. She tried to emulate his steps.

The next number was a ballad. Lumaca grasped her, held her close and proceeded to step on her feet.

'Aah!' he whispered. 'You are a real woman. It is so wonderful to hold the flesh of a real woman in my hands. You are a vision of loveliness!'

Dianna wished with all her heart he would talk about art. She tried desperately to think how to open thc topic. His breath smelled of onions and the unrhythmic gait was just too much. Her illusions crashed around her. She looked around desperately for Plomer, to signal that she really would like to be rescued. But he was dancing with a young woman in purple.

The eyes that met hers were, in fact, those of the devil. They were sympathetic and they followed her.

The ballad ended and she wrested herself away from Lumaca's grasp, thanked him, and started to leave the grassy dancefloor.

But Lumaca caught hold of her hand.

'Really, Signor Lumaca!' Her displeasure rang clearly

in her voice. She knew for certain she had risked everything. He held her tight. She was about to tell him he was an oaf and thereby ruin her artistic career for ever when the red devil stepped in.

'May I?' he asked, in English.

'How old-fashioned of you!' squealed Lumaca, not releasing his grip. 'We don't do that kind of thing – '

'I think the lady might like a little old-fashioned treatment,' said the devil. 'Let's ask her.'

'Ha! Ha! Ha!' bellowed Lumaca.

'Yes,' said Dianna. 'I would like it.'

Lumaca's face fell but he had no choice but to leave them.

The slender young devil took Dianna lightly around the waist and led her round the dancefloor. He was a natural, expert dancer. Dianna relaxed in his arms. She felt very sad, though, and lost. She pulled herself together and made conversation.

'Are you Italian?' she asked.

'No,' he replied. 'Austrian.'

'Oh,' she said. 'You were very kind.'

'I could see you needed rescuing from the satyr.' He smiled at her. On his upper lip the most absurd painted moustache curled on to his cheeks.

Dianna giggled.

He whirled her around the edge of the dancers.'You ought to be careful,' he said. 'I don't know how to put this kindly but I feel it's my duty to tell you that he has ulterior motives.'

'What do you mean?' asked Dianna in alarm.

'Your friend who brought you to the class did you no favours. She boasted to everyone last week how rich and gullible you were. I fear that's why he's making such a fuss of you.'

Dianna knew in her heart it was true. She had sensed it. But perhaps there was some rivalry between this boy and the master – perhaps she was in the middle of it.

'I don't remember you at the class. Are you a student of Signor Lumaca's?' she asked sharply.

'I have been modelling for him,' he said.

'Were you the model today?' she squeaked.

He nodded.

The thought of her earlier rendition of his penis brought a hot flush not just to her cheeks but to her body as well.

They danced into the centre of the crowd.

'So all the compliments about my talent; they were just flattery?' she asked, bravely.

'I'm afraid so,' admitted the young devil.

'I think I had better find my son and go home,' she said sadly.

'Oh, not yet,' he blurted out.

Dianna felt remarkably comfortable with him. She swallowed her mortification and followed him in the dance.

'You *do* have talent.' he said suddenly. 'If you work hard you'll be able to develop it. But he has no right to fill your head with nonsense in order to fleece you.'

Dianna looked up into the young devil's face. His eyes were serious but gentle.

'I might ask what a model knows about an artist's talent,' she said defensively.

'Times are hard.'

The tune ended.

'So you are an artist yourself?' she asked.

'I'm trying to be,' he replied.

'I think I want to go home,' said Dianna. 'I'm suddenly tired.'

'Are you deflated?' he asked.

She smiled tightly. 'Exactly.'

'Better safe than sorry,' he said.

'Thank you. Thank you for everything,' she said miserably.

The devil's eyes suddenly lit up. 'I'm responsible for

this. I can't let you go away now. I've got an idea. Come with me! I'll show you something special!'

'What do you mean?' Dianna felt cynical.

'If you have to ask, then you need showing,' he said mysteriously. He held out his hand to her. 'It's free.'

She found herself taking the offered hand. 'I'd better tell my son I'm going.'

'I'll meet you by the gate,' he said.

Plomer seemed to be having a jolly time. She told him she was going off with the red devil and he frowned but she told him firmly that she was old enough to make her own decisions and left him. Luckily Signor Lumaca was looking the other way as she hurried towards the gate. The devil was waiting. She said goodnight to the porters and thought she caught a gleam in one's eye. But she didn't care. She stepped out into the deserted street and he took her hand once more.

She felt a delicious sense of adventure and excitement as they walked through the narrow, dark and quiet streets. She had never done anything like this before in all her forty-odd years. Even as a girl in college in Boston she had been conventional, never going alone with a boy anywhere. She suddenly thought of all the people she knew back home. None of them knew where she was or what she was doing. 'I feel so free!' she said.

He smiled at her and for one awkward moment she thought he was going to kiss her. The realisation that he might want to kiss her hit her like a warm wave. She was glad he didn't though; not just then.

He took her down by the river and along its banks until eventually they turned into a residential street. The houses were old, and although in their prime they had probably been beautiful, they were now run down. The neighbourhood made Dianna nervous. It wasn't the kind she would normally go into.

'Here!' he said, turning into a courtyard. 'Come and look at this.'

In the centre of the exquisitely picturesque old stone

courtyard was a small garden full of flowers. There was one bench in it and beside that a plinth with a woman's head on it. It was beautiful.

'It's a Michelangelo,' he said.

He thinks I was born yesterday, thought Dianna. Florence was full of supposed masterpieces.

'Look closely, here.' Sure enough, etched into the weather-beaten stone was a small 'M'. Dianna gasped.

'Think of it!' he said. 'Just sitting here! Touch it!'

She gingerly put out her fingers and touched the stone. She wanted to please him. Even if it wasn't a masterpiece, she sensed he believed in it.

'Don't be so shy! You can't do this in a museum!' He laughed and took the stone in his two hands as if it was a lover's head.

Dianna placed both her hands on the stone, close to his. She felt the strongest urge to touch him too; to touch the contours of his face, framed by its absurd red headdress. His dark hair poked out and curled on his forehead.

'I live just up there,' he said softly and he pointed to an iron staircase in one corner of the courtyard. 'Would you like to come up?'

She nodded.

He went up the iron staircase first and unlocked the wooden door at the top. They stepped into a studio. There was a half-finished still life on the easel. It was very good, she thought. She looked at it while he went into his kitchen to get some glasses. Dianna had never been happier. Perhaps she had a guardian angel, she thought. How many people like her had this kind of experience? The stories she would be able to tell! But perhaps she never would tell stories about this. The prospect was as strange as snow in July, but none the less it excited her.

'I only have grappa,' he said, carrying the bottle. 'I hope that'll do?'

'Oh yes,' she replied. She was acutely aware of the

shape of his body as she sat down on the couch next to him.

'Will you show me the rest of your work?' she asked.

'It's very kind of you to ask,' he said. 'Why not come tomorrow in the daylight? Then you can have a really good look and tell me what you think of it. I expect people to give me their opinion if they look.' Dianna was so flattered that she blushed. 'You are girlish,' he said, looking at her rosy cheeks.

'Is that a compliment?' she asked, coquettishly.

'Not particularly.'

'Oh!' She was dismayed.

'It's just an observation,' he said. 'You have something very youthful about you. Don't misunderstand me. I'm not obsessed with youth. I prefer maturity in a woman.' He gave her the glass of clear liquid he had poured and smiled at her. His eyes sparkled beautifully.

As he drank his drink he stretched back on the sofa, his legs apart. Dianna couldn't take her eyes off his thighs in their red, skin-tight costume.

'May I kiss you?' he asked, suddenly.

Dianna squeaked.

He took it for an assent.

His lips were soft and lovely. Afterwards, he sat back and looked at her. 'Are they real diamonds?' he asked, touching her necklace.

'Why would a young man like you want to kiss an old woman like me?' she asked, ignoring his question. She had a feeling of dread in her stomach.

His face crinkled into a question. 'Don't you understand the allure of an older woman to a younger man?'

'No,' she said.

'It's your experience. As well as your beauty.'

She didn't feel at all experienced. More profoundly, she felt like a failure. It was on the tip of her tongue to tell him that her husband didn't find her attractive anymore. But she stopped herself.

'Let me take off your shoes,' he said, and he bent down, ready to slip them off.

Dianna smiled shyly at him and nodded her head.

As he slipped them off very slowly and even pressed the leather to his cheek, Dianna decided that there was nothing so appealing as a man bending down and taking your shoes off.

He sat back up on the couch again and laid his hand on her shoulder and caressed it. His fingers travelled lightly to the buttons at the back of her dress under the cape and started undoing them. She sat very still as the fabric loosened. She was terribly aware that underneath she wore her corset. But at least it was her favourite one, in vieux-rose batiste with lastex panels. He unhooked the cape and peeled the dress away. Her lovely creamy shoulders and her cleavage were bare.

'I want you to keep your diamond collar on, to remind me that you belong to someone else. I shall lose my head otherwise,' he said.

She suddenly realised she didn't know his name. But it didn't matter. In fact, as he pressed his hand into her back and drew her to him, kissing her on the lips, she decided she didn't want to know until afterwards. To make love to a nameless devil in red was perhaps what she had come to Florence for. She felt like some hapless innocent in a Marquis de Sadc extravaganza. It was the devil costume that fired her imagination. She trembled for what might happen to her.

'How do I get into this?' asked the horned one.

She showed him where the hooks were in the front of her corset.

He unhooked them and her magnificent breasts tumbled out. She kept her eyes closed so that she wouldn't see him cringe at her rolls of fat.

'My God, you are beautiful,' he said.

She stole a look at him. Did he really mean it? The hardness of his sex pressed against her leg. Perhaps he did.

He kissed her breasts gently at first, and then he lost himself in their luxurious abundance and his mouth became more insistent on her sensitive nipples, biting and pulling so sweetly she really felt aroused.

She opened her eyes fully and watched him. The little horns on his head-dress bobbed up and down and she almost laughed. It was heavenly.

He unhooked more of the corset and kissed her belly. He uncovered her pubic hair and buried his face in it, moaning with pleasure. As he did, he got himself a face full of sex. Her legs spread as his head prized them apart. She felt the rude excitement of his wet tongue.

His devotion to the task was complete. He seemed determined to get the best from her. She had never been licked like this before; never felt a man so bent on giving her pleasure so selflessly. If he didn't stop she might orgasm right away. Good grief, she thought! She had never done that with Plomer Two, nor, heaven forbid, with Niccolo. She could never bring herself to be so unladylike in front of her husband, nor in front of her servant. She always went into the bathroom afterwards and did the fast fingerwork she had discovered as a young bride. But this . . . this devil. What was the point of him, if not to give her something she had never had before?

Her $200 dress lay crumpled at her ankles. She frowned at it.

Suddenly he stopped. Her sex was dripping wet. He pulled her gently up. Her face brushed the outline of his red sex inside the clinging fabric of his devilish costume. He picked up the bottle of grappa and the glasses, then marched her from behind, very gently, into the bedroom. He kissed her by the side of the low bed and then poured her a very large drink.

'Drink,' he ordered. 'Drink and forget everything. Forget who you are. You and I are all that matters. Here and now.'

'I'm not experienced,' she whispered. 'I'm not what you think.'

'Perhaps you are and you don't realise it,' he whispered back, almost purring in her ear. 'You know what you want. You know how to get the best of me. You just haven't tried yet.'

Oh my God, she thought. I could ravish him, eat him up, devour him.

His devil costume was fitted with a zip at the back. He turned around and asked her to undo it for him. He stood up as she brought the zipper down to his buttocks. The dimples on either side of his spine inspired her to kiss him there. He turned around, slipping the sleeves and the bodice away from his skin, then he stood before her in his nakedness. He was lovelier to behold here than as a collection of curves in a class.

The grappa went through her veins like fire and she stopped thinking. She kissed his flat stomach because it was there. She was much too shy to kiss his sex. She gave herself to his caresses. His hands stroked her shoulders, and reached and played with her breasts. He gently pushed her on to the mattress.

Despite his slenderness next to her own big body she felt fragile. She felt loved. She felt warm and incredibly beautiful. Her sex felt as if it was waking up after a hundred years without the smallest prick. She raised her hips to push on to his hand.

'Yes,' he murmured, 'yes.' He kissed her mouth so tenderly that she suddenly warmed all through and crisped at the edges like a marshmallow on a two-pronged fork. She felt such a great rush of passion through her whole body that she knew the big IT was going to happen with him and she wasn't going to be able to stop it. She didn't need to. This was her chance.

Her rolling, pink cushioning flesh tingled all over as he climbed between her thighs. He spread her wide, opening her sex. The last vestiges of shame melted from her in milky white fluid.

He took his prick in his hand and put it inside her. It surprised her and made her gasp. Not because it was a prick but because it embodied all his passion. His passion for her was the biggest surprise of her life – the kind of surprise that makes the heart leap, the mouth open, the eyes goggle.

She came like an express train passing and her body fluttered like grass on a railway embankment for some time afterwards. As it was happening, she forgot him. As it disappeared into the distance he gave an enormous heave and came.

It was dawn when she said goodbye to him and got into the taxi in the Piazza Signori. He had kissed her dozens of times, stopping in the bluish dawn streets every hundred yards or so. He didn't want to part from her. But now he had to.

He waved and she watched him out of the back window. The streets were almost deserted except for early tradesmen and a group of tired young revellers, sitting by the fountains.

The motor taxi rumbled across the river and climbed up to her villa.

Chapter Ten

Cia's hand shook as she signed for the money at the little telegraph office in the bar. The bar owner seemed to take an eternity to count the notes and Cia began to imagine he was stalling her. She kept her new handbag clutched in front of her on the counter. Inside, in the middle section, the pistol was loaded.

At last he pushed the money across the counter. She said goodbye and walked out into the sunshine. She walked along the main street of the village without hurrying. Every fibre of her being wanted to run but she could not arouse suspicion. A woman swept the pavement in front of her house. A ripple of brown dust edged towards the kerb. As soon as Cia reached the outskirts, she flew.

It had been three days since the shooting. She had spent them in a secret room behind the wall in the ladies room. Tellino had opened it by pressing the clitoris above the vaginal fire. At another time Cia might have been amused by this, but all she could do was cry.

The room contained very little except a bed and a stock of books that were too esoteric to be found accidentally. The sexuality of the biblical patriarchs, for example, was laid bare between the leaves of one. Another taught the seven paths to true orgasm based on tantric principles. A single dim lightbulb was the only lighting in the room, there being no windows. The dark corners were left to the imagination. The room was warm though, heated by the constantly burning vaginal fire.

Tellino had been very kind, spending as much time with her as he could. For the first two days they both lived in hope that Giordano would come back for her. Cia's mind refused to believe the awful truth of his abandonment. For Tellino, the shooting was not a surprise. Sooner or later it had had to come. No-one so active in the anti-Fascist movement, going in and out of Italy under their very noses, would have been disregarded indefinitely, even if it meant Blackshirts crossing international borders. There were so many spies on the state railways.

What *was* a surprise was his escape to France. The only possible tie that could have been strong enough to make him abandon his work in Italy was with his son.

Gradually Cia had just had to accept that things were as they were. But her nerves were so on edge, the thought of going to the village to get her money was terrifying. She had wanted Tellino to go with a letter of authorisation, but he had gently made it clear to her that although he wished he could, if he linked himself with her in public he might be risking his life.

The role of outlaw, even in her distraught state, appealed to a corner of her personality. The pearl-handled pistol helped. She felt as if she were carrying something very potent.

When she got home, there was a stranger sitting at Tellino's table. A man. Her heart threatened to spew out of her mouth.

'This man is a comrade,' said Tellino. 'He got a message to help you.'

Cia sat in an empty chair and looked at the man hopefully. He had a pleasant, gentle face.

'Who was the message from?' she asked quietly. She

wanted desperately for him to say Giordano. She almost heard him say she had to meet him somewhere.

'I can't tell you. I'm sorry,' said the stranger. 'But I am here to drive you to Lausanne.'

Cia stared blankly at him. What was she going to Lausanne for, she wondered?

'There is a Simplon Orient Express to London tomorrow at two,' he explained.

So that's that, she thought. She only half-listened to the conversation between the two men.

Eventually, Tellino told her to go and get her belongings. As she left the kitchen, she was aware of the concern of the two men. Their faces were so worried they scared her. What dangers would she face on the journey?

She opened her travelling bag and took out the red Chinese silk and held it to her face. She thought of Giordano singing his heart out and laughing. She was certain he had loved her then. He had no more thought of going back to his wife then than flying to the moon. She wondered about leaving the fabric in the hope she might leave the heartache behind. But if that would work, then maybe if she took it he might follow her.

The car drove out of the village. She kept looking back. Beyond the clumps of pines was Giordano's house. She peered out but it was impossible to see it.

'Do you know what happened?' she asked her driver. His name was Franz. He was Swiss.

'No,' he said, 'and I don't want to. No-one knows everything. That way no-one can tell everything to anyone else.'

'I see.'

The scenery was glorious. The road was a small one, connecting villages. The landscape was almost like a body in its summer softness – the swell of the mountains, the sudden view of a valley. There were outbreaks of dazzling Alpine flora by the side of the road.

In contrast, the city was hideous, although it was so

clean it didn't feel like a real city. Franz pulled to a halt outside a pretty hotel in one of the streets off the main square.

They went in together and she was surprised when she realised he was staying too. His room was next to hers, overlooking the street. So, he was to be her body-guard as well. She felt secure.

Once in her room, Cia decided to take advantage of the modern shower. She bent her head under the jet and let the water massage the back of her neck and her shoulders. It felt lovely. She looked at her dark triangle of hair through the trickle of water, then at her thighs.

Damn Giordano for going back to his wife! she cursed. Bastard! It would serve him right if I leapt into bed with Franz. Maybe that's not such a bad idea – show the cad I won't be saving myself in the vain hope of seeing him again.

She burst into tears. He probably wouldn't even care if she slept with Franz or anybody. He wouldn't care.

Dianna awoke mid-morning after her night with the anonymous young devil. For the first time in more than a year her waking thoughts were not filled with dread. She leapt out of bed, humming a tune, and rushed downstairs to cat. She was starving.

Plomer was still eating. He gave his mothcr a smile.

'You were late too?' she asked. 'Did you have a good time?'

Plomer went pink. 'Yes,' he said. 'I did. I wasn't that late ...' He changed the subject. 'Louisa Penhaligon has called this morning twice.'

'Oh, she's fishing for news of the party. Well, to hell with her,' said Dianna, taking a spoonful of eggs from the sideboard.

Plomer smiled. 'Has Louisa lost your favour?'

Even as he spoke, the telephone bell was ringing somewhere in the house. Its tones reached them with muffled insistence.

Niccolo entered the room a moment later and plugged the telephone into the wall.

Dianna took the receiver.

'Darling,' said Louisa. 'There's an awful upset at the Palazzo Fiancata. The count left all his money to Cia Finnemore.'

'No!' cried Dianna.

'He did too. But how was the party? I'm sorry I was so silly yesterday. I was a teensy bit jealous. How was it? Do tell!'

'Lumaca is a slug. He's nothing but a gold digger. He can't even dance,' stated Dianna, matter of factly.

'Now hold on, Dianna,' said the confused voice on the other end of the line. 'Signor Lumaca is a greatly talented artist. He's – '

'He's an oaf, with bad breath and roving hands,' interrupted Dianna. She heard Louisa splutter. 'And you set me up as a target, Louisa Penhaligon. I thought you were my friend, but you went round telling everyone how rich and gullible I am. You threw me to the wolves. Is that a friendly thing to do, Louisa?'

'Of all the nerve!' shouted Louisa. 'I didn't telephone to listen to this abuse!'

'Well, get lost then!' screamed Dianna. She put the phone down. 'I guess that's that,' she said.

'That was a brief social blossoming.' Plomer grinned at her.

'There are other ways to blossom,' she replied dreamily, helping herself to some crisp white rolls.

'I've had a letter from Harry Walcarp-Etting,' said Plomer. 'Inviting me to sail in the Clyde and the Cowes regattas again this year. Would it offend you if I went? Cia will be at Cowes. I thought – '

'God!' cried Dianna suddenly. 'Louisa said Cia has been left all the di Ravanello money and the title and everything! He changed his will the very minute before he died. You did say you sent that money to her in Switzerland, didn't you?'

'Yes,' replied Plomer.

'Good,' said Dianna.

'Mother, you hypocrite!' exploded Plomer. 'She's come into money and suddenly you've changed your mind about her! You won't send her money when she needs it but now she doesn't . . . that's disgusting.'

'I'll thank you kindly not to use that language,' sniffed Dianna, 'and I don't see your point. Of course one treats people with means differently. Money makes Cia an equal. Without it, she was a servant.'

'She always was your equal and mine,' argued Plomer. 'It's the money you respect, isn't it? Not the person.'

'You sound like a communist,' said Dianna, tucking into her eggs.

'So what?'

'Are you going to give away your inheritance then and grow potatoes?'

'Don't be ridiculous!'

'Aha!' triumphed Dianna. Plomer glowered at her. 'All I'm saying,' she explained, 'is that if you want to be a communist, you may as well be one wholeheartedly.'

'I didn't say I was a communist. You said I was a communist,' wailed Plomer.

'And I say treating people with no money as equals is pure horseshit.' Dianna enjoyed a good set-to sometimes.

'Except if they're a handsome young artist,' Plomer burst out.

Dianna blushed. 'And what is that supposed to mean?'

'Look, I have no idea why we're arguing. You seemed so happy. And now this absurd argument has made me say too much.'

'You're damn right it has,' fumed Dianna. She was outraged. She sat silently, chewing.

'I'm sorry,' said Plomer, after a little while.

'I forgive you,' Dianna responded. 'If you will forgive me too. I probably over-reacted to your involvement with Cia.'

Plomer gritted his teeth. 'So you wouldn't disapprove of me going to Cowes?'

'Of course not, dear.' Dianna smiled. 'I might even come myself.'

'Well, I suggest you make up your mind fairly soon. Accommodation is always such a problem in Cowes.'

For Dianna it rather depended on the devil, although the call of English society – all those lords and dukes and kings and whatnot – was perhaps just as loud as the song of lust. She thanked God, silently, that she was forty. Imagine being this sensually stimulated at twenty, she thought. You'd give up everything – and that was plainly daft!

Later that day she climbed the iron steps to his studio once again. She felt a little self-conscious in the daylight, but to hell with the world, she thought.

The devil seemed delighted to see her. His paintings were standing against the walls. There were a lot of them stacked up, but he had turned most of them around to face the room. There were three of the same young woman, naked. Dianna tried to ignore the little stabs of jealousy that she felt in her heart.

'That's my old girlfriend,' he volunteered.

Of course. Dianna smiled calmly and felt very Bohemian. Of course, artists were always libertines. She might even end up sleeping with his friends as well.

There was a delightful painting of the courtyard and the little garden, complete with its 'Michelangelo'.

'It has to be that one,' she said.

'Of course. I hoped you would pick it.'

Perhaps, thought Dianna, he might paint a portrait of me. Then she would buy that as well. She was too shy to ask, especially as he had taken her in his arms and was kissing her.

'You're not wearing your corset,' he said.

'I didn't feel like it,' she whispered.

He smiled. 'Well, that's good. I quite liked it though. I liked the way you burst out of it like a butterfly.'

'Butterfly!' she scoffed.

'My butterfly!' He kissed her.

'I don't know your name,' Dianna said.

'Wilhelm. You would call me Bill.'

'I like Bill.'

'Then I am your Bill.'

'Bill, how old are you?' She couldn't resist it.

'Thirty,' he replied. 'No longer young.'

'Ha!' she laughed.

But he stopped her laughter with gentle entreaties to go into the bedroom.

The feel of his body sent a thrill through her that made her want to get out of her clothes immediately. Dianna felt so naughty making love in the afternoon. With Niccolo she had merely fucked, without the huge pleasure that this boy brought her. He constantly told her how beautiful she was. And his hands stroked away all the pain that she had begun to feel was normal since Plomer Two had deserted her.

'What are you thinking about?' Bill's voice cut into her thoughts.

'Nothing,' she murmured.

He looked disbelieving, but he didn't intrude. He took her into the bedroom and stripped her without further ado.

This time he left her shoes until the last, and she watched the rapture on his face as he took them off. He held each shoe briefly to his lips, kissing them and breathing in their scent. She watched him with curiosity.

His hair was silky. She stroked his head as he spent an age at her feet, kissing them gently. He kissed her shins. His mouth travelled upwards, giving her kneecaps a playful bite.

He licked her thighs and finally her sex. And then he left it, wet and wanting him, and rubbed her breasts with all the vigour of his youthful delight in them.

God, she thought, if she had enough of this treatment, her breasts would stand up on their own again and she could ditch her corset permanently.

And then he penetrated her, piercing her self-satisfaction and frightening her just a little. She tensed and he lay still. He kissed her mouth and stroked her hair. He moved inside her again and clung to her as if he was determined to become part of her. The strength of his feelings was infectious. She lost herself.

Angelina's second visit from the killer was just as violently frightening as the first. She was drinking coffee on her balcony.

He held her around the throat with one arm and jerked her head from behind.

'So, you think I'm a fool?' he hissed. 'This has been reported stolen and no-one will touch it. Do you think you can cheat me? Cheat death? I am death, you stupid woman!'

He dropped the belt buckle into her lap.

'I didn't tell them *you* had stolen it!' she gasped. 'I blamed Gianni!'

'They didn't arrest Gianni, you stupid cow. He's on his honeymoon!'

He pulled her up on to her feet by her neck, choking her. Then he pulled her backwards into her bedroom.

'We are going to the bank, now! You will buy your life.' He threw her across the room.

She raised herself. 'At least turn your back,' she pleaded.

'No!' he barked. 'Get on with it!'

She slipped her wrap off as she stood up, leaving it like a snake sheds its skin. She could feel the tension as she stood naked in front of him. She smiled at him, though her teeth were chattering.

'Get on with it!' he sneered.

They went to the bank and she wrote out a cheque for 20,000 lire and waited while the teller checked it. The teller returned with a manager who told her discreetly that this cheque was good but that the bank needed to review her finances in the light of her father's death.

'What do you mean?' asked Angelina loudly.

The manager's shoulders shrivelled into his neck and his lips pursed. 'We ought to discuss this privately.'

'Why? I demand to know what you mean!' trilled Angelina.

Other customers in the marble-halled bank turned to look at Angelina. Seeing a woman in an expensive, tailored white suit, they turned back to their business with their ears open for gossip.

The manager coughed. 'Come with me,' he said.

He met her at a gap in the security glass and he walked out to her, shutting a half-door behind him. She sat down opposite him at a very big oak desk. A glance behind her told her that the steely-blue-eyed killer was scowling but waiting. I like that, she thought, keeping him waiting. It made her sex wet, taking this risk. She sat down and pouted at the manager.

'Your allowance is in abeyance, until the will is sorted out,' he said. 'That's all; nothing to worry about.'

'I don't think you can do that,' she said. 'You are under instructions which you should carry out until you receive new ones.'

'Well,' said the manager, through his nose. 'It's bank policy. We have to safeguard ourselves in case of error.'

'What exactly do you mean? What kind of error are you hinting at? Speak straight to me, man. I can't understand this double talk,' growled Angelina.

'Well, there are rumours of your disinheritance.'

Angelina kept her calm and asked very loudly, 'Do you mean this is the kind of bank that acts upon rumours?'

The man's face froze. 'I am just asking you to be careful until your father's wishes become known,' he said curtly. 'I don't think there's anything to be gained by making a scene.'

Angelina glared at him and then wiped the glare off her face. She softened. She sighed. She crumpled.

'Won't you tell me what I can do?' she breathed.

The manager's gaze rested lovingly on her breasts.

She fell back in the chair and mopped her brow. 'Oh dear!' she whispered.

'Are you all right, signorina?' he asked.

'I felt a little faint, that's all,' she said.

She crossed one exquisitely stockinged leg over the other and made sure her skirt rode above her knee. She watched his gaze. It travelled down the curves of her leg and up again.

She waited a moment. Then she said, 'Won't you help me? What time do you finish work for the day?'

'S-six o'clock,' he spluttered.

'And what do you do when you finish work?'

Oh, it was brilliantly predictable. He couldn't resist. She knew damn well he went home to his perfect little wife somewhere and played perfect little domestic games and he was just dying to escape.

'I usually go to the Piccolo Bar, for a cocktail . . . before I catch my train,' he said.

'Can I meet you there?' she whispered.

He got up hurriedly. 'Thank you for coming in,' he said, looking around. 'I hope we will continue to do business.'

Pathetic, thought Angelina, as she collected her cash. I bet he's never had anyone like me! I'll ruin the little dog.

She walked out of the bank with Blue Eyes, paying him the 20,000 as soon as they turned the corner and there was no-one about.

He took the money. 'I like your style,' he said.

She raised her eyebrow at him. 'You didn't seem to earlier.'

'I don't mean your sex, thank you. I know where it's been.' His mouth twisted with contempt. She glared at him. 'It's your manipulative skills that I admire,' he continued. 'If you ever want to do business, you can find me in Via Schiamazzao.'

'What kind of business would I do with you?' she asked.

He laughed. 'Haven't you noticed? I kill people. I can torture them too, or threaten them.'

She stared at him. 'You can be bought off too easily,' she said, rising to the occasion.

'Not if the price is right,' he replied.

'Do you have a name?'

'Call me Ninnolo.'

She watched his slender, black-suited figure disappear across the piazza and then she turned to go home. The idea that she could have anyone she wanted killed was a new one. Who could I have killed? she asked herself. Gianni? A stab of pain froze her heart. No, not death for him. Despite everything, never death. Some slow tortu-rous wreckage of his marriage. Why hadn't the bloody police done anything? The cold truth was frustrating. She guessed that the *podesta* had had some say in the decision not to arrest Gianni. Perhaps she could have the bank manager tortured if he didn't make sure she had money in her account. What about her mother? She often felt like killing the dumb bitch. If there wasn't enough money to go round after all her father's whims then that might be a viable option.

Then the bombshell hit her. If the rumours were right, the cause of her woes was the *putana* Cia Finnemore. If Cia hadn't entered the picture, the *podesta* would have arrested Gianni, surely, no matter how much so-called disgrace the family had suffered. Florentine nobility looked after its own. That bank manager wouldn't have been so mealy-mouthed . . .

Everything would have worked as smoothly as it always had done if that little strumpet –

Now if she was dead . . .

But that would mean sending the blue-eyed Ninnolo

all the way to England to dispose of her. That would cost a fortune. How much? A million?

Angelina spent the afternoon at the beauty salon. She asked for a complete body massage. The woman who did it was a tall, strong woman with horse hooves for hands. Angelina was pummelled and rolled and pounded. She turned over on to her back. The woman was softer with the front of her, except the thighs, which she pinched and rolled mercilessly. She massaged everywhere but her breasts and her vagina. Angelina kept her eyes closed for much of the time and thought. But when the masseuse worked below her breasts, Angelina opened her eyes and caught the woman looking at her tits.

'Will you massage them for me?' she asked sweetly.

The masseuse hesitated for a second. Then she massaged them in the most professional manner. Angelina dripped into the fluffy towel she was lying on.

She went to the Piccolo Bar at six. The bank manager was sitting at the bar. He looked nervous, hot and very, very excited. She ordered a champagne cocktail and watched him pay for it. The money he took out of his pocket was damp.

It wouldn't be difficult to seduce him, she thought, especially after the third glass of champagne.

His tongue grew loose with the alcohol. He was fifty and he had never slept with anyone other than his wife, he told her, looking lasciviously at her thigh.

'I sleep with whoever takes my fancy,' she told him. 'I sleep with men, women, anyone.'

'What about me?' he snorted. 'Would you sleep with me?'

'Are you any good?' she asked him.

'Of course I am,' he said, squeezing her breast furtively.

'Put your hand up my skirt,' she demanded.

'What – here?!' he growled.

'Yes,' she said. 'Come on.'

He looked around. There were a few other people in the bar. They weren't taking any notice.

'What if someone sees us?' he whispered. 'I can't be seen.'

'You didn't worry about that when you touched my breast,' she said, and she opened her thighs a little way.

He looked around again and then he slid his hand underneath her skirt and touched her.

At that very moment the barman caught her eye and smiled.

'I must talk to you about my money,' she said. 'I know it's silly!'

'No. No. I'm sure it's not silly. Tell me what you want to know,' he said.

'Business is not my forte. I'm a passionate woman. I get into trouble because my passions are so *un-con-troll-a-ble.*' She pronounced every syllable very distinctly.

'I can take care of business for you,' he slurred.

'It would make me feel so safe if you did. All I need is an itsy bit of money to eke out an existence. I'm not material. I can exist on very little of everything but love,' she breathed into his face.

'Oh!' he groaned, touching her hair. 'What a woman you are. So very much a woman. Tell me what your woman's heart wants to know.'

Jesus, thought Angelina. How did he get to such a responsible position? 'Well, if I knew that there was enough money in my account in this uncertain period, I would be so very grateful to whoever saw that it was done. And it would be good for the bank too because the awful truth is that my terrible father was delirious when he made his last will.'

He frowned, drunkenly.

'Oh!' she said. 'Don't think I just want you because you are my bank manager. I've had my eye on you for a long time. If you did something for me it would just be a sign that you were a nice man; that you wouldn't just use a girl and then drop her.'

He swallowed it. 'I can do it.'

'It would mean so much to me. Not because of the money, but to know you thought of me as worth it . . .'

'Of course I think you are worth it,' he said. 'I'll do it tomorrow. I promise. Will 250,000 lire be enough to make you feel secure? What's the matter?'

Angelina had arranged her face in a picture of sorrow. She ignored the amount for now.

'Tomorrow? Can't we do it now?' she pleaded.

'What?'

'You must have keys! Can't we go back to the bank and make the arrangements? We could . . .' She looked quickly around the bar. Then she reached for the bulge in his loose trousers and squeezed.

'Why, that's outrageous!' he hissed, but his eyes lit up.

'It would be so much fun,' she whispered. 'It really doesn't matter about the money. It would just be so much fun to do the naughty thing in the bank, in your office.'

'Vixen!' he whispered, and he nibbled her ear. 'You are terrible.'

'But you like me, don't you?' she asked.

'I certainly do,' he said. 'Especially when you pout your little lips like that.'

Chapter Eleven

It was nine o'clock when they left the bar. It was dark. 'You go to the back of the building,' he said, 'just in case I'm seen. I'll let you in.'

She left him opening the big glass door. It seemed as if she waited an age in the narrow street opposite the art school. She stayed hidden in the deepest shadows of the porch of the back door. Eventually she heard the click of a key and there he was, grinning. She slipped inside.

He kissed her against the wall in the dark corridor and slid his hand up her skirt. She let him have a good feel of her damp pussy but then she stopped him. 'Have you done the business?' she asked.

'Not yet.'

'Let's do it. I would feel so much more relaxed if I knew it was done. I would be much more able to enjoy myself and let go.'

'I bet you're wild when you let go,' he leered.

'Me!' she declared innocently. 'I don't know. I'm helpless when I'm inflamed with passion!'

He looked as if he might melt. His gills twitched. He squeezed her breasts again. His hands were surprisingly strong. He pressed his hard sex against her leg and groaned loudly.

Angelina acted as if she were bored. She started whistling. He stopped and loosened his tie.

He was panting as he led her through into the main banking hall. There was no light except a dim glow from the streetlamps outside, that shone through the material of the vertically slatted blinds. She sat on one side of the desk they had occupied earlier in the day, while he sat on the other and wrote out the necessary paperwork. When he was writing the noughts she leaned across the desk.

'It would make things so much easier for me if you put just one more little little nought . . .'

He frowned.

She pouted.

He added the nought, bringing the transfer to two and a half million lire. He backdated it.

'There. Now, you just sign there and I'll enter it tomorrow.'

She signed it. 'Please enter it now or I won't be relaxed at all,' she said. 'Oh, please!'

'But the paperwork! I have to erase things. I – ' he began.

She undid the buttons of her blouse. He reached across the desk for her breast but she made sure he couldn't get at her.

'Wait there,' he said.

She watched him go behind the partition, and suddenly had the urge to go and open all the blinds and show the world what they were up to, bare breasts and all. It had been too easy. He was far too gullible. Any excitement she had felt was ebbing away now her plan was about to reach maturity. She toyed with the idea of refusing him sex altogether. Then she realised that people were passing by outside. Of course! The bank lay en route to the restaurants and the opera. Every so often she saw a glimpse of a sleeve or a skirt through the slats of the blinds. If she could see them, then surely they could see her.

She took off her clothes and draped herself over the desk to wait for him. She amused herself with fantasies of being caught by a passer-by, or his wife perhaps, come looking for him! Angelina thought she would probably seduce the old cow too.

She heard the door to the back office click. 'Madonna!' he exclaimed when he saw her.

'Is it done?' she asked, picking up a pencil from the blotter.

'Yes. Yes.' He was taking off his tie as he approached her. 'Oh, you are so beautiful!'

He, on the other hand, was not beautiful at all. He had a paunch. His chest was pale and hairy. But Angelina was aroused enough by the possibility of being glimpsed to want him. Then, when she thought that his kisses – slurping all over her body – would never cease, he took his pen from the blotter and began to twiddle it at her vagina. She heard him cackle as she felt the cold steel and she was aroused by his foible.

'I want to stick all my pens inside you,' he said, and he grabbed about five from the tray on the desk. 'Will you let me?'

Angelina watched as he took out his cock and began to rub it furiously. He had an enormous cock. She took the pens from him and inserted them herself, exaggerating the arousal she felt, all the time watching the way he masturbated himself.

'Come and do it on my secretary's desk,' he said.

She took out the pencils and put them back neatly in the tray, then she followed him behind the counter.

'Is there any money anywhere?' she asked.

'No,' he said, smiling. 'Naughty! There's not much anyway. Most of it is in the safe.'

'Let's go to the safe!' she said. 'Is it a big one?'

'Oh, yes,' he groaned, 'but do it here first. Please. Here. Sit in my secretary's chair. Be sexy.'

She sat in the chair and spread her legs.

'Do it to yourself. Please!'

She put her finger into the soft folds of her pussy and massaged her clitoris.

'Yes. Yes,' he said, pumping his cock like a madman. 'Oh, I like that.'

She eased her finger right inside her. 'Do you fantasise about your secretary doing this?'

'I fantasise about every woman that comes into the bank,' he told her.

'Do you play with your cock under the desk, you naughty boy?'

'Sometimes,' he admitted, breathing heavily.

'Come here,' she ordered. She stood up on the chair and sat on the typewriter, her legs open. 'Come here and play with me again.'

He rushed at her breasts and kissed them, then jabbed his fingers inside her. His knuckles hit the keys and a couple of letter-arms pinged her buttocks.

He pushed the typewriter away, sending it crashing to the floor. He climbed on to the table and pulled her to him, kissing her desperately. She licked his lips and pushed him flat on the desk. He was a silly little squirt of a man and she felt like having her way and leaving him gasping.

She straddled him and took his prick in her hand, watching him writhe on the blotter in agony. 'Yes! Yes!' he moaned.

'Oh yes,' she growled. She eased his cock inside herself and pushed down on him, feeling the whole of him inside her. She pushed against his pubic hair and his paunch. It got better. All the while she kept glancing towards the blinds at the other side of the room. She worked his wet shaft like a demon, building a rhythm. Papers went flying from the next desk along as their bodies edged their way along the row. All the while he moaned underneath her and then he jerked frantically, pushing his great cock so far inside her she cried out.

The bank furniture all around them – the glass, the

marble, the chandelier, all in repose and humming with money – was witness as she stretched and struggled.

And then she realised that something was wrong. The grimace on his face had turned to real agony. He clutched his left arm. He clutched his chest and gave a horrible gasp.

He lay still. She leapt off his prick. It was still stiff. She listened for a heartbeat on his chest. There was none.

'Jesus!' she muttered. He'd fucking died! But the awful thing was his cock was still hard. It was seeping too. She suddenly felt a great curiosity about whether or not it would come of its own accord. It presented itself as a unique experiment. She took hold of it. It was warm. It would be a Christian act. She'd be sending him to his maker in a better frame of mind if she did. She shuffled it quickly. One-two-hoopla! It did! An arc of sperm ejaculated and petered out, like a fountain switched off at night by some municipal hand.

She tried not to panic as she searched for her clothes and dressed. He lay still on the desk, dead as a stone. She searched his clothes for his keys. They were still warm. She found his wallet as well and helped herself to his money. She looked one last time at the body. Then she crossed herself.

A quick rifle through the teller's drawers confirmed that he had been telling the truth. The money was in the safe. But she was too scared to go down to the safe and risk an alarm going off.

She half-expected one to ring as she opened the back door. But there was no sound. There was no-one about. She fled.

Dianna stood in front of Wilhelm feeling very self-conscious. He was looking at her critically, trying to decide where she should pose. It has been his suggestion in the end. Dianna was overflowing with pleasure.

'I can't tell, really, until you are naked,' he said. 'Get undressed.'

It was a bit brutal for her. She had imagined a dreamy mood to the whole experience but he was serious today. This was work. How could she get him to see her as a woman, as he usually did? It was to the advantage of art as well. She wanted to be painted beautiful, not merely as a collection of lines. It was a matter of confidence actually. She felt cold; she didn't like the feeling. She would look disgruntled on the canvas. She half-thought of saying it was a bad idea today – but she wanted the portrait. They had agreed that this one was for her, for her private collection. But he would paint what he wanted, he told her. There was to be no flattery. At the time, in the love stew of the sheets, that hadn't worried her. He was always so passionate about her beauty in love. But now he was just cold.

She slipped open the first two buttons and smiled at him – seductively she hoped.

He looked at her intently, like a bird when it spots something edible in the ground. She undid another button and wiggled her breasts.

'Stripteaser!' he laughed.

She stopped. She felt silly.

'No, please, carry on. I would like to see the exhibitionist in you. Strip for me.'

So she wiggled as she pushed her blouse off one shoulder, then the other, without undoing all the buttons. It rested coyly on her breasts without exposing them, while she undid her skirt. She let the skirt fall around her ankles. She stepped out of it and whirled it around her head before throwing it over the chair. She undid her blouse but she held it to her breasts with one hand while she slid the bottom of it up her belly, exposing her flesh there. She pushed her pelvis forward and then she let her blouse go and stood still, just in her knickers. She undulated her shoulders so that her breasts bounced provocatively. She turned around and, pulling her knickers up between her buttocks, she bared her beautiful, pink, undimpled, enormous, fatty arse.

'*Brava!*' he cried, approaching her from behind.

She felt his sex stiff between her buttocks.

'The customers mustn't touch,' she said.

'Hmmm,' he murmured. 'I like to break rules whenever I can.' He kissed her passionately and bundled her on to the couch. 'If you are a cheap stripteaser then I can take you without ceremony, without nicety.' He opened his fly in one swift movement, wrenched aside her knickers, and slipped inside her, leaving her gasping.

She was thrilled by this little game, right through to the bone. She felt so free, so released from every convention, that she came almost immediately.

He waited a little while, giving her a few tranquil moments. The studio was airy and light, and a slight smell of turpentine reached her nostrils.

He put one finger inside her wetness, then two, and slid them gently in and out. She tensed. She was too satiated to welcome the invasion, or so she thought. But his fingers were so gently insistent that she gave herself to another swell of pleasure. It began in the roof of her womb. Her skin, from her head to her toes, tingled with feeling. A current ran up her backbone as he climbed on top of her. Her breasts felt light as air as he lay on her. He slipped his cock inside her once more and began to move. He raised her legs so they lay heavily over his shoulders and her sex was inviting from her clit to her arsehole.

He was graceful yet strong, and the muscles in his arms and shoulders stretched in the service of an agonising pleasure, defined by veins.

She lay suspended, dream-like, feeling only the rhythmic sliding of his soaked cock. Her whole body focused on the sliding and the crushing of his body. Do anything to me, she thought. Anything. And then she burst into a million splinters of melting crystal.

Afterwards, they lay together on the narrow couch and she had the mood she had craved.

Eventually he spoke. 'Are we going to start work

today or shall we leave it until tomorrow?' He seemed to be talking as much to himself as to her. Then he smiled. 'I'm lazy. I work in long spurts and then I could just lie around for days and days dreaming, especially with you beside me.'

'Let's start today. Yes.' she said. She wanted to encourage him not to be lazy. She felt a motherly gentleness towards him.

Eventually he got up, dressed, and opened the door to the outside and made some coffee. She lay naked, languorously watching him as he sharpened pencils and positioned himself to study her.

She sipped her coffee and reached for her purse. She took out a comb.

'Oh no!' he said. 'Please. Just like you are, tousled. You look beautiful.'

She almost purred. She really felt it now. She lay so still while he drew, she even drifted into sleep on a mist of happiness. When she awoke he was setting up an easel.

'Hello,' he said. 'You're back. I think I may as well start on the painting. I have a good idea of what I want to do.'

This time she insisted on combing her hair. She had to go to the toilet before they started, so she wrapped herself in one of his shirts and crept down to the communal bathroom on the floor below. She listened to the sounds of ordinary family life going on in the apartments around her: the bark of a mother to a naughty child, the clattering of a family lunch, the creak, creak, creak of a bed . . . Dianna thought it all absolutely charming. She had always lived in a detached house, even if, as in her childhood, it was not in one of the best of neighbourhoods. So to hear people, strangers, right there in the corridor, and to have the possibility of meeting them on a landing, was all quite charming and mysterious. She ran up the stairs back to the apartment.

If she wasn't mistaken she was losing a bit of weight. She felt young again.

She settled herself back on the sofa, and lay still while his brush strokes kissed her flesh alive.

She had been in her pose for about an hour when the sound of footsteps running up the iron stairs outside jolted them both out of the subconscious, working state. He quickly threw her the shirt she had discarded. She didn't have time to put it on. She had just about laid it over her body when a figure appeared in the doorway.

He was a red-haired man, stocky and dressed in paint-spattered corduroys. Dianna was thrown into acute confusion by the fact that she was separated from nakedness, with two men in attendance, only by the thin cotton of Bill's shirt.

The stranger beamed at them both and apologised for interrupting. He was a neighbour, another artist, and he had come to tell Bill about a commission he'd won. He was animated and excited. Bill offered him a drink.

Dianna rather liked him. Most of the time he sat in the chair opposite her, although he had a tendency to leap up and do a circuit of the room without warning. If she wasn't mistaken, he was aroused by her.

Oh, she thought, it was thrilling to be an artist's model. Her body felt like common property but in a nice way. The appreciation of artists, whose very existence was enslaved to beauty, made her feel like a queen. Never before, not in all her time as the wife of a powerful man, with all the flattery that could bring, had she felt so marvellous, so sexual, so desirable.

When Fausto left she asked Bill if he thought he had been able to see anything of her. Bill sat in the chair Fausto had recently vacated. 'I can see enough,' he said, and he returned to his work.

All Dianna could think of while she lay there was him looking at her sex. She began a daydream for herself: first Fausto, unable to control his desire, came and sat on the couch and touched her. He stroked her thighs and then he buried his head in her sex and ate like a pig. Bill joined in. Dianna closed her eyes and saw the two of them standing her up, one behind and one in front. They pressed against her naked body, sandwiching her between them, their hands busy-busy, their cocks searching her crevices. Dianna opened her eyes and gazed at her own flesh – at her breasts, at her pubic hair – and breathed heavily, thinking about it, while Bill worked on solidly, appearing not to notice.

After an hour he stopped, announcing that they had done enough for the first day. He washed his brushes while Dianna lay in a kind of stupor of desire. He returned from the kitchen sink.

'Come to me,' she whispered.

The force of her arousal delighted him. She had no conscience, no inhibitions. She took him into herself like a serpent enclosing prey, almost coldly, yet every pore of her skin seemed to be ablaze. Her clit hit his pubic bone and fed its mad desire. She crushed his body to her breast; smothered her face with his; kissed him to death.

He sat on the rag-rug by the couch watching her recover. She panted.

'I feel smug,' he said.

'Why?' she asked.

'Because I brought you alive. If it weren't for me you wouldn't be who you are now.'

She reached out her hand and gently stroked his hair. As she touched his head she felt unutterably tender. She could cry for all the lost years, she thought.

She lay in bliss for a little while and then she took back her hand. She was going to have to break it to him at some point that she would be leaving Florence in a few weeks. Not now though. Not in this gulley of absolute tenderness.

He sensed something. 'It won't last for ever,' he murmured. 'We're lucky.'

* * *

'I'm afraid we don't have much information yet, sir,' said the clerk behind the glass.

The station concourse was busy and confused with people waiting for the Express.

'How long is the delay?' asked Franz.

Cia stood behind him, peering at the clerk round his broad shoulder.

'We're not sure,' said the clerk. 'We're waiting for news. It could be hours.'

'What's the reason for it?' asked Franz.

The clerk shot a look at Cia. 'There has been a suicide.'

Cia's heart gave a lurch. 'Where?' she asked.

'North of Milan,' he replied. 'As soon as I have any more information it will go up on the departures board.'

Cia and Franz made way for the next people in line, who asked the same questions.

'Let's go to the bar and wait,' suggested Franz.

The bar had one door on the concourse and tables outside on the street. They sat outside in the afternoon sunshine.

Cia felt cold.

When the waiter had gone, she expressed what was on her mind. 'It's Giordano,' she said.

'What?' Franz frowned.

'I have the strangest feeling that Giordano didn't go to France. He went back to Italy and now he's dead,' she explained.

'Giordano would never commit suicide,' said Franz. It was the first time that he had admitted to Cia that he knew him personally.

'No, of course not,' she agreed. 'But he could be murdered.'

'It's impossible,' said Franz. 'You're imagining things.'

'Won't you tell me what you know?' she pleaded.

'I wish I could,' said Franz, 'but I don't know anything.'

Cia knew he was lying.

The waiter set a half-bottle of white wine and two

glasses on saucers with serviettes in front of them. The glass of the bottle was opaque with condensation. Franz poured the pale liquid into the two glasses. They drank in silence.

Cia saw nothing of the streetlife going on in front of them. She was seriously wondering about seducing Franz to make him talk. The idea didn't arouse her, although he wasn't without his attractions.

'Do you have to let anyone else know where you are if you are delayed?' she asked.

'No,' he answered.

A young woman sat at the table next to them. Cia watched Franz's gaze flicker over her figure. Ah! she thought, he's hungry. What was especially nice about him was his neck. For some reason it appealed to her. His shirt collar was loose and this small detail made her wonder what he looked like without his shirt.

'Are you married?' she asked him.

'No,' he said.

'Girlfriend?'

'No.'

'Have you ever experienced the pleasures at Tellino's place?'

He frowned at her and then stared at the news-stand.

Cia sighed. All through the drive, at dinner and at breakfast, he had been quite chatty.

'I'll get a newspaper,' he said, and he walked over to the stand.

She watched him. He carried himself attractively. Women glanced his way.

He returned with a lunchtime edition and scanned it. He seemed to be the most interested in the sports page. Cia sat silently, a bit irritated. Then all of a sudden it dawned on her. Perhaps –

'Do you think I'm attractive?' she asked, point blank.

He looked at her with something like fury in his blue eyes. Then he softened. 'Of course I do,' he said.

'But I'm off limits?'

He grinned. 'You certainly are.'

'I needn't be,' she said.

'You don't know what you are saying.'

'Of course I do.' She felt she did too. She wanted to go back to the hotel and spend the rest of the afternoon in bed with him. She would weedle everything that he wasn't telling her out of him, like Mata Hari. She liked the idea of herself as a *femme fatale* in the service of finding Giordano again.

'I don't think so. Don't get me wrong. You are a beautiful woman, and under different circumstances I'd be flattered to think you were trying to seduce me. But you're unbalanced. I couldn't take advantage of you now and still call myself a gentleman.'

Cia was furious. His words stung her. What did he think she was? A fool? She knew what she was doing! She wanted to slap his patronising face!

Some French people sat down at the table behind her. The man bumped into her back. *'Pardon Madame,'* he said. Cia's attention was distracted. She nodded at the man and smiled a tense little smile. When she looked back at Franz he was still looking at her intently. His face looked worried. She felt tears spring to her eyes. He reached across and laid his hand on hers gently.

'What do you want to drink?' asked the man behind them in French. He was talking to a beautiful female child of about eight with silky, straight dark hair and huge dark eyes.

'Du vin blanc,' replied the girl, looking at Cia's glass.

The man ordered a bottle of white wine and a bottle of water. 'Oruela,' he said to the woman who was obviously the mother of the child, 'do you have any cigarettes?'

The woman passed him a packet of American cigarettes. The child wandered to the news-stand and looked at the magazines. 'Imagine throwing yourself under a train, Paul,' said the woman. 'The poor woman must have been desperate.'

Cia and Franz looked at each other. Franz turned around and spoke in French. 'Excuse me,' he said to the man. 'Have you heard recent news about the Simplon Express?'

'It's been delayed by a suicide,' said the man.

'Is there news of how long?'

The man shrugged.

'I think something came up on the board just now,' said the woman. She said it to both of them.

'Thank you,' said Franz.

He got up and went to check, leaving Cia alone. She didn't know whether to laugh or cry. They said it was a woman. Thank God. It couldn't be Giordano. But if it wasn't him then he was in France with his wife. It was black and white to her.

She listened to the conversation of the couple behind her. They were going to Berne. Their child returned and they fussed over her. They obviously adored her and they adored each other. Cia felt incredibly lonely. Giordano had changed her for ever, but he had gone and the aching pit was still there inside her, almost as if he had never existed. Almost. Not quite. Now she felt worse.

'It's on its way!' said Franz. He was a little breathless. 'It'll be in in ten minutes! Don't ask how; I don't know!'

Cia gathered up her things and stood up. She said goodbye to the French family.

'*Bon voyage*!' said the woman, kindly.

'You can take this with you,' said the child and she handed her a fuchsia from the glass on their table.

The woman looked intently at her child.

Cia was about to say she couldn't, but the flower smelled wonderful.

'Take it,' said the woman. 'You really must.'

Chapter Twelve

The ferry docked in Cowes on the Isle of Wight with a bump and a gregarious group of young yachtsmen on the dock whooped at their friends on deck, oblivious to the fine drizzle soaking their skins. Cia felt an acute sense of failure. There was no-one to meet her. There would be no-one at Finnemore. She felt like a middle-aged spinster, an object of derision. And how was she going to survive once Plomer's money ran out? To touch the ground was to feel thoroughly deflated by circumstance.

She made her way through the crowd, past the Fountain Hotel, into the high street. There were new shops, she noticed, selling yachting clothes. The whole of Cowes was brightening and stocking itself up as it did every year in the weeks before the regatta when the world, at least the rich world, was at Cowes. There were no groups of men standing idle on the streets as she had seen in London. Here there was an atmosphere of hope, almost as if the depression was over. If only it were her hope too.

She took the seaside route home. The first thing she noticed was that the new Caryatid Apartments had been finished. They were very modern and sleek. She could imagine the huffing and puffing about the building among the old farts at the Royal Yacht Squadron. The thought almost made her smile.

The Royal Yacht Squadron castle itself stood on the point, its windows strangled with unclipped ivy. If you were a man it was more difficult to become a Squadron member than sit in the House of Lords. If you were a woman, you were completely excluded. Last year a wag had hoisted a pair of pink, crepe-de-chine panties up the flagstaff. Cia remembered them fluttering in the breeze. And then she did smile.

She walked past the unprimed cannons of the Squadron, then rounded the point and at last Finnemore came into view. She glimpsed its rotting roof over the high hedges and her heart leapt to see the beautiful old place. It was a feminine house in some way. It was big but it wasn't a monster. It was elegant. Its three chimney stacks were still standing, thank God. So was the gazebo, although the untamed growth of the shrubs and bushes obscured much of it. But it was a good feeling; an omen. If that old gazebo could still stand after being neglected for so many months, then so could her life. Yes, she thought, so could her life. She had sat in the gazebo with Grandma often, when her mother had first sent her away, and she had learned all about the Solent tides, about Grandpa who was dead, about everything. Cia quickened her pace.

She opened the green gate and walked up the path to the front door. It had been a long time since she had used her key. The house was dim inside, and spiders' webs joined walls to ceiling as if holding the place together. A stranger in the house might have imagined a skeletal hand coming out of the woodwork and grabbing her ankle –

But Cia was completely blasé about ruin. She had always lived with it. The main stairs swept upward into the denser shadows of the interior. A huge portrait of Great Grandmama, Lady Finnemore herself, looked down, smiling a very pale smile. Below the stairs, the old butler's mirror that she had loved to gaze in as a child because of the way it made everything seem small like a fairground mirror, was covered in dust. Everything had been still for so long that it seemed incapable of movement. Off the hallway to the right and to the left there were a number of slumbering doors, to drawing rooms, the dining room, the library.

Cia didn't open any of them. She went straight through to the back of the house where she and Grandma had long since set up in the old servants' hall and its adjoining rooms.

It was growing dark. She put on the electric light and the comfortable, cluttered living room sprang into half-life. There were two small bedrooms here in the back, as well as a huge scullery and a modern bathroom. They had that and the electricity put in with the last lot of stocks and shares they had sold, luckily, the year before the crash.

She plucked a key off its hook and opened the back door with it, letting the air in. In the scullery stood her trunk! She hugged it, then realised what she was doing and laughed at herself.

There were no curtains and the big old windows acted like mirrors in the gathering twilight. The glass was ancient and imperfect, so that her clothes seemed painted on her with an unsteady hand.

The mattress on her old bed didn't seem damp but the sheets she got out of the linen cupboard did. There were newspapers in the basket by the kitchen stove dated the year before, untouched. The torch didn't work but there were matches by the stove. She went out to the woodshed. There were spiders everywhere but she gritted her teeth and packed a box full of logs to take inside. She dragged the box a little way and then something made her look up. She saw immediately what it was. A light had gone on in the turret window of Tennyson House, up on the hill behind Finnemore.

It was another good omen, Cia decided. Tennyson House was Edna and Rudy's house. When she and Edna were kids, that turret light was Edna's signal to Cia down below. Three flashes and the coast was clear to sneak out and meet on Princes Green. It didn't flash.

Perhaps they were home. The fleeting glimpse of Rudy she had had at Milan came back to her. Everything was all right. The last few weeks had never happened. She wondered who was up there.

She awoke the next morning intoxicated by unremembered sensual adventures in dreamland. She was sexually aroused to the point of gasping desperation. Her whole body seemed bewitched and her sex itself was cream between her legs. She had no fantasies about anyone. All she had was a belly full of need. It was so strong that as she came to consciousness, she conjured herself up a phantom with a stiff cock. He remained a phantom for some time – an anonymous sexual being, with hands and lips anxious to please every inch of her flesh. He was infinitely better equipped than any earthbound being because he was tailormade by her. He had hands so big he held her whole arse in his palm. He wrenched open her legs and his mouth sucked her whole body, from her clitoris to her lips. His tongue, hot and red inside her, licked her womb, while his fingers rolled her clitoris.

He had soft, silky hair that covered her face and stirred her senses like the perfume of a morning flower. He breathed; he whispered sweet everythings. But he didn't have a face.

Only at the moment of truth did his face come into vision. In the midst of one of the most violent, thigh-stretching orgasms ever to take her over, Cia saw Giordano's dear face. She heard his sweet voice; even felt his thrust.

He seemed so real to her she cried out. She sat up in bed, alone, and her heart felt bitter.

By the side of her bed was her travelling bag. She reached inside it and pulled out the small, pearl-handled gun. It was cold. She held it against her naked breast, not knowing why.

She took out the little box of bullets. Then she opened the bedside cabinet drawer and stashed the weapon away. Then she got up and made herself some black tea.

She felt better when she got up and dressed. She cleaned the rooms at the back, she opened windows, and made lists of things to do. At last she went out and bought herself a newspaper, a chicken, some milk and a bar of bitter-sweet chocolate.

She spent the afternoon writing letters of application for housekeeping jobs. But she didn't post the letters. She didn't want to go out again. She felt insular. She didn't want to see anyone. Neither did she want a bloody housekeeping job, she admitted. The weather had worsened – it was raining hard now. She lit a fire, took down a novel from the bookshelves, and read it from cover to cover, stopping only to break off pieces of the dark chocolate. She crawled into bed at two in the morning. The servants' quarters were warm as toast.

She dreamed that she was stopped at customs and tried on the spot for concealing Giordano under her skirt. He came out, laughed in the face of the customs officers, took her hand and pulled her on to a passing train. The train gathered momentum and they made love in the carriage, tearing each other's clothes off in a mad frenzy of passion. Their love was so powerful it blew the roof off the train and she woke up, blinking in the darkness.

Outside on the window sill some neglected geraniums squeaked against the window pane.

There was a bar at the end of the Via Schiamazzao with two spindly tables and chairs outside on the dusty pavement. Angelina walked in. The owner looked up from his conversation with another man at the bar.

Angelina ordered an expresso. 'I'm looking for a man named Ninnolo,' she said.

'He was in this morning,' the owner told her. 'I expect he'll be in again.'

The other customer was looking her legs up and down. They were shown to advantage by the way she perched on the stool. Her dress had a split in it that went right up to the top of her stocking. She had given up white. Her dress was an Elsa Schiaperelli. It was hot pink, and she had toned it down with white leather pumps and a soft white leather peakless cap. She had had the colour of her hair changed too, back to something like its original lush chestnut brown. She was trying to blend in, dressing prettily like any other girl.

'I need to leave a message,' she said.

'Here.' The owner gave her a notepad.

She wrote: 'Time to work together.' She didn't sign it. Surely he would know it was her?

He surprised her that evening by ringing the bell and being let in like an ordinary human being. A servant showed him into the white room. She was looking at fabric samples in the latest colours for upholstery. She was dressed in a black charmeuse lounge suit, with the Cadenti di Ravanello crest screen-printed across her back.

'What can I do for you?' he asked.

'I've reached a decision, Ninnolo,' she replied.

'And what does that mean?'

'I want you to go to England,' she said slowly, 'and kill my so-called half-sister, Cia Finnemore.'

'That'll be expensive.'

'I stand to lose half my father's fortune if she isn't killed.'

'What's the legal position?'

'What do you care?' she sneered.

'I don't. I want to know if the money she is due to inherit will come to you if she dies.'

Angelina stared at him blankly. 'I assume so,' she said. 'Who else would it go to?'

'It's worth finding out, don't you think? There's no point in spending my time and your money killing her unless you stand to inherit in the event of her death?'

Angelina's heart swelled in her breast. 'Thank you,' she breathed. 'Thank you. You could have just taken my money and gone off to England '

'I don't like messy jobs,' he said, screwing up his nose.

'How will I find out the legal position without arousing suspicion?' she asked.

'That's your problem.' He turned to go.

'Wait! Couldn't you do it for me?'

He hissed.

'I could give you a retainer?' she suggested.

'What kind of money are we talking about?' he asked.

'I was thinking about a million lire for the killing but I could add – '

He roared with laughter and then, just as quickly, he stopped. 'I wouldn't touch it for less that fifteen million.'

'That's outrageous! That's half what she'll inherit!'

He shrugged.

'You would have killed me for a pittance!' protested Angelina.

'I have different terms for different people. I have a sliding scale. You're not Gianni.'

'And you're not reliable. I'm supposed to be dead!'

'Shall I tell you why you were able to buy me off?' he said, looking her straight in the eye.

'Yes, do.'

'Because you are worth much more than him.'

'It's that simple?'

'Yes.'

'Five million,' she bargained. 'And that's to include the legal niceties.'

'Twelve,' he argued. 'It's not much to pay for your inheritance, including your title.'

'What?'

'I assume she could claim your title on your mother's death.'

Angelina hadn't thought of that. This man had the kind of brain that she could use.

'Ten,' she said.

'Eleven.'

She needed him. 'If I pay you eleven million lire I want you to find out where Gianni and his bride have gone for their honeymoon.'

'No,' he stated simply. He looked at himself in the mirror above the mantelpiece. 'I'm a killer, not a sneak. Besides I know where they've gone. Some of your money went towards their trip.'

Angelina was speechless. But she was enthralled.

'Do you fuck women?' she asked.

'What's that got to do with anything?'

'Just wondering, that's all.'

'I don't mix business with pleasure.'

Angelina's sex thumped. Aha! she thought, a challenge.

Eleven million was a lot to gamble on her own sexual magnetism but she was narcissistic to the point of foolishness. She might not have to pay him everything.

'You'll have your eleven million,' she announced suddenly. 'When you deliver.'

'Fine,' he said. 'I'll be in touch.'

And with that he went, leaving her alone to think. She desperately wanted to find Gianni. He was the first man ever to overpower her completely. She would find him, she vowed.

Cynthia Rowbotham's dress shop was at the top of the high street in Cowes, near the corner of Beckford Road. Its windows were bevelled glass with gleaming wooden frames. There were two windows, each dressed with a black backdrop setting off a headless wire mannequin. Cynthia was pinning a dreadful beige three-piece into one of them.

Cia walked past the shop and drifted up to Beken's the photographer's. In its windows were pictures of The Big Class. *Velsheda, Brittania* and *Candida* were all in one: graceful, millionaires' yachts, 85 feet on the water line, defying gravity with their 200 foot masts. The sheer size and beauty of them inspired Cia; it always had. She never tired of looking in Beken's windows.

She spotted *Pearlita*. Rudy Wycke had built *Pearlita* years ago. It had made his name as a boat builder, as well as his personal fortune. Now there was a man. She wanted a man. She wanted the oblivion of sex.

But her thoughts were more on making a living than making love. Her gaze shifted to her appearance, reflected dimly in the window. Was her hair straight, she wondered? Then, with a grimace of impatience, she turned away from the glass.

The door of Cynthia's shop opened with a jangle of chimes as Cia pushed it. The chimes crashed on her nerves.

'Why Miss Finnemore!' cried Cynthia. 'So nice to see you back in Cowes. How can I help you?'

'I'm afraid I haven't come shopping,' admitted Cia.

'No,' said Cynthia. It had been a long time since any of the Finnemores had bought one of her gowns. She looked at the bag that Cia was carrying. 'How can I be of service?'

'Would you consider buying two gowns I had made in Italy?' whispered Cia.

'Let me see them and I'll make you an offer,' said Cynthia.

They were two of the evening dresses that she and the tailor, Signor Volpe, had made together. They were both heavy crepe, one with batwing sleeves, studded with rhinestones, the other sleeveless and pinched under the breast with a satin rosette. Cia hated to see them go but she only had three pounds left from Plomer's money. She had kept two evening gowns – one to sell eventually perhaps, and one, a midnight blue, which she would never part with if she could possibly help it.

Cynthia's eyes lit up briefly before she put a veil over her glee. She offered Cia a pittance.

Cia gratefully accepted the money. She pocketed it, rolled up her bag, and was about to leave the shop when the door chimes went again and the small, ill-lit shop was flooded with sunshine.

The woman who entered was wearing a pair of canary-yellow trousers with at least thirty-inch bottoms. She wore a crushed silk white blouse with a turned-up collar. She could have been a fashion plate but her breasts were far too large and she exuded a sensuality in her walk. She had red hair and a wide mouth that opened in a huge smile when she saw Cia.

'Zounds!' she cried. 'You're back!'

Cia couldn't help but laugh. A vague hint of some delicious perfume wafted from the woman's skin as she hugged her. 'Zounds, Thora?'

'Belle,' said the redhead. 'I'm called Belle and "zounds" is terribly in, didn't you know?'

'Oh I say, darling,' said Cia, sticking her nose in the air. 'My lingo's obviously a season out of date. I've been in Italy, you know, and of course we say *ciao* rather a lot.'

Belle poked out a long, red tongue and snapped it in again. 'I knew you were in Italy. Ran into some American at Monaco who knew you.'

Cia giggled again and then, for some reason, she shivered.

'Can you wait while I have a fitting? Then we can have a natter,' said Thora Belle.

'OK,' agreed Cia.

To Cia's surprise Cynthia Rowbotham was obsequious to the point of fawning over Thora . . . Belle. Times had obviously changed with her old school friend.

Belle disappeared behind the curtain.

Thora Snook, now apparently Belle, came from the

cottages in St Mary's Road. Her family were numerous and poor. Cia had gone to school with her. Grandma was a Fabian and believed schooling should prepare you to communicate with all the social classes. Mostly, the girls at St Mary's School had been from workers' cottages and Cia had had a great education. The children were tough as mainsail sheets. Thora was the only one Cia still had something in common with. Thora hadn't married either. Most of the other working-class girls had a fleet of children by the time they were twenty, and soon ended up looking like their mothers.

Thora, though, had disappeared off. That's what her mother had said when Cia had gone to the house. *'Disappeared off! No notice. No nothing!'* – as if she were a lodger. When she turned up – a full seven years later – she told Cia she was amazed her mother had even noticed she'd gone.

Thora made light of her family. But she had masked deep emotion when she had told Cia and Grandma about their lives. Grandma had noticed it and thought Thora was probably not the father's child. Grandma had had a nose for that kind of thing.

The last time Thora had been in Cowes was a few weeks after Grandma's funeral. Thora had shown up out of the blue yonder and they had talked about Grandma for much of the afternoon. It had been a heck of a relief for Cia – as Thora had said – because people who visited her always tried to skirt the subject of Grandma in their obsessively polite conversation.

Thora had been working as a stenographer in London at that time and she wore sensible dresses and brogues. This, then, eighteen months later, behind the curtain, was a different woman. A married woman, perhaps, with a rich husband?

'So, how was Italy?' Belle stared at her. 'Tell me – I really want to know.'

Cia couldn't think of what to say in front of Cynthia. Dianna Fitchew had christened Cynthia's 'Gossip City'.

'It changed me,' she said, at last.

Belle's head disappeared and suddenly Cia felt uncomfortable. She found it hard to breathe. A sense of panic rose from nowhere and started to grip her. She wanted to cry.

I'm having hysterics! she thought. She half-raised herself off the couch. This was awful. She had an overwhelming urge to leave the shop immediately. But she couldn't bring herself to get up. Was she going mad? She decided to sit tight and try and concentrate on the painted sign on the shop door; try and focus her mind. She traced the outline of the 'R' and she saw Giordano's face in the loop.

'I'll be with you in a moment, Cia,' called Belle.

The sound of her friend's voice almost brought tears to her eyes. Mercifully, there was a flurry of curtain and within a minute Belle whirled her out into the street.

'Let's walk home together,' said Belle.

A young lad, who Belle called Jimmy, followed in their wake and carried the purchases they had made. The high street was not busy but there were a number of familiar women shopping. By the way they snubbed Belle, Cia guessed that she was no married woman. No-one stopped to talk to them at all.

In the greengrocers they came upon Sapphire Critchley-Rawnipton, the admiral's niece, buying a mountain of potatoes. It was impossible, in such close quarters, for either party to ignore the other. But Lady Sapphire managed it. She passed the time of day with Cia as if Belle didn't exist.

Belle got so ruffled she stormed out of the shop mumbling something about not having to buy her own fucking vegetables anyway.

Cia bought hers and walked quickly to catch up with Belle. They walked in silence to Castle Rock, the large house owned by Rosa Lewis, former mistress of King Edward VII, where, to Cia's astonishment, Belle sent Jimmy in with her parcels.

'I'm just staying here until the apartment at the Caryatids is finished. We're having it done by a Parisian decorator . . . Are you busy today, Cia?' she begged. 'Can I come to Finnemore? There's a crowd in.' She nodded over her shoulder at Rosa's.

'Of course,' said Cia. 'I don't think I want to be alone.'

In the comfortable clutter of the old servants' hall Belle flopped into a chair while Cia made the tea. 'Are you all right? You looked awfully pale at Cynthia's.'

'Something came over me. I felt . . . I felt hysterical suddenly.'

'When did you get back? Are you exhausted from travelling?' asked Belle.

'It might be that,' Cia replied despondently. 'I hope so. I thought I might be going mad.'

'Not you! Not bloody likely!' said Belle. 'Cia, I'm so pleased to see you. You see the way the buggers in this town treat me. You'll probably get some shrapnel through walking along in broad daylight with me. Will you mind?'

'Don't be silly,' laughed Cia, taking out the half-pound of cheap tea she had bought. She was wondering what Belle was. A film star? Or a kept woman?

Belle screwed her nose up. 'Haven't you got any proper tea?'

'There's nothing wrong with this. It's much cheaper,' said Cia sharply.

'We used to drink it in St Mary's Road,' said Belle. 'Are things that bad? What were you doing at Cynthia's, by the way?'

'Hocking a couple of dresses,' Cia told her.

'Grandma's?' asked Belle, incredulously.

'No, mine,' admitted Cia. 'My own designs.'

'Your own designs? God, you always were clever. Did you have to sell everything?'

'No, not by a long shot.' Cia grinned. 'I've got a trunk stuffed with them! I went a bit wild in Italy.'

'Jolly good. Let's see!' said Belle.

Cia put down the tea and fetched an armful of clothes from her mostly unpacked trunk.

'Zounds!' cried Belle, more than once. 'You're a genius! Would you design something for me? Oh, please say yes! It would help you out! I'd love something unique for Cowes Week. Something to wear on Sven's yacht. Cynthia's no good at day wear. Her stuff is all too staid. That beige frumpsuit in the window, for example. I was going to go up to London, but who can be fagged?'

'I'd love to design something for you,' said Cia. 'And who's Sven?'

'Sven Lipgliec. I'm a kept woman, Cia. I'm living in sin.'

Sven Lipgliec was a Latvian banker. He was at least fifty but he was charm itself.

'He must be ancient by now!' said Cia.

'He's not that old. He's only fifty-four! He's still very energetic.' Belle's face broke into a lustful smirk.

'Don't you mind that he's married?' asked Cia quietly.

'They divorced a couple of years ago. Everyone's divorcing these days, haven't you heard? The King said they ought not to have renamed the Big Class the J Class to conform with the universal rule, they should have called it the A Class, for Adultery.'

'Mr Wit,' sneered Cia. She didn't really dislike King George. She was actually feeling an unreasonable stab of jealousy towards her friend. She was glad to see her happy but she was miserable that Giordano hadn't loved her enough to divorce his wife.

Belle pursed her lips. She always had been a royalist.

'Is Sven going to marry you?' asked Cia.

'He's asked me.' said Belle, glowing, 'but I'm in no rush. I'm just enjoying being in love with him. It's just . . . oh, it's wonderful! If I was his wife I'd have to have lunch with the bankers' wives and they're all extremely boring. I like it just as it is. The only horrible part is that the Sapphire Critchley-Rawniptons of this town are so obsessed with other people's private lives. They're so puerile. What does it matter if we're not married? We're buying a beautiful apartment at the Caryatids. You must see it, Cia. It'll be ready soon.'

Cia smiled. 'Has he got a big dick then?' she asked.

Belle howled with laughter. It was their private language. They always asked each other that. The game was not to tell.

'In South America last winter it was so hot he had the bath filled with ice so we could fuck in there! I wouldn't have minded,' hooted Belle, 'but there was a bloody orchestra serenading us down below and I was freezing! In the end I insisted we put a blanket over the ice. Then it was just darling . . . the cold on my back and the heat of him on top of me. My cock was drooling. Oh Cia, it's super to talk to you. Who else can I talk like this with? Rosa, I suppose, but I find her too intimidating actually.'

'*Your* cock?' asked Cia.

'Oh, I've adopted that one. I heard a black woman singing it at the Bal Negre in Paris. It means the lips of your vagina, you know, like a rooster's head. Cock-a-doodle-Yeeeow!'

When they'd stopped laughing, Belle continued more soberly. 'Look, you won't repeat any of this?'

'Cross my heart and hope to die,' said Cia. She was impressed. Her friend must really be in love.

'He likes to put chocolate sauce all over me and lick it off,' said Belle. 'And he puts chocolate bars, you know, up there.' Cia was grinning from ear to ear. Belle paused. 'Are you laughing at me?'

'No,' lied Cia. 'Well yes, I'm laughing at your coyness. What's "up there"?'

'In my cunt,' said Belle. 'He likes to put chocolate in my cunt and eat it. He likes anything sweet, actually. He piped buttercream up me once and I squeezed it out. I like a man who likes a face full of cunt, I really do.'

'I saw some interesting things in Switzerland,' said Cia. She told her about Tellino's.

'God!' cried Belle. 'I love the sound of that. So what were you doing at this den of iniquity in Switzerland then? Come on, you've told me nothing about yourself much. You must have had lovers.'

'Giordano took me there.' Cia stopped. Saying his name brought tears to her eyes.

'Giordano? Who is or was Giordano? Are you crying? Oh Cia!'

'He was so wonderful, Belle. I can't believe he turned out so . . .' she stopped, trying to recover herself a bit. 'Sex with him was just . . . indescribable.'

'Oh, come on, you can do better than that. Did he have a big dick?' asked Belle, her tongue firmly in her cheek.

Cia smiled weakly. 'He was so sensual, so passionate. I thought he really loved me at the time. I still think he did then, although now I'm trying to believe he was a prick all along. You know that feeling when a man takes you over, as if you are communicating on a different plane? No words, just love. Christ.' Cia's voice cracked.

'What on earth happened?' asked Belle.

'It lasted about a month. Then he went back to his fucking wife,' sobbed Cia.

'Oh God. I'm sorry.'

'The Fascists came for him in the middle of the night,' she blabbed. 'We escaped and then he left me at Tellino's and rowed off back to France where she lives.'

'What did the Fascists want with him?'

'He was a communist. He wrote anti-government pamphlets.'

'Well I'm not surprised he turned out to be a bastard. Communists are all bastards.'

'No, they're not,' said Cia. Suddenly she wanted passionately to defend his ideals even if she was near to hating the man.

'Cia, that's mad! They're nasty people. Can't you see that? They murder innocent people!'

'Have you met any?' sneered Cia.

'No,' admitted Belle, huffily. 'But look what they did to the Romanovs!'

There was a brief silence between them.

'Oh, for Christ's sake,' continued Belle. 'We're not going to let politics come between us and that's that. Did he really hurt you?' Cia's eyes filled with tears again. 'Well, I don't understand how you can still think of communism as a good thing, then,' finished Belle.

But Cia was really crying now and her friend reached out and held her close, patting her back gently like a baby's as the tears emptied from her. 'You're as beautiful as you ever were,' she said. 'You'll find someone else in no time.'

Cia blew her nose. 'I don't think there's much hope at my age, not here,' she said. 'Englishmen run a mile from a passionate woman. You know that. They even run if you have an original idea!'

Belle sat up straight. 'Original ideas . . .' she began.

They finished the sentence together. '. . . are the driving force of progress!'

'Oh Miss Isard, where are you now?' sighed Belle. 'Now there was a woman! When you think back you realise how far ahead of her time she was. Imagine teaching a gaggle of slum kids, except you of course, about ideas! We were supposed to be drilled in the three Rs. I knew she was special even then. I had erotic fantasies about her in bed at night while my two sisters were snoring on either side of me. Oooh. Just me and her in some gorgeous country garden in the nude whispering poetry to each other . . .'

'You didn't tell me at the time!' Cia was shocked.

'There were plenty of things I never told you,' said Belle mysteriously. 'Wait a minute – I've just thought of something. Why does it have to be an Englishman? You know who's free now, don't you? Rudy Wicked! He's a Jew but he's lovely to look at and he can't be a communist – he's rolling in money.'

'You're not anti-Semitic as well as anti-communist are you?' asked Cia.

'No I'm not! Sven thinks this racial purity stuff in Germany is terrible. I'm just saying he's a Jew. Jesus, you're nit-picky. You need a lover, pronto!'

Cia smiled ruefully. Belle always took on the colour of her lover's politics.

'That's one thing I know about myself. I need sex like a bloody flower needs rain,' she said.

'Well, you've always fancied Rudy. Now's your chance,' said Belle with glee.

'Don't be daft,' laughed Cia. 'He'd never look at me!'

When Belle had gone, Cia thought about drawing. The drawings she had done in Switzerland had just about survived the journey. While she was retrieving them from her bag, she unpacked the red Chinese silk. She unravelled it and suddenly she saw the progression of the story in it. The story of the goose. And in the last panel the goose was gone.

She gave way again to tears. She cried so much she could have filled buckets.

When she finished crying she sat down with a cup of tea and thought about Giordano more clearly, and not only about him but about herself. It was as if he had died.

She knew what grief was like: its twists and turns, and how it made you a bit barmy. Grandma's death had taken her a long time to get used to. But that was real. The affair with Giordano, on the other hand, had been so brief. Why should it have affected her so? She picked up the silk and held it to her cheek for the umpteenth time. Was it all so intense because she had been scared and in the middle of nowhere, with a stranger? Or had she really been in love?

She put it down again. That avenue of thought was useless. What did it matter? It was over. Somehow, deciding that made her feel better.

She unfolded the drawings. Looking at them critically took her out of herself for a glorious half-hour. It gave her the power to draw again. She decided to set up a workroom in the small dining room on the first floor, where Grandma had kept her sewing machine. The room needed cleaning.

A long time later she made herself some dinner and listened to Reginald Dixon at the organ of the Tower Ballroom in Blackpool on the radio. When the concert was over, she undressed for bed.

When she was naked, the impulse to take up the red silk again was so strong that she held it up next to her pale body, letting the geese fall over her.

Outside, everything was dark beyond the uncurtained window. It was as if the whole world was dark and silent without the music. She could see nothing of the tiny patio, the small back lawn or the high, privet hedges – only herself and the wavy reflection.

She wound the fabric around herself as she had done before, that night a million years ago in Switzerland when he was in the bath. But now the fabric did not redden her skin. She wound it loosely. Her reflection in the old glass looked like an old self. She let the fabric fall. She sighed heavily. That self was gone.

Chapter Thirteen

'But you were looking forward to my going!' protested Dianna. 'You said that love doesn't last, people change.'

He had! He had! Now he was retracting his words. Their short month together had flown by and she was as sorry to leave him as he obviously was to see her go.

They were sitting, naked, in the easy chair, she between his legs. The view of Florence lay serenely in front of Dianna's open thighs.

The villa, however, was not its usual self. There were packing cases and trunks in most of the rooms. Plomer had gone off to Scotland to sail with *Pearlita*'s new owner, Harry Walcarp-Etting.

'I'll miss you,' said Wilhelm.

'I'll miss you too,' she assured him. 'You don't know how much.'

'You'll have all those society parties to go to that you love so much. I'll have nothing.' He pouted.

'You'll find yourself a new girlfriend soon enough.' She felt no jealousy. She wanted him to be happy.

'I've become used to having someone around. Perhaps I'm just feeling lazy,' he said.

'You know what I love about you?' laughed Dianna.

'What?' he asked. 'My good looks? My genius?'

'Your frankness. Your openness. Men and women of my generation don't talk this way to each other.'

'I keep telling you, we're the same generation. We're only ten years apart.'

'But my husband is ten years older than me, so you're a generation away from him. That's what I mean, really.'

'Will you go back to him eventually?' he asked.

'Yes,' Dianna admitted. 'I will, eventually. I expect we'll live like brother and sister.'

'Promise me you'll take a lover?' said Bill. 'Don't let yourself go to waste.'

She turned her head and kissed him. He responded passionately, climbing around her on the chair and kissing her all over – every single part of her – until she squealed out with laughter.

Somewhere in the house down below, a door slammed furiously.

Dianna noticed it, in passing, but she was too busy to care. His head was between her legs now, his slender body kneeling on the floor. She stroked his head and his tongue reached for her clitoris and licked it.

She sat with her legs wide open, all of Florence below. What more could any sane woman want? She had real doubts about giving this up. But she had set the ball rolling and she was going and that was that. The portrait of her was done. She was superstitious about it. She had to go now, taking it with her, to remind her of what she could be.

She was so glad to be able to part loving him, having him love her. There had been a strange few days, when he was coming to the end of the portrait, when he seemed not to approve of what she had become under his awakening fingers, of her growing sophistication in the art of love –

A stab of pleasure stopped her thinking. She raised her legs so that her knees touched her shoulders and slid down in the chair.

'Mmmmm,' he whispered, and he stroked her sex from the tip to her tail over and over again. He never seemed to tire of stroking her. She had complete confidence in their sex now. He knew her and knew what she needed. He had known it always it seemed, as if he knew her body as well as he knew his own.

He applied more pressure to her and she became wet. He took her moisture and massaged it into the pink flesh of her cunt. She closed her eyes and gave herself to the feelings.

He left her cunt and kissed her thigh. He kissed the crooked back of her knee. Standing up, he kissed her calf, her heel, the sole of her foot, her toes. The sensation made her giggle with pleasure.

'You have such beautiful feet,' he said, taking her foot in his hand and stretching her leg out. He put the sole of her foot on his cock and pushed lightly. 'Did you know that some men find women's shoes so erotic they'll use them?'

'What do you mean?' Dianna asked, opening her eyes. His cheeks showed a slight blush and it intrigued her. 'What do you mean?' she repeated.

'The shoe is an intimate belonging,' he explained. 'I have read of a man stealing a shoe from his lover and taking it home to use in her absence.'

'Show me what he would do,' she whispered. She knew he wanted to – she could tell by the blush. She was so excited. Imagine discovering something secret about him, now, right at the end. God, he was lovely. 'My shoes are in the cupboard, there.'

He gently placed her foot back on the floor and went to her shoe cupboard. There were only about ten pairs left, the rest having been packed away in a trunk.

'Which shall I use?' he asked.

'Take your pick,' she said. 'I will give you them as a present. You can use them when I'm gone.'

He spent some time choosing. She turned round to look at him. His back was curled so that the bumps of his spine showed through his skin. He looked so vulnerable. His back seemed to go all the way down; his buttocks had disappeared underneath him. His shapely legs were crunched against his chest and his exquisite, brown feet balanced him. He reached for her pale blue satin evening slippers.

They had quite high heels and a wide peep-toe. She loved them, but she knew she was going to love giving them to him – after he'd done whatever he had to do – even more.

He stood up and walked back to her with them in his hand. His cock was still quite stiff. It bounced. She never tired of it.

He lifted her left foot again. 'You have to wear them for a little while,' he said. 'So that they are warm with your heat.'

As he placed the shoe on her foot she thought of Cinderella. 'Why, it fits!' she giggled.

'Something you never knew about Prince Charming!' He grinned at her.

When she had both of them on, he spoke. 'Will you walk around in them for me?'

She held out her hand and he helped her up. She began her parade up and down the room, naked, in pale blue, peep-toe heels.

He swivelled the armchair around and watched her. 'God,' he breathed, 'there's nothing like the movement of a woman's hips in high heels.'

Dianna sashayed across the room towards him and lifted one foot. She slowly put the sole of her shoe down right on his prick. He groaned with pleasure and his prick grew huge, but it was too difficult to keep her balance and she took her foot away.

He stood up grabbed her and leapt on the bed. 'Fuck me,' he said. 'With those shoes on. Put it there again. Go on.'

Dianna sat at the end of the bed looking at him while he lay with his legs open, his cock stiff. The secret darkness of his arse filled her senses with strange passion. She put the sole of the shoe gently on his cock. The heel touched his balls and she tried to be careful, but he seemed insensible to any danger. He pressed his cock against her shoe and her foot wobbled. He thrashed around in an absolute frenzy. She had never seen him so excited.

After a while he raised his head and peered down at her split sex and groaned all the more loudly. 'Do it to me! Come up here and fuck me. Here!'

She scrambled up him and took his cock in her hand. It was like a tower of sex, bursting. She was wet. She straddled him and pushed it inside her vagina.

'Bring your feet up here!' he pleaded.

She put her feet on his shoulders.

'Dig your heels in!' he cried and he screamed with a mad pleasure as she did.

Her clitoris was touching only air. She watched his incredible pleasure and took pleasure in it herself, but there came a point where she could stand it no longer. She took her legs back, lay on top of him, and pushed into his belly in a frenzy to match his own. Her heel scraped at his calf as her orgasm shuddered through her body and he burst with pleasure.

'I still want to know what you would do if I weren't here!' she told him later.

They were down in the kitchen. Niccolo appeared to have jumped ship. They were preparing a meal from the larder.

Bill stopped slicing the salami. 'Just the thought makes my knees go weak again,' he said, grinning.

'Well, I won't mention it again until you've put that knife down!' she replied, laughing.

She kept her word. When they sat down to supper though, Bill asked her to go and get the shoes and wear them. 'Please!' he cried.

So she wore them under the table and towards the end

of the meal she rubbed his leg with one, then the other. They drank a good deal of wine and went back upstairs to bed so they could be naked, except for her shoes.

Angelina put the newspaper on the seat of the train as it drew into the station at Pisa. For two weeks she had read the bloody newspapers every day, but she had found nothing, absolutely nothing, about the bank manager. No-one had come looking for her either. She was beginning to think she might have got away with any involvement. It was a relief.

She got down from the train and swayed along the platform. Male heads turned. She never went anywhere without men's heads swivelling. *Mosci,* they were. Flies. If she were Contessa di Ravanello, she would employ this type of man to file her nails and they would think themselves lucky.

She had heard nothing from Ninnolo about legalities, and her days and nights had been filled with nothing but a growing obsession. How dare Gianni stay away so long on honeymoon, on her money! And how she needed him! What she would do to him for being so ruthless . .

She had finally found a hairdresser who knew where they were reported to be. Daft bitch had told her for nothing during the course of a trim. Angelina's hair was very short now – the number of hairdressers she had had to visit.

A telephone call had done the rest. Gianni and Petra were on the register at L'Increspa Rosa, an extremely cheap hotel in Pisa not far from the tower.

Angelina made her way there. It was a sweet little honeymooners' paradise. It had pale pink flowers in profusion hanging from baskets on either side of the door and trailing from window ledges. It had no shutters, but Viennese-style curtains, rouched and sweetly tied with ribbons. The ground floor window sills displayed a collection of little china figures with sweet smiles and a pink galleon with roses stuck in the barrels of its cannons.

'Yeuch!' spluttered Angelina. It was just the place to take a daft little peasant girl.

She went in and asked for Mr and Mrs Gianni Vittima. The happy couple were out, she was informed by the landlady. The woman's face was writ plain with a question. Why would anyone come looking for a honeymoon couple?

'Signora,' said Angelina, 'be warned. This so-called couple are thieves. They were my employees and they have left my house along with several precious items. I don't even think they are married.'

The landlady shot an alarmed glance at the occasional table in the centre of the lobby. On it was a glass configuration of lovers in a kiss. It was in the style of Murano, and although it was an imitation she clearly valued it.

'Be warned,' repeated Angelina, and she left the landlady with a worried look on her face.

She retired to the interior of a small cafe on the other side of the street and waited for Gianni and Petra to return and get thrown out. But when they didn't appear by the time she had drunk two cappuccinos, she got restless. What the hell, she thought. The damage was done. No need to die of boredom.

She walked to the end of the street. In front of her she could see the tower, leaning. There were numerous visitors all ogling in wonder; some taking snapshots, some going up inside the thing. There was a professional photographer at the bottom, taking a picture of a couple. He had covered them in bird seed and there were doves covering their shoulders, sitting on their heads. Angelina couldn't believe her luck. It was Mr and Mrs Gianni Vittima.

Gianni saw her at the very instant she saw him. His face contorted in anguish as the camera snapped, and he was captured forever thus. Angelina smiled and blew him a kiss. She unbuttoned her blouse as he paid the photographer and struggled to get Petra to walk the other way. Angelina leaned on the leaning tower, keeping Gianni in sight. He kept looking back. Angelina felt gratified that he found her so irresistible he couldn't take his eyes off her.

Eventually, he manoeuvred Petra around the tower to the entrance. Angelina went the other way, and when Gianni was in view she carefully lifted the hem of her blue crepe dress, sliding her skirt up her leg.

'Signorina?' said an American voice behind her. 'Are you looking for a little business?'

She looked at the tall American in dumbfounded amazement. She had to crane her neck. He was possibly the biggest man she had ever seen.

'I'll pay five dollars!' he said, pretty sure of himself.

Angelina spat at him. He swore at her and wiped his face but in that couple of seconds she had lost sight of Gianni and Petra. She looked around wildly, then she looked up.

There was a file of people going up the stairs inside the tower, passing by the loggias like ducks on a shooting booth. She spotted the happy couple in among them because she recognised Petra's dress. Gianni was virtually pulling her by the hand.

Trust him, she thought. He tries to escape me but he traps himself at the top of a tower. He wasn't all that bright really. She paid for a ticket and entered the tower, following the stream of tourists up the narrow stairway.

At the top she stood at one side of the belfry watching Gianni and Petra at the other. She enjoyed Gianni's discomfort. Petra was obviously beginning to get a bit annoyed at his attempts to usher her down quickly.

In fact, it didn't take long for Petra to realise something was wrong. When she finally saw Angelina her response was completely calm. She left Gianni and walked over to her enemy.

'Are you going to make a scene in public?' she asked.

Angelina was lost for words for a second or two. The peasant was absurdly self-assured.

'I dare you,' continued Petra. 'You'll find yourself arrested and taken into an asylum, I expect. Your reputation for madness is growing.'

Angelina raised her hand to slap the bitch's face and then she saw Gianni start for the stairs.

'I think your husband is running away!' she said gleefully.

But he wasn't. Two Blackshirts were at the top of the stairs. They stood surveying the crowd of people, their backs stiff, their faces blank. Gianni approached them.

Fucking bastards are everywhere, thought Angelina. She knew she had no chance. She steeled herself and walked away from Petra, past the Blackshirts, past Gianni. She glared at him. She saw something weary in his eyes. She felt frightened of that more than hatred. She hurried.

She went back to the cafe and ordered a glass of wine. She didn't have long to wait this time before the happy couple returned to their hotel. Angelina decided to eat something while she waited to see if they were thrown out. Sure enough, 45 minutes later they emerged, carrying bags. She paid her bill quickly and followed them at a discreet distance.

Three hours later she watched them go into the apartment block in Florence and then she returned home to wait.

The maid announced Gianni about an hour later. Angelina trembled slightly as she fluffed her hair in front of the mirror while she waited for him to reach her.

And then, at last, he was there in her room. He closed the door behind him.

'You are determined to make my life hell, aren't you?' he said quietly.

'Oh Gianni!' she cried, and she flung herself at him.

He took her by the shoulders and pushed her away to a distance of a couple of feet.

'What do you expect? You paid to have me killed!' she protested.

'I was desperate,' said Gianni. 'I am desperate, still. I'm trying to create a life for myself and all you want to do is destroy it!'

'I just want to be part of it,' she pleaded. She reached up to touch his face.

He didn't stop her. A current of electricity seemed to spark between her hand and his body as she let her hand fall to his chest.

'You shouldn't excite me,' he growled. 'You can't push me without taking the consequences.'

'I want you,' she said, 'I want the consequences, whatever they are.' She moved her body closer to his.

Gianni's resolve was clearly melting. Angelina excited him beyond all reason. He reached for her, took her in his arms and kissed her. Her body was so thin, her flesh was loose on her bones. She was so different to Petra whose soft roundness of form quivered in submission every time he touched her. He could almost feel the will beneath Angelina's skin, strong as iron, hardening in triumph. He was the only man who had ever broken her. She was irresistible to him.

His kiss tore into her lips. His body smothered her own. She felt light as air as he lifted her and took her to the couch and lay her down. His body crushed her, driving everything but the glorious weight of him from her thoughts. She lay like a queen as he opened her blouse and ate her breasts. His hand slid under her waist and he raised her hips. He took her knickers down with the other hand and grabbed a cushion. He put it under her arse so that her cunt was tilted in the air and then he played with it – for almost an hour.

He watched her sink deeper and deeper into a trance as he played with her rosy sex. He manipulated her skin with his fingers, he pulled her hair gently. He massaged her sex with the whole of his hand, the heel of his palm pressing her arse. Then he started with his mouth.

He licked her and licked her and sucked her until her sex felt like lava. Angelina cried for him. She cried like a baby, trying to hide her face behind her hands. She gave up and just cried. The torture of it was so sweet.

He left her to undress and she watched him in the still white room; brown from the sun, firm as a man could be, the bulk of his shoulders enormous as he walked towards her.

She lay motionless, her body helpless and heavy, and her sex the centre of her universe.

He penetrated her quickly, reaching her cervix in two thrusts. She threw her legs around his torso. Her heels rested passively on his bouncing buttocks. His momentum took her along, lifting her with each thrust until the beginning of an orgasm twisted in her womb.

He rammed into her more quickly, trying to crash though resistance that was no longer there. Her orgasm came, long and twitchy, and he felt so triumphant at drawing a moment of complete and utter gift from her again that he exploded and filled her.

He left her quickly afterwards and went home to Petra. He faced her across the kitchen table at her parents' apartment. The old folks had gone to bed.

'I know where you've been,' she said, her voice breaking. 'And I don't know what's the matter with you.'

He said nothing.

She cleared her throat 'Do you want to leave me?'

'No,' he said.'No, never that.'

'But you want her too?' she asked, in a whisper.

'Yes.' He hung his head.

Petra got up from the table and put the bottle of *Aqua Minerale* she had been drinking in the cupboard where it was kept. Then she walked out of the kitchen, saying nothing more.

Gianni was exhausted. He waited a few minutes, to

give her time to undress and get into bed. Then he followed her into the bedroom.

He climbed into bed beside her and put his arm around her. She took his hand and put it to her face. He could feel her tears on his hand and he moved closer to her. He kissed her hair and her neck.

Petra tried to be immune to him. She tried hard. But she couldn't. She had no choice but to respond. She loved him. She turned to him and met his lips, meeting his body with her own.

He lifted her nightdress and caressed her rounded thighs, then pulled her body close, feeling her luscious warm breasts close to his chest. He felt her hairy sex. She was damp. His own sex began to harden. He opened her legs.

In the darkness of their bedroom there was only one thought in Petra's mind as she climbed on top of her husband's body and took his sex into her own. The thought shone like a beacon. Tonight she would get pregnant.

Cia felt nervous about going to a big party – she hadn't been to one for a long time. She was getting used to her own company. But that wasn't the only reason for her nerves. She wandered from the bathroom to the bedroom, dragging her towel behind her. Well, she thought, to hell with the awkwardness of it. She wanted to go out. If Dianna Fitchew caused a scene tonight she wouldn't gain anything by it.

The invitation to the Wyckes' party had arrived a week ago, on the same morning as a letter from the di Ravanello lawyers in Italy.

The news that she might inherit nearly £500,000 took a while to sink in. The thought of what she could do with such a huge sum thrilled her. All her troubles would be over; life would be infinitely more comfortable. But she promised herself she wouldn't get too used to the idea because the letter also said that the family had initiated proceedings to contest the bequest and Cia knew the determination of her half-sister only too well. The hearing was set for two weeks time – and she was advised to either be in Florence or have someone there to represent her.

She could afford to do neither. She had written back explaining her position and had put it out of her mind as much as she was able.

Belle, who was always up on what was going on, had told her as soon as Dianna had arrived with Lady Walcarp-Etting and her son Hector. Harry Walcarp-Etting and Plomer were sailing to the Clyde but the ladies, dutifully escorted by one son, had come overland and would travel on. Belle would be at the party alone too because Sven was going up to the Clyde. The weather was too chilly up there for Belle. She was philosophical. The events of the sailing year were as regular as the moon and the tides and yachting widows got used to the absence of their men. Besides, Belle maintained, she didn't want her man on her heels all the time.

When she had bathed, Cia combed out her wet hair into the shape it should be when it was dry and put on some eye make-up. Many of her dresses were still in the trunk – there just wasn't the room in her wardrobe. She took out a green cocktail dress and ironed it carefully. It had a high mandarin collar with a little button at the neck and a slit at the side. With her hair waved sleekly, her face powdered and her lips red as raspberries, Cia looked as if she was ready to burst from a succulent green pod. She wore no stockings, having sandpapered her legs smooth and drenched them in moisturising oil that she had bought with an advance from Belle for her clothes.

She picked ten of Grandma's old roses from the garden and made a bunch for Edna. She left Finnemore by the side gate. The evening was warm and sunny. A couple of marines passed her and gave her appreciative looks which made her glow.

Tennyson House rose in a series of decorous eaves and leaden windows behind a more modern front, with American-style bays. On top of all this stood the turret, with its battlements and its fine views of the Solent.

The huge glass doors of the front bays were open on to the sloping front lawn. Old stone steps wound up to the house. Cia entered the house through one of the bays and immediately a servant offered her a glass of Pimms from a lacquered tray. Cia took it and followed the servant through the house to the back.

There were a lot of people on the terrace and scattered on the lawn at the back. Their voices, mainly the men's, drifted on the evening air. Glasses clinked. Beyond them, the Solent sparkled in the evening sun.

The men were predominantly naval types. Some were in uniform, and a few were in evening dress. Mostly they were tall, straight backed, and very English. Almost all the women were in evening gowns. Cia's short green pod drew one or two looks, but Cia had the confidence that comes with knowing you look stunning.

Edna was on the terrace, dressed rather gaily in a low-necked turquoise gown. The colour gave a real sparkle to her dark features. Edna was small and curvy and her twinkling spirit gave her an aura of playfulness that some men just adored. She beamed when she saw Cia. She was standing with a couple of old sea dogs of immense height and whiskers, a tall fierce-looking grey-haired woman and a handsome younger man. She left them to greet Cia.

'Cia, you came! I'm so glad! I've been neglecting you. Rudy keeps telling me he's seen you but you didn't come up and I've been so busy with the race committee.' Edna was the only yachtswoman ever to have been invited on to the committee.

'I haven't seen Rudy,' said Cia. She was puzzled.

'I suppose he must have seen you out shopping or something,' said Edna. 'He has been going out more, thank God.'

Cia was more than flattered that Rudy had noticed her. 'I must ask you something. Were you and Rudy in Milan on . . . it must have been the 26th May?'

'Golly!' said Edna, after thinking about it a bit. 'We were there on that date!'

'I saw you at the railway station. I tried to catch up with you but I lost you. I was on my way home.'

'That was months ago! Well, weeks, at least. No – months!'

'I was robbed of all my money. I missed the train.'

'Well, thank heaven you're in one piece,' said Edna.

'I'll tell you all about it another time. Is Dianna Fitchew here?'

'I saw her and Belle disappearing off into the walled garden a few minutes ago. They seem to have hit it off.'

'How is Rudy?' asked Cia.

'Awful,' replied Edna, lowering her voice slightly. 'He hasn't come down.'

'Oh,' said Cia. She was fiercely disappointed.

'He's still distraught over Nora's death. I think it's so drawn out because he's hardly ever had to wrestle with something he doesn't understand. You know how easily he always does things. Her suicide seems inexplicable to him, what with all the other implications. He vacillates between hating her and wishing she were alive. I don't. I hope she rots in hell.' She paused.

'We came home via Milan. We were on our way back from a sort of round trip which I insisted on. We were sailing for a while in Monte Carlo with Harry Walcarp-Etting. Rudy seemed much more himself when he was sailing *Pearlita*. But he's not himself now, that's for certain. Could you imagine him not coming down to a party in the old days? At least he goes out occasionally now. It was bloody awful before our trip when he wouldn't even come down from the turret room. I thought we were going to have a lunatic on our hands. I resolutely went up every day . . .'

Cia switched off, momentarily, from her friend. So it

must have been Rudy up there the night she arrived back. She suddenly felt happy. It was a strange feeling.

'Anyway, I must introduce you to people,' said Edna. She dropped her voice again. 'The new Lady Walcarp-Etting has got some fire in her belly, I tell you. She used to be married to the Earl of Eachester. Hector's her son. He's Earl now, of course, since his father died. He doesn't act like any other earl I've ever come across. Not half so stiff. They're off to join the circus.'

Cia grinned. Some yachtsmen called the Big Class a travelling circus. King George, with an eye on public opinion, put the race committees under an obligation to set courses as close to the shore as possible, especially on the Clyde where *Brittania* had been built. The people came out in their thousands to watch their *Brittania* and the rest of the class with all their glittering guests on board.

'Come on,' said Edna. 'I'll do the honours.'

The old sea dogs had gone westward. The grey-haired woman and the handsome younger man had been joined by another youngish, portly man who swayed with drink. He was talking about how the communists would be overrunning the lawns one of these days if they weren't all locked up in jail soon. His wife, a bottle blonde with a ridiculous bow in her hair repeated the end of his sentences.

Lady Walcarp-Etting primed her cannons. She came about and blasted the social-climbing non-entities right out of the water. Edna tried to man the social lifeboat as the mortified couple clung tenaciously.

This left Cia and the young man to make their own introductions.

'Call me Hector,' said Hector, the Earl of Eachester. 'The colour of your dress is wonderful. I think that's one of the best dresses I've seen in a long time.'

Cia was so surprised at an Englishman actually noticing a dress that she didn't know what to say for a moment. But he was so easy they were chatting away like old friends within a few minutes. He was a bit of a misfit, he told her. He could never please anyone, least of all his mother.

Cia listened to him with increasing amazement. It was most unusual for anyone to open up so quickly. She found herself thinking how pleasing his face was. It was so animated it fascinated her.

'Dear me,' said Lady Walcarp-Etting, as the social climbers slunk away.

'They're local dignitaries. I had to invite them,' explained Edna.

But Cia wasn't listening to them. Hector had completely closed up, like a shop for the night, at the re-entrance of his mother into the conversation. It was incredible.

Lady Walcarp-Etting frowned at her son. Then she turned to Cia and beamed. 'My old feet are absolutely killing me,' she said. 'Will you excuse me, my dear? I'm sure we shall meet again but can I leave you in the company of my son?'

She walked away and Edna made excuses and left them too.

'She's always giving me orders,' complained Hector.

'Please don't feel obliged . . .' said Cia.

'Not at all. Not at all.' He smiled softly at her. 'Some orders are easy to follow.'

He really did have a lovely face, thought Cia. He was plainly flirting with her. Well, well, well, she thought.

A little while later, some yachtsmen claimed Hector's attention and Cia wandered down the lawn to the walled garden. She might as well face the music now as later. The garden was tiny – a small private space where you could forget the world.

'Cia!' squealed Dianna, and she got up from the bench. Her skin glowed, her eyes sparkled, and her whole body had a happy demeanour. She flew at Cia and hugged her.

Belle turned around and over Dianna's shoulder she gave Cia a grin.

'You look wonderful,' Cia told Dianna.

'I've lost weight. Oh Cia, I've got absolutely loads to tell you. But how are you, my dear? I was a silly fool to let you go, although I hardly had time to miss you. Isn't it wonderful news about your inheritance!'

'I'm not counting my chickens,' said Cia. 'How did you find out?'

'That stupid woman, Louisa Penhaligon, told me.'

Cia gawped at Dianna. The goddess Louisa had obviously fallen from her pedestal.

'I don't want too many people to know about it. The contessa and Angelina are contesting it. I'll feel silly if it doesn't materialise.'

'I have a feeling it will,' said Belle, getting up. 'You deserve it.'

When Belle had gone back to the party, Dianna told Cia all about Wilhelm. 'It's opened up a whole new world for me,' she declared. 'A world of sensation!'

Cia listened to the glowing accounts of Dianna's sex life. It was impossible not to forgive this bubbling, lovable woman. It was as simple as that.

After dinner there was dancing – for the more energetic – to an excellent band, and Cia's disappointment at not seeing Rudy was mitigated a little by the attention Hector paid her.

In the interval she and Belle went up to Edna's bedroom to freshen up.

'So Hector's very interested in you . . .' mused Belle.

Cia smiled.

'Wouldn't it be wonderful if you were to become Lady Eachester? It would be so right after all the women in your family living without a title all these years.'

'Hold your horses!' cried Cia. 'I've only just met the man.'

'But you can't deny – '

They were interrupted by Edna's entrance. She closed the door behind her and burst into tears.

'Whatever's the matter?!' cried Belle and Cia at the same time.

'It's Rudy. He's going to kill himself with sorrow. I just asked if he wouldn't come down and he shouted at me.'

'You mustn't be upset,' soothed Cia. 'I'm sure he didn't mean to. Grief does really strange things to people . . .'

'Cia, why don't you go up and try to persuade him to come down for a minute? He was asking if you were here.'

'Um . . .' mumbled Cia gormlessly. He was asking after her!

'Good idea,' said Belle, smirking.

Cia grimaced at Belle.

'Oh go on, Cia! Please?' begged Edna.

And so, against her better judgement, Cia took two glasses of champagne and made her way along the corridor to the west end of the house and up the winding stair to the turret.

She heard the strange noise about halfway up the stairs and stopped, holding on to the rope bannister fixed to the outer wall. After a minute the noise seemed to stop, so she continued upward very quietly.

The stairwell opened out into a small room where, among books and charts and drawings, Rudy sat, his broad back towards her, crumpled, his head in his hands between his knees, sobbing his heart out.

Cia's chest wrenched. Her impulse was to fly over and put her arms around him but she could not intrude on such a moment of extreme privacy. She turned, quiet as a mouse, and went back down the stairs.

At the bottom she steadied herself. Shocking though it was to see him cry like that, she knew that he would feel better for it. Something would change once he had given vent to his feelings.

She drank one glass of champagne straight down and took the other one downstairs where she rejoined the party.

It was almost two o'clock and some of the guests were departing.

'How was he?' asked Edna quietly, when she got a chance.

Cia suddenly felt the need to protect him from the possibility that Edna might fly upstairs and try and stop the sorrow that needed to be expressed. 'He's OK,' she said.

Luckily, Edna didn't get a chance to ask more questions. Some more of her guests were leaving.

Hector grimaced when they were alone again. 'This business about Rudy is terribly dreary, isn't it? Edna seems perfectly fraught.'

Cia's back suddenly started to ache with all the standing. 'I'm tired,' she announced, ignoring his remarks.

'I feel like quitting too.' He beamed at her. 'Shall I walk you home?'

'It's just down the road,' said Cia, shaking her head. 'There's no need.'

But he looked hurt. She relented. It was rather rude not to accept his offer.

Lady Walcarp-Etting, still going strong, beamed at the pair of them when Hector announced he was walking her home. Cia was bemused.

They walked down the dark road to Finnemore and Hector chatted happily until they reached the gate.

'So it's you who lives here! This is a lovely old house. Very witchy though. I thought it would be some old dame's place,' he said brightly.

'Perhaps you'll come and visit me? Then you can see the inside.' She said it more out of politeness than anything else.

'I'd love to!' he cried. 'Shall I come tomorrow?'

'Yes,' she said. 'Why not?'

She closed the door behind her and fumed. That remark about Rudy being dreary had incensed her. She grumbled to herself the whole time as she undressed.

Chapter Fourteen

Sunday wore on and Hector hadn't turned up. Cia was relieved. The light was perfect all day in the upstairs dining room. She spent most of the day cutting and sewing toilles.

About five, just when she was thinking she'd give up and have tea, the doorbell rang. It was Belle, with some fresh crab. Ten minutes later, Dianna arrived with some pastries and the three of them were just about to take a tea tray out to the gazebo when Edna arrived, empty handed and looking strained.

Edna started making excuses when she realised Cia had company but she was drowned out by Dianna and Belle's insistence that she stay. Cia grabbed an ancient bottle of Sutherlandshire single malt whisky and some cigarettes before she followed her guests down the front lawn.

Cia had cleaned the gazebo up. It just about held the four of them round a glass-topped wicker table. They drank tea and ate the crab with bread and the pastries. The summer afternoon waned and the Solent changed colour in the sun beyond the road in front of the house.

The other guests at the Wyckes' were the subject of much discussion.

'Anyway,' said Edna, 'I don't think they'll be going up to the Clyde.'

'They're not. Did you hear that awful row, too?' Dianna blushed. 'I wasn't eavesdropping. You couldn't help but overhear – '

'It *was* loud.' Edna butted in to soothe Dianna's embarrassment. 'There's been a change of plan. She came and asked me if she could stay longer. She's developed a cold and the weather up there is so changeable.'

While the other two discussed the weather and the Clyde, Belle leaned over to Cia and whispered, 'So the earl's going to be in the vicinity. I bet you find out pretty soon whether *he's* got a big dick.'

Cia snorted.

'What are you two laughing about?' asked Dianna.

'Dick,' improvised Belle.

'Dick who?' asked Dianna.

Edna was grinning.

There was a moment's silence.

'We have a game we . . . we've played it since we were very young,' said Cia. 'When we talk about our men – lovers – we always try and prize information about the size of their penises out of each other.' Dianna raised her eyes heavenward. 'It's silly, I know. But to show we're grown up and sophisticated – at least I think that's why we do it – we avoid actually telling. It's a game.' Cia paused. She felt as if she were deep in some private world. It was hard to explain.

Edna helped her out. 'As far as I remember, that bit about not telling came about *after* you'd sampled a few. It started long before that.'

'I didn't know you knew about it,' said Belle.

Cia unscrewed the top off the whisky bottle.

'I'd love some,' said Edna. 'You thought I was too young to know what you were talking about, but I wasn't.'

'Yes, please,' said Dianna to the whisky. 'You youngsters! Don't you know that size doesn't matter. It's what they do with it that makes the world go round!'

Belle held up one of the heavy-bottomed whisky tumblers as Cia poured and looked at Dianna expectantly.

Dianna took a cigarette from the box. She lit it and took a long drag. She blew the smoke out in a stream and held the stick between two elongated fingers.

'I was with a young man in Florence who did something truly extraordinary with his,' she said. 'Oh God, I must get it off my chest! You're women of the world, aren't you? You won't be shocked?'

'Probably not,' said Belle, looking at Edna.

Edna stuck her chin out at Belle and looked at her with fiery eyes. 'I'm not as shockable as I was when I was fifteen!'

Ignoring their rivalry, Dianna told them about Wilhelm and her pale blue satin peep-toed shoes.

'. . . and then,' she continued, 'I reminded him he was going to tell me what he would do if I wasn't there.

'"Give me the shoe,"' he said finally.

'I took it off and he got very excited because it was still warm. He even liked to sniff it! Can you believe it? Sometimes, if we'd been walking, I nearly died with embarrassment. But he never seemed anything but completely besotted.

'Anyway, he unbuttoned his fly again and got out his pretty cock and slipped the shoe on to it! And then he pulled the heel up and down so that the shoe went up and down, up and down.

'I couldn't just sit there on the side of the bed, looking at him do it, so I rolled on to the bed next to him and watched it from a different angle. The tip of his cock peeked out of the toe every time. I tell you, it was so strange it really aroused me. It was purple!'

The girls giggled.

'The thing was, it wasn't funny at the time, although

it does sound it now. At the time it was his seriousness, his absolute abandonment that made it what it was.'

'I know what you mean,' said Belle, nodding. 'I had a lover, a very long time ago, who used to like to wear my underwear. If I think about it dispassionately it just seems absurd, but at the time I used to get really aroused by it; more, I think, by his arousal than anything else. He was just so helpless, too. Men can be so free sexually. They think nothing of letting themselves go. We have to teach ourselves to be.'

'I was offered money for sex at the station in Milan,' said Cia. 'At first I was horrified. Then I had a drink and my inhibitions went and I was quite aroused by the idea of being just sexual – uncomplicated perhaps – for a short time.'

'I bet you're glad you didn't though, now?' asked Edna.

'I am,' said Cia.

'I wonder why? I wonder if that has anything to do with the actual act or just with the larger perspective, the condemnation, implicit or explicit,' said Dianna.

'I bet you've never seen two cushions fucking.' said Cia, lightening up.

'What?' cried Edna and Dianna in unison.

Cia told them about the furniture at Tellino's and the orgies in the garden. They loved it. They sat wide-eyed, listening. An atmosphere settled in the gazebo, of intimacies shared.

'But what are you going to do Dianna? Are you going back to America as you planned or are you going back to Florence?' asked Cia, turning to her friend.

'Oh, I'll go home,' said Dianna. 'In September. But I won't let myself rot at home. I'll find a lover, although whether I'll ever find one like Wilhelm . . . As long as I'm discreet, I don't see why I shouldn't have one as well as Plomer Two.'

'Don't get found out,' said Belle.

Dianna took a slug of her whisky. 'I think you're very brave, living with Sven and not marrying him. It's tantamount to a declaration to the world that you're interested in sex.'

'I'd have a much easier time of it if I married him. I will, I assume. But I don't feel like giving in now.'

'Don't let anybody else's behaviour influence your decision whether to marry him or not, Belle,' said Edna passionately. 'Marry him if and when you want to.'

'And what about you, Edna? Do you have a lover?' asked Belle.

'I'm too busy.' Edna avoided the other women's eyes.

'Hmph.' said Dianna.

'I have actually, but he's . . . he got fed up because I'm so busy. He's gone up to London,' said Edna.

Cia and Belle were the most surprised by her admission. They'd always suspected it but Edna kept her mouth shut most of the time. By this time though, she had drunk two large whiskies. Cia poured her another one and the bottle did the rounds.

'How long has this been going on? Why haven't we ever seen him?' asked Cia.

'We didn't want to make it public. I have the same reservations about marriage as you, Belle. And as soon as it's out in the open everyone will be wanting to know the date and so on, if there is one. To be truthful, the thought of dressing up in a bloody tutu and doing all that ceremonial girly rubbish puts me off entirely.'

'Run away,' suggested Cia. 'Do it in secret.'

'While it works, marriage can be wonderful,' said Dianna. 'Mine worked for nineteen years and it *was* wonderful. It changed – but I wouldn't have missed those years for anything. I wanted to trash them all a few weeks ago but now I feel differently. I've grown up. If Plomer Two gets elected to office, I think we could be a good partnership. I'm going to make him give me something interesting to do, like setting up an arts foundation.'

'So you can find another artist!' giggled Belle.

'I love artists. They're so wayward!' laughed Dianna. 'But I won't restrict myself to a particular profession. I'm sure all kinds of people have wonderful peccadilloes. I think I'll hunt them down and publish a pillow book. Women in China have pillow books that they pass on to their daughters. We need more sexual knowledge in Western culture. Knowledge is power.'

They drank a toast to that one.

Belle crossed one superbly shapely leg over the other. 'I've been daydreaming about doing something for Sven during Cowes Week – giving him a crew party. I've had an outrageous idea.'

'What is it?' asked Cia.

'I'd like to have a woman covered in fruit and cream and chocolate . . . and served up as the dessert!'

'Yourself?' asked Cia.

'Well, no. I know them all . . .'

Dianna groaned. 'I'd love to be the woman . . . if my identity were never to go beyond the four of us!'

'You could wear a mask,' said Belle tentatively. 'But the practicalities . . .'

'I'm sure they could be overcome.'

They talked it over.

'What I need is someone to seduce my brother,' whispered Edna loudly, close to Cia's ear. Cia's womb did a somersault inside her pelvis.

'Perhaps I could hire a prostitute. I could go to Rosa Lewis and ask her to find me one. I don't think he's had sex for a long time, you know. Nora was having the affair with Steven Kent for a year before her death. Rudy knew about it. We spoke about it once and I gathered that their sex life was dead.

'He would never actually go to a prostitute. I know that for a fact. But sex would do him the world of good.'

'If he wouldn't want a whore then it would be mad to give him one. Surely he'd be better off with someone who loved him,' said Cia sharply.

'But he doesn't socialise! How on earth is he going to meet anyone?'

'Are you talking about Rudy?' asked Belle, returning to the conversation.

'I was saying I'd like to hire a whore to give him a good fuck,' slurred Edna.

'I think I know a slut who'd fuck him,' replied Belle, grinning.

Cia winced.

Edna noticed. She looked at Cia. 'Oh, I couldn't use one of my friends. And Cia's not a slut! You shouldn't call her that.'

'It's a term of endearment, I think,' said Cia.

'Are you still fond of my son?' asked Dianna.

'Yes, of course, but – '

'What's this?' cried Belle and Edna together.

'I broke him in,' said Cia, laughing and blushing at the same time.

'That was nice of you,' said Belle.

'It was nice, full stop,' laughed Cia.

'And that is *never* to go outside this room,' insisted Dianna.

'Of course . . .' said the others.

'I didn't understand it at the time,' said Dianna bravely, 'but now I'm glad it happened.'

'I think Hector's smitten with Cia,' said Edna.

'Me too,' agreed Belle.

'Your name came up during the argument he was having with his mother this morning. That's what made me prick up my ears,' said Dianna.

'I think he's the one that's decided not to go to the Clyde. He's going to stay here and woo you, dear,' Edna told Cia.

'I'm not sure I like him' said Cia firmly.

'Why ever not?' asked Edna.

'There's just something not – ' Cio began.

'You seemed to be getting on fine last evening,' argued Dianna. 'And Cia, think of the *title*!'

'Oh God,' laughed Cia. 'Honestly!'

'Would you be more specific? The earl in question seems eminently suitable for marriage,' slurred Belle. 'I think she ought to explain don't you, girls?'

Cia didn't want to tell Edna or Dianna why Hector had annoyed her, because it was on Rudy's account. She decided to deflect.

'You lot really take the biscuit. You talk about your own disillusionment with marriage and then as soon as an earl pops up you want *me* to be a guinea pig!'

There was a pause for thought.

'We keep on dreaming. It's woman's eternal conflict,' said Belle. The others looked at her quizzically. 'Could I have just a smidgeon more of that excellent Sutherlandshire malt?' she slurred.

Belle insisted on taking Cia out to dinner at her favourite restaurant on the waterfront after Edna and Dianna had left, swaying slightly, to Tennyson House for theirs.

'So,' said Belle, as they drank their after-dinner port by the big plate-glass windows overlooking the black sea. The pair of them were full of good food and drink. 'Has Plomer Fitchew got a big dick?'

'Actually,' replied Cia, 'he's got a massive dick!'

'Gotcha!' cried Belle.

'Game over, I think.' laughed Cia.

It was still early when they left; only 10.15. The darkness was soft and warm outside. They turned the corner in the high street just as a Tatra zoomed round the corner. It was a highly polished, black, low-slung beast of a car with the back wheels half-hidden by seamless, muscular steel.

'That's Hector's car!' said Belle.

The man in the driver's seat was difficult to identify in the darkness. The car disappeared in a roar.

'Roadhog!' yelled Belle.

* * *

The Tatra drew up at the Ryde ferryport about twenty minutes later. Even stationary, the car looked as if it was moving, it was such a dynamic shape. Hector jumped out and ran for the last ferry. He just caught it.

As the boat steamed out to sea, he stood on deck in the darkness with the breeze blowing in his face. Damn his mother. Damn her, he thought.

He didn't know yet whether he would obey the old witch. The morning's argument and the frostiness between them all day pained him. His feelings were utterly confused. He liked Cia; that was all. He knew he would have to marry. No doubt Cia would be a good companion. But he wished his mother would allow him to come round in his own time instead of forcing it. Would he ever be able to though?

Forty minutes later the ferry docked. Hector made his way down the gangplank along with the other passengers. There weren't many people travelling at that time of night. Hector turned towards The Hard. He hurried with the assurance of someone who knows where he is going, and turned into the maze of streets by the docks. He slowed his pace. If he didn't find what he was looking for he would spend the night in a pub he knew, the Rose. It was up ahead, a long way off, at the other end of the narrow street, and the soft, distant sound of voices drifted in the night air as someone left. The sound of a ship's foghorn blasted as she left the dock.

Hector knew the man was the one he was looking for as soon as he saw him. He had just left the Rose. He was brawny, tall and dark. He swayed, obviously a bit drunk. But by the way he looked at him, Hector felt it was safe.

'Have you got a match?' asked Hector, going up to him. He didn't stand too close in case he was wrong. Just in case, because the man was big. He was so big, Hector got a hard on just thinking about him. He shook a bit as the fellow got out a box of matches and lit his cigarette. The madness of his need! He cursed it. But it was the risk that thrilled him too.

The stranger caught his eye. 'Is that all you want?' he asked.

'No,' whispered Hector.

The man looked up the dark street. 'What then?'

'I have nowhere to stay,' said Hector softly.

'What's a bloke like you doing without a bed for the night?' asked the stranger, looking Hector up and down.

Hector was instinctively certain it was safe but he still trod carefully; there was only a touch of flirtation about his reply. 'People have unusual needs sometimes.'

The stranger looked deep into Hector's eyes. Then his gaze flickered up and down the dark street once more. 'Touch me,' he whispered.

As Hector reached to touch the bulge of the stranger's cock in his trousers, fear screamed through his mind. He could be a plant. He could be a policeman. He could be a queer-baiter. The fear always screamed like that. You never knew.

But the stranger was aroused and hard.

'Cor,' he said. 'We'd better stop, mate. My gaff's round the corner though – you can come with me if you want.'

Hector's knees were so weak with anticipation they barely held him up as he walked beside his man. They could have passed for a couple of pals out from the pub but the secret dimension of the reality made Hector's skin glow. Oh, how glorious it would be to walk alongside such a big man in daylight, in the open!

They passed a couple of tarts, much the worse for drink, who tried to pick them up. Suddenly one of the girls looked hard at Hector's friend.

'I know you,' she slurred. She turned to her friend. 'No use wasting our time here. They're a couple of pansies.'

Hector looked back and gave them a smug grin as they turned the corner.

'Dirty bastards,' came the tart's voice out of the darkness.

'Here, watch it. They could have the law on us,' said the big fellow.

'I doubt it,' said Hector. 'I don't expect they're best friends with the law.'

'You never know. They haven't got no thieves honour with us. If they wanted to put a favour in the bank they could easy go to the law.'

Hector's face dropped. 'I'm sorry,' he said. 'I'm so sorry. Would you rather not?'

The stranger grinned. He had nice teeth.

'They don't know where I live,' he whispered. 'Besides, I think you're a little peach.'

Round another corner the big fellow opened a door, right on the street, with a key. Inside, the passageway was lit gloomily by a fringed lampshade high in the ceiling, and the floor was covered in clean, brown linoleum. They were halfway up the stairs when a door opened on the ground floor.

'Cooee, Mr Ewing!' called a landlady's voice. 'Are you coming or are you going?'

'Bit of both if I can,' whispered Mr Ewing, giggling. 'Hello, Mrs! Just brought a mate over for a drink.'

'Nice,' said the landlady, looking up the stairs at Hector's legs.

'Cor,' said Mr Ewing, as he closed the door of his room behind them. 'They all fancy you, don't they, the tarts?'

Hector blushed.

The room was sparsely furnished, with a cooker and a sink at one end and a single bed by the window. The curtains were clean and blue. There was a picture of a mournful Christ over the mantelpiece and a collection of literary novels underneath it.

'Can't say I blame them, though.' Mr Ewing reached for Hector's waist. 'Come 'ere.'

Hector let the bear of a man draw him in. He reached up for the kiss of his lips and the bliss of it. At last! The magic of another man's body pressing against his own saturated every cell in his body.

They were always gentle, these giant men that Hector found. He was lucky, perhaps. One day he may not be. This one was no exception though. He caressed him like a mother caressing her child. He undressed him.

For Hector, the undressing was almost the best part of it. He ran his fingers through his lover's hair as the man slithered down the bed and took his cock in his mouth. Hector spread his legs and gave himself up.

He ran his fingers down the broad, hairy back. Hector marvelled at the hair on the man. It was soft and dark. His body was so different to his own small, pale, hairless one. He watched his lips eating his sex. His concentration, his desire, was all his.

Hector twisted his slender body and reached for his lover's sex. He encircled it lovingly with his fingers. The man groaned with pleasure and thrust his moist hardness into the loving fingers. His hair was dense and damp.

Hector wriggled down the bed and between his lover's legs. Their twin cocks met and pressed together. The man put Hector's cock between his legs, closing his thighs around it. Hector's cock inched between soft buttocks.

'You're lovely, you are,' breathed the giant and he covered Hector's face with kisses.

The giant lay on his front on the bed afterwards. His buttocks were paler than the rest of his body and his legs were long, long, long. Hector curled up, resting his face on the hair that graced his lover's lower back.

Mr Ewing turned his head. 'I could do with a drink of something,' he said.

'No sooner said than done.' Hector sprang to his feet. He would do anything for this man.

The cups and glasses in the cupboard were spotless. 'Water?' he asked.

'Yes,' said the man on the bed, turning to look at him.

Hector turned on the tap and the clear water gushed

into the glass. Mr Ewing propped himself on one elbow to drink it. 'Come and cuddle me,' he said.

Hector's face lit up. He was so happy. But the next moment he was sad. He felt seedy. What kind of man did this with strangers?

'Are you going to stay the night with me?'

'What about the landlady?' asked Hector.

'It's all right. It wouldn't enter her head.'

Hector snuggled into the single bed and made the most of his stranger.

In the morning Hector woke up to the sound of light rain. A grey sky blanketed the world. They made love once more.

Hector climbed over Mr Ewing's body like a wild child, taking what he could.

Mr Ewing didn't ask to see him again. Hector was grateful for that. They said goodbye, quickly. Then, just as he was walking out the door, the giant pinched Hector's bum and laughed at the surprise on his face.

Hector walked through the drizzle, back to the ferry, with a smile in his heart.

Chapter Fifteen

'There's nothing more I can do,' said the doctor. 'Perhaps a priest?'

'No,' said Tellino. 'He doesn't believe in God.'

'People change their minds,' the doctor argued.

Tellino looked at Giordano's pain-filled face. 'Not him,' he said, with complete certainty. 'He'd hate that.'

They went downstairs and Tellino gave the doctor a glass of wine at the table. He paid him. The kitchen was changed; it was emptier. In the corner, a big rubbish bin overflowed with old jars, the clutter of years.

'I might as well wait,' said the doctor. 'It won't be long.'

Tellino's body was stiff with fear. He wished Giordano would hurry up and die. Then he cursed himself. What a thing to wish.

Giordano hadn't got very far. The remainder of the squad that had been sent to kill him had finished the job the day after Cia left, or so they thought. Giordano had survived in the forests for some time with two gunshot wounds, one in his body and one in his leg, going gangrenous. His will to survive was strong. It was only when he had got back, and had lain in a bed with care and attention lavished on him, that the will seemed to have left him. Tellino didn't understand it.

He went back upstairs to the bedroom at the very top of the house. No matter what he did to freshen it up, the room still stank. Giordano was mumbling something.

More than once, as he lay delirious, Giordano had talked about Cia. He loved her. He had said it many times. Tellino had promised him he would write to her and his son, once it was over – not before.

Tellino knelt and listened to him. The soft, cracking voice made no sense this time. The sound went on and on. Then it changed. The throat rattled.

Later, Tellino sat for a long time in the darkness looking at the body lying in the freshly dug grave on the slope behind the house.

He couldn't bring himself to bury Giordano in the earth. It was too final. He climbed in and out of the grave twice, and felt the pulse. Even though the doctor had certified death, Tellino waited for a miracle. He sat remembering the way the lifeless face had smiled, frowned, argued until dawn.

As the light began to change, he picked up the spade.

In Florence, the lawyers were arguing. Angelina and her mother sat outside the judge's room waiting. The corridor had marble floors and leather seats for them to sit on. There were identical busts of Mussolini on plinths at either end of the room.

The judge's door opened and the contessa jumped up nervously. The two lawyers emerged and shook hands grimly. The count's lawyer walked off down the corridor.

'I am afraid we've lost this round, Contessa,' said theirs. 'But we will appeal.'

The contessa sat down with a bump. 'Is there any point?' she said wearily.

'Of course there is. We can't give up, can we?' he appealed to Angelina.

His crotch was level with Angelina's eyes. There

wasn't much to be seen, given the looseness of his trousers, but somewhere in there was a soft swell. She was looking for it. She thought she saw it. But then it wasn't, after all, his cock, but merely a fold. What an elusive little thing it was. The lawyer himself was embarrassed at the direction of her gaze.

Suddenly she stood up and grabbed his balls hard. She squeezed. 'All the more money for you, you useless pig!'

'Owww!' squealed the lawyer.

She twisted. 'If we don't win the appeal then you don't get paid another penny. So, you make the decision to appeal or not on that basis.'

'We might win!' squeaked the lawyer.

Angelina let him go. She didn't care if there was an appeal or not. There was no point. She had a better plan.

'You don't know anything about the death of a certain bank manager, do you?' said Ninnolo.

'No,' said Angelina in a furious whisper.

Ninnolo laughed but only with his mouth. His steely-blue eyes remained blank.

Angelina suddenly noticed his high forehead and the way his blonde hair seemed sculpted on to it. His lips were thin pink lines. She realised she hadn't seen him properly in such broad daylight before. He looked completely unnatural, as if a person had been melted down and rebuilt. He disgusted her.

They were walking across the Ponte Vecchia. The gold in the jewellers' shops on either side of the bridge gleamed softly in the windows.

It had been at Ninnolo's insistence that she was walking with him to the station where he was catching the train for England. It was a stupid idea.

He had established that she would inherit in the event of Cia's death. Angelina had given him his fare and expenses.

He stopped at the golden boar in the market square and stroked its nose for luck.

'You look very nice today. I always think people look better when you are just about to say goodbye to them,' he said. Angelina sneered at him.

'If I had really meant to kill you that time, I would have fucked you first,' he said. Her guts twisted inside.

'I thought, when I put two and two together, that you might understand me. Did you enjoy it when he died?'

'You are sick,' said Angelina, turning to go.

He grabbed her arm and led her on. At last they reached the station. The train was in. It was merely a matter of him getting aboard.

'Wait until it leaves,' he said.

'Why?'

'Because I want you to.'

'You've got a damn cheek,' she hissed at him through the open window of the compartment. 'I'm paying you a fortune. It's not for me to take orders from you.'

He smiled. 'You're a natural to take orders. You debase yourself daily.'

Angelina glowered at him. The train gave a jolt and began to move.

'See you soon.' He blew her a kiss.

Her distaste and anger didn't last long. How could it? She was going to see Gianni. She almost skipped across the piazza in front of the station. She was wearing blue today, and her dress had a bow on the front, at the waist. There were bows on her shoes and one in her hair. She passed by the back of her bank as she walked towards the Piazza Signori, and she stopped skipping and walked in a ladylike manner.

Gianni had a souvenir booth below the steps of the Uffizi. He was serving a couple as she drew close. She watched him at work. What a beautiful man he was. His head and shoulders were all that were visible behind the hanging merchandise. Strings of glass rosary beads with tin crosses hung around him in their dozens. Cushion covers embroidered with 'The Birth of Venus' in gold thread fluttered in the breeze. On the front of the stall, legions of miniature plaster Davids and Towers of Pisa stood with painted ashtrays and scallop shells painted with flowers.

Angelina ducked round the side of the booth. She took a quick look around and, sure she had not been seen, slid under the canvas and into the booth. Gianni's legs and backside stood in the private green gloom.

The English couple were deliberating over two miniature Davids. They were both exactly the same but the man was convinced there was a difference. Gianni stood patiently, smiling, helping them to spend their miserable 50 lire wisely.

Angelina slid her hand up the inside of his thigh.

He spun round and looked at her. He frowned.

She knew immediately by the way he looked that something was wrong. 'What is it?' she begged.

He held up one finger and said 'Sssh!'

Angelina sat on the little stool and waited until the tourists had handed over their money.

Gianni bent down and gave her a little peck on the cheek.

She responded by grabbing his balls, gently.

'Don't,' he said.

'Why not?'

'I have to talk to you,' he said. He looked out of the booth before turning to her again. There was a lull in exits from the Uffizi.

'Petra thinks she's pregnant,' he said.

The bitch! thought Angelina. What a fucking trump card!

'It doesn't matter,' she said. 'We can still carry on as we are. What's the difference?'

Gianni stared at her. 'The difference is I'll be a family man. I *want* to be a family man. We're going to save up and rent a small house in the country, so the child can grow up with nature.' He paused. 'We've had a wonderful time, you and I. But things change.'

Oh God, thought Angelina, not again.

'Look,' she said. 'You thought getting married would change things but it didn't, did it?'

'It might have done if you'd left me alone in Pisa,' he said. 'I hardly thought about you at all until you turned up.'

His words stung her. She had a moment of doubt. Was it worth it? Why was she continually chasing this man? But it was only a moment's doubt. She would never stop wanting him. Never. Ever.

'Listen, I'm rich. I could buy that country house now. Why should it be small? Why not a big place with a vineyard?' Gianni's eyes showed interest. 'We could all live there,' she continued. 'Me, you, Petra, the children. She could grow vegetables. She could cook, do the housework. I've always fancied viniculture myself. I could take care of the business. Petra could take care of the house and you – ' she stroked his sex, gently, ' – you could be master.'

Gianni smirked. His sex was growing hard.

'You could be master,' she repeated. 'You'd have us both, all the time. When you got fed up with one you could go to the other. You could even have us both together . . . if you wanted to.'

His sex filled with blood and sprang up hard.

Angelina squeezed it.

He groaned.

The doors of the Uffizi opened and a party of Americans drifted out. They began to wander to the booth, distracting Gianni's attention. He moved away from her to stand at his selling position.

'It's a dream,' he said gruffly over his shoulder. 'And from what I hear, you're not going to be as rich as you thought.'

'I've taken care of that,' said Angelina. She

manoeuvred her stool close behind him, so that her face was level with his divine arse. She bit it playfully.

A woman in a straw boater picked up one of the scallop shells.

Gianni looked down at Angelina. 'How have you taken care of it?' he whispered.

'I've sent Ninnolo to kill my big sister,' she said quietly.

'How much are these?' enquired the woman. She was holding up one of the little naked Davids.

Gianni coughed. 'The small ones are fifty lire. The bigger ones are one hundred.'

'God, I could buy heaps,' said the woman to her friend. 'Do you think Roberta would like one for her . . .'

Angelina reached through Gianni's thighs and cupped his balls in her hand.

'She may do,' said the woman's friend. 'but I think little Deborah should have one too if you get one for Roberta.'

Angelina got off the stool and knelt. She twisted her arm up and reached the buttons of Gianni's flies. She pulled at the fabric. She undid one.

Gianni grabbed her hand in an attempt to stop her.

'Could I have a look at the bigger one?' asked the customer.

Gianni had no choice but to leave Angelina to her own devices as he picked up a big David from the back and handed it to the woman.

'His thing is very lifelike,' said one.

Her friend giggled. 'Is it suitable for the children? What do you think, Elizabeth?' she asked, as another woman joined them.

Pop. Pop. Pop. Pop. Gianni's fly buttons came undone under Angelina's fingers one by one. His trousers loosened and Angelina pulled them down. She massaged his warm sex through his pristine white underwear. A little damp patch appeared on the cotton. She crawled round to the front of him. She unhooked the elastic waistband over his sex and pulled his underwear off him. He had an enormous erection. It was bigger than she'd ever seen it. She pumped him.

The customer Elizabeth thought the cushion covers were rather nice and she wanted to see one closer. Gianni picked up a wrapped one and took it out of its tissue paper. He looked down, just in time to see Angelina's mouth enclose the tip of his cock.

Angelina took him in her mouth and sucked. She sucked. She bit a little, she licked, and she sucked again up and down the slithery wetness.

'Have you got a blue one?' asked the customer.

It gave Gianni the excuse he needed. 'I've got some under here,' he croaked and he dropped down below the stall.

Angelina kissed him violently.

'Take your knickers off,' he whispered. 'When they've gone I'm going to fuck you.'

He grabbed a little tissue packet labelled, in Petra's handwriting, 'blue' and stood up again.

Angelina took off her knickers and wrapped them around Gianni's cock as the customer said she would take it. Angelina pumped his cock as he took the money and put it in the cash tin.

But the discussion about the little David's cock was still going on and some of the men of the party had been drafted in.

Gianni stood grinning at them weakly, as Angelina, leaving her knickers hanging on his shaft, went round to his backside and started playing with his arsehole. She pressed her finger into the unyielding muscle. She pressed harder. It yielded. She pushed her finger inside him.

'Excuse me a moment!' he cried, to his customers.

Angelina rescued her finger as he crouched down.

'Dirty bitch,' he whispered.

Angelina's body quivered with complete abandon.

He pulled her under the stall and laid her unceremoniously on the concrete. She opened her legs wide and her dress slithered up. Gianni covered her body with his and penetrated her as the murmur of his customers droned on and on. He fucked her hard, harder than ever, driving her backbone into the hard ground. She almost cried out with pain. She closed her eyes to the slats of the stall above her and concentrated.

'I'll take three,' called a voice.

Between Angelina's legs, Gianni's body gave one huge thrust as he came.

He got up, ran his fingers through his hair, and smiled at his customers.

'I'll take three,' repeated the woman in the straw boater. Gianni wrapped them and took her 300 lire.

Angelina was still gasping under the stall, her dress still round her waist. Gianni bent down and cradled her in his arms. 'My pretty,' he whispered, and he slid his fingers into her pussy.

They were interrupted again by one of the men in the party returning to the stall and calling out.

'You serve him,' whispered Gianni.

'I can't,' hissed Angelina.

'Go on,' he replied. 'Just see what it's like.'

Angelina stood up. Her legs were shaky. 'Can I help you?'

Gianni slid two fingers inside her cunt and found her clitoris with his thumb.

'Can I get one of those pink rosary beads?' asked the man.

Gianni grabbed a little packet from the pile in a carton under the stall with his other hand and gave it to her. As she handed it to the man, Gianni pressed his lips to her clitoris and sucked it.

The customer opened the packet and looked inside. 'That's fine,' he said, and he reached in his pocket for change. 'I still can't get used to this money. Would you take it from this?'

Angelina's sex was wet and it was all in Gianni's

mouth. The sensation was so wonderful. Her sex felt heavy and enormous. The man in front of her smiled and waited, his hand outstretched.

Her orgasm was starting! It was happening! Right there in front of a stranger. It crept from her sex up through her belly. She pushed down on Gianni's face. His tongue went inside her and her clitoris rubbed against his nose.

'Ohh!' she groaned. The man's face in front of her disappeared for a split second as her orgasm tumbled down, down, down.

'Miss?' asked the man. 'Are you all right?'

Angelina reached over the stall and took some money from the outstretched palm.

The tourist wandered off.

'Oh, my love!' cried Angelina, as she crumpled next to Gianni under the stall.

Gianni was laughing. He laughed and laughed and laughed until tears came to his eyes.

'What?' cried Angelina. 'What?!'

'I love you,' said Gianni, touching her face.

'Then you'll persuade Petra to fall in with my plan? For the vineyard?' she asked.

'I'll try,' he said. 'Why not?'

She kissed him passionately. 'And if not, then you'll leave her?'

'We'll see about that,' he said.

Cia was beginning to weaken. Everyone else was so thrilled that Hector had been taking her out, and he was so very sweet, that it was impossible not to like him.

She had changed her mind about his superficiality. He had an offhand way of expressing himself, that was all. Underneath it, Cia suspected a deeply passionate nature.

And driving in the beautiful Tatra was such fun, so sexy. So was going out every evening after a hard day's concentration at cutting and sewing. She got the chance to wear lots of the dresses in her trunk. Why shouldn't she just enjoy herself? If it led somewhere, then . . .

He never failed to compliment her on her clothes, which was charming. She thought his old-fashioned gallantry was delightful. He hadn't laid a finger on her either.

There was a knock on the door. She checked her hair in the mirror and went to answer it.

'Ready then, my industrious Cia?' said Hector. He looked lovely in his linen suit.

She laughed. 'I finished the skirt today.'

'Top hole!' he said. 'Will you show it to me?'

'No,' she said. 'I can't really. Belle wants to be the first to show it off.'

'Come on then. I hear this restaurant is wonderful.'

She watched his long legs slide into the driver's seat of the Tatra and thought how she always loved long legs. He started the engine and it purred as he manoeuvred the car out into the road. She almost purred too.

They drove slowly through the town and out past the new suburbs, into the country where they sped up.

'Can you navigate?' he said, over the sound of the engine.

The summer fields were green and beautiful. She had an idea. 'What I'd really like to do is watch the sunset,' she told him.

'Aha! I know enough of the island to know just where to do that. And it's on the way!' he called. And he drove on.

He certainly loved speed. She liked that. She liked the risk-taking he did. They had that quality in common. She stole a glance at his crotch just as he slowed the car and made a sharp turn.

He parked the car on the top of the cliff. In the perfect stillness Cia could hear the crash of the waves on the beach.

'Oh, this is glorious!' he cried, and he clambered out of the car and walked off towards the edge. 'Look at that!'

She hurried towards his tall, slender form. She stood next to him. Out on the velvety sea a moment of magic was unfolding. The last of the sun's rays were split in two by a small pink cloud. Two beams hit the sea some distance apart.

As they watched, the cloud slowly floated away and the two beams travelled together to become one, momentarily, before the sun dropped below the horizon.

'Why haven't you married?' asked Hector, suddenly. 'Although, if you think it's none of my business then tell me so.'

'I don't mind you asking,' Cia replied. She felt instantly very nervous though. Her legs were tingling, almost as if they wanted to run fast. 'I haven't wanted to marry anyone who has asked.'

He smiled. 'That's a perfectly good reason,' he said.

'What about you?' she asked.

'I haven't felt ready,' he told her.

'If I did ever get married,' quipped Cia. 'I'd do it in red silk.' She almost continued: 'With the geese flying about it.' The urge to talk to him about Giordano was suddenly strong. She took a deep breath and willed the urge away.

'Do you think I'd find a husband who would agree to that kind of wedding?' she asked.

'I think it'd be terrific,' he laughed. 'Surrealist! It would have to be in Paris or something. Away from . . . all the family and everything.'

'I haven't got any family,' Cia said, quietly.

There was silence for a moment. The sound of the waves dragging stones drifted upwards.

'What do you think marriage is all about?' she asked.

'Friendship,' he answered, quickly. 'I think it's a lifelong friendship.'

'That sounds nice,' she said. Nice with you, she thought. 'But what about passion?'

'Passion?' He cleared his throat. 'I don't think it lasts.'

Cia kept her eyes averted from his, and looked at the sea. The silence between them was quite peaceful now. He must be the most old-fashioned man she had ever come across, she thought. She couldn't imagine marrying anyone with such a matter-of-fact approach to passion, however true it was that it didn't last.

But, she thought, perhaps passion was all over for her anyway, after Giordano. Her heart beat fast as she looked up into Hector's face. Surely he would kiss her?

But he looked scared. He was forcing himself to smile. 'Come on,' he said, 'I'm starving.'

Cia was just about to follow him back to the car when she saw her out on the sea, rounding the point, her sails glowing pink in the echo of the departed sun. The magnificent yacht was under spinnaker, travelling at speed.

'It's *Pearlita*!' cried Cia. 'I'm sure it is!'

Hector ran back. He squinted. 'Do you know, I think you're right. What terrific eyesight!'

They stood and watched as *Pearlita* sailed gracefully towards Cowes.

'Thank God,' said Hector, with feeling, and he flung his arm around Cia's shoulder and kissed her on the nose.

Cia grunted at the small clock on her bedside table. It was only 8.30 and they had drunk quite a lot of wine the night before. Who the hell was pounding on her door? She slid out of her solitary bed and put on her silk wrap. She scratched her head and yawned as she turned the big old key in the lock.

'There's a storm forecast,' said Rudy. 'I think your roof ought to be patched up.'

Cia blinked. He was carrying a huge roll of canvas and a toolbox.

'I'm not up yet. Um . . .' she mumbled.

'Doesn't matter. I'll get to work. Do you have a key to unlock the ladder?'

Cia stumbled into the scullery and rummaged in the drawer for the padlock key. She was in a sleepy daze. It never occurred to her to wonder how he knew about the ladder or why he was there. He just was. He was Rudy, the boy next door.

He had put the roofing materials down in the porch and was standing in the living room. He was just over six feet tall. His hair was dark and quite long on the blue neck of his shabby cotton sweater. He wore tough khaki shorts that stopped just above his knees, revealing beautifully shaped, downy haired, brown legs and ankles. He wore no socks and a pair of old deck shoes.

Cia's whole body came alive in the split second that she had to look at him from the doorway before he turned. Her sex seemed to spread a message through her abdomen, round her hips, to her breasts. Her nipples grew hard and perspiration dripped from her armpits and trickled down to her waist.

He turned. He had the most beautiful brown eyes. The skin around them was pale, a little puffy. It gave him an air of always being sleepy, like someone who has made love all night. He had always looked like that, even as a boy.

She held out the key.

'Thank you,' he said.

He stood still for the briefest moment, as if he was going to say something. Then he thought better of it.

Cia slipped into her work clothes – a pair of heavy cotton trousers and a comfortable cotton vest that showed off her shoulders. She felt absolutely beautiful. She was fiddling around under her bed for her shoes when she saw him push the ladder up the side of the house. Next minute his legs were disappearing up the rocking rungs.

Cia made herself some coffee and toast and sat down at the low table in the old servants' living room to have her breakfast. The coffee woke her up. Up above her head she could hear the tap, tap, tap of Rudy on the roof. She picked up her coffee cup and walked through to the front of the house. She had a sudden desire to see the sea.

It glittered, turquoise, in the sun before her. What a beautiful day it was, she thought. There had been several like this. But today seemed the best.

She could still here the tapping above. Rudy was on her roof! He'd come to fix her roof! Rudy! She suddenly felt how glorious it was to be young, to be alive, to be her.

The tapping stopped.

She listened.

She heard the letterbox clatter at the back. He must have finished. Oh no! Not already! She flew into the back, just as the tapping started again overhead.

She picked up the letter that had fallen on the mat. It was from Italy. It wasn't a typed envelope. Her name and address were written in a spidery hand. It crossed her mind that it could be something hateful from Angelina. Or perhaps . . .? She tore it open and looked at the signature.

She read Giordano's name on the first page. She read quickly. And then she read the words again because even though she knew they were true they didn't seem quite right. She couldn't see them properly through the film of tears that clouded her eyes. She read the whole thing slowly once more and and a great wave of pain and anguish filled her. Her mouth opened in a silent scream and she clutched her stomach. The letter fell to the floor as the sound of her own voice ripped her apart.

Up on the roof, Rudy heard the unearthly scream. He scrambled to the edge and skinned down the ladder, landing in the back yard with a thump.

He burst into the living room. Cia was crumpled on the floor between the armchair and the low table.

'Cia! What is it?'

She didn't respond – she wasn't capable of it. She clutched her knees. She was howling like an animal.

Rudy pushed the table out of the way. He knelt down and took her into his arms. He held her tight as she rocked. He stayed with her on the floor for a good twenty minutes until she sat up, gasping. She looked round wildly.

Rudy stood her up gently and went to the kitchen for some water. She drank it down, tears streaming down her face. He took the glass from her and walked her into the bedroom.

'Lay down,' he said.

She lay on the bed and he sat on the edge.

'What's happened?' he asked.

Cia sat up. Her eyes were red. Her hair was all over the place. Her nose was swollen. 'My friend died,' she said, simply. Rudy swallowed. 'Oh, Rudy!' sniffed Cia, and she moved towards him and leaned against his body.

He put his arms around her again, tight, and she hugged him close, her legs curled under her like a child.

'Was he more than a friend?' he asked.

Cia looked at him with eyes shining with tears. 'Yes,' she said.

She breathed deeply and drew back from him.

'There's some malt whisky in the scullery,' she said. 'I think I could do with some.'

He fetched it and poured two glasses. 'I'd better not go up on the roof again,' he said grinning.

'Why do people's lives have to be wasted?' she asked.

He shrugged. 'Tell me about him,' he said, after a minute.

'I really loved him,' said Cia. 'I met him in Switzerland . . .'

It took her all morning to tell the story, in fits and

starts. She told it backwards and forwards and just when she thought she'd said it all, she remembered something else. She began to smile at the memories, as the whisky balanced her. After a while, naturally, he began to talk about Nora and how he had felt when she died.

And then somehow, suddenly, their bodies were close and the words dried up and there were only heartbeats. His lips brushed hers, like the soft wing of a butterfly closing as it lands. She breathed in the indefinable sweet smell of his skin.

And then he really kissed her and the utter bliss of the lips she had loved her whole life spiralled through her softly, completely. He drew her close to his body with his hand in the small of her back and she felt lighter than air. The kiss went on and on and on for ever. And then it stopped too quickly.

They drew away from each other reluctantly. She wanted him so much, her body was clammy with desire. He looked at her.

'Can you walk?' he asked.

'Huh?'

'Can you stand?' he said, jumping up.

She swung her legs off the bed to the floor and slowly stood up.

He hugged her. She could feel his sex, not rampant, but swollen, on her belly.

'Come with me,' he said. He took her hand.

He only let go of it to pay for the sandwiches he bought in the little shop on the beach. The woman wrapped them in paper.

Cia stood in a daze and the woman's glance at her suddenly made her self-conscious. She must look a state. But the woman smiled.

It wasn't far round the point to the Tennyson House jetty. Rudy took some cushions out of the locker and threw them into the boat. He helped Cia in and she sat hugging her knees. The crushing memory of that other boat, on the lake in Switzerland, was physically painful.

Rudy pushed the boat out on to the water and hoisted the sails in the breeze. They flapped noisily.

'Grab that sheet!' he called.

She pulled the rope and fastened it.

The boat sped along, the activity and the breeze whipped through her, clearing her head.

A long time later, when they had dropped anchor and eaten and were lying on the cushions sheltering under the deck from the sun, she said, 'What made you come today?'

'The roof,' he said. He paused. 'I hear you're fond of Hector?'

Cia shook her head so vigorously it made her a bit dizzy. 'No! No! Not that way,' she told him.

'All the women in my house think you're about to get engaged,' he said.

'Never!' she said.

He smiled broadly. 'Promise?' he said.

'Oh no!' cried Cia. 'I mean yes!'

He stroked her hair. 'Love me Cia,' he whispered. 'Love *me*.'

It was a plea. She could hardly believe it was true and yet it was. She looked tenderly at his lovely, yearning face. As if he needed to beg her!

Chapter Sixteen

Rudy wanted her to stay at Tennyson House for the night.

'I want you to feel safe,' he said.

They could have made love on the boat but they hadn't. Cia felt no urgency as yet. Something told her that a little time would only make him sweeter to the touch.

She had no wish to be alone with the thoughts of Giordano. Giordano dead; her feelings had crystallised into anger. Why should such a man have to die young?

It was Saturday and there were a lot of people staying. Dinner was a big sociable affair. Plomer was there, with the other yachtsmen from *Pearlita,* and so there were three lovers, at various stages of success, solicitous of Cia's well-being. The attention warmed her.

It was Hector who sat beside her. His mother sat opposite and Cia felt a little guilty, knowing, as she did, that her friendship with Hector would never go any further. She felt guilty because, for some strange reason, the woman seemed desperate to have her as a daughter-in-law.

The talk at dinner was predominantly of sailing and the Clyde. *Pearlita* had done well and the mood was boisterous.

As soon as she had eaten, Cia suddenly felt she could take no more and she retired early, going up with Edna, who was working flat out towards Cowes Week, now only six days away.

At dawn, Cia woke up with a start and struggled to recognise her surroundings. Her waking thoughts were all of Giordano. She felt impotent, frustrated. Couldn't she have done something to save him?

Eventually, her need to pee prevented her from lying in the shady room any longer with her thoughts grinding round in a circle.

She opened the door of her bedroom. The house was completely quiet. Her memory of the house was indistinct. She knew the bathroom was at one end of the landing, but there were doors at both ends. She turned to her left, towards the nearest one, and she turned the handle quietly, just in case.

She knew, as soon as she opened the door a little way, that it wasn't a bathroom. She would have closed it again immediately, but the sight of two pairs of male feet hanging over the end of the bed hit a chord. She had known this, she realised, somewhere in her mind, all along.

Lying on the bed, in an embrace, were Hector and a man Cia recognised from dinner the night before called LJ.

She closed the door quietly and retraced her steps back down the corridor to the bathroom at the other end.

It took her exactly five minutes, as she chewed over what she had discovered, to get angry. No wonder his mother was so desperate to see him married. Cia was furious with the pair of them! Not only her vanity, but her sense of fair play was outraged. What kind of marriage would that be for any woman?

Friendship. He'd said it himself. But how could you be friends with a man who hadn't the courage to be himself? She was so annoyed she forgot to thank her lucky stars.

She put on her dress and was leaving her room when Edna galloped down the stairs. 'Cheerio!' she called.

Cia closed the door of her room behind her, quietly, as LJ emerged from Hector's room, trying to look nonchalant, as if he'd just been paying a pally visit to organise the day. Cia nodded tersely.

Rudy was sitting on the terrace, drinking coffee. He offered her some and she sat down. Now, looking at him, she remembered her lucky star. Poor Hector.

Suddenly, out of the blue, Rudy said, 'Do you think people can always be forgiven for their faults?'

'It depends whether they act on them,' she replied. A look of consternation flew across Rudy's face. 'I've just discovered something about Hector,' she continued.

'Oh, yes,' said Rudy, as if he knew.

'Did you know?'

'Yes.'

'Does everyone know?'

'No,' he said. 'It wouldn't occur to most people. I wanted to tell you but I couldn't bring myself to – '

To rat on a friend, thought Cia, on another male.

'He was going to ask me to marry him, I think. That would have been a sterile sort of marriage wouldn't it?' she said. Rudy frowned.

'I think I need to get out of here, before Hector comes down.'

'Would you like company?' he asked. 'I usually go for a walk at this time.'

They joined the road at the side gate, just as a tall, odd-looking, blond man, apparently walking past, nearly tripped on the kerb. They offered him assistance but he was all right.

'I couldn't think what else to do but turn up at your house and stake a claim,' said Rudy, as they walked along the coast road.

Cia stomped on. She felt like a piece of land. Damn

men, she thought. They stick together, some of them literally. They talk about you as if you're property.

'If Hector and his mother *hadn't* been scheming, would you have felt the need to stake a claim?' she asked. Her voice was laced with sarcasm.

He reached for her hand. 'Oh, yes,' he said fervently. 'Yes.'

Well, she thought, I'm not sure that's the truth.

There was a bend coming up. In front of them, before the turn, was woodland that sloped down to a tiny beach.

'Race you!' said Cia. It was a euphemism for *fuck you*.

Rudy laughed. But his laughter turned to bemusement as she raced off.

Cia scrambled down the slope, whooping like a tomboy, beating him to the bottom by a hop, skip and jump.

She sat down on the sand, picked up a rock and threw it at the sea.

'I remember you coming down the cliff like that when you were eight years old!' laughed Rudy, sitting down next to her. 'You and Edna had persuaded your grand-mother and my mother that you ought to be able to wear trousers, I think, and the first thing you did was follow myself and Dick St James down the cliff.'

'You were angry with us,' she replied.

'We didn't like girls much in those days,' he admitted. He paused. 'But we grew out of it.'

Cia laughed.

'Phew!' said Rudy.

He pulled off his sweater. His back, in the thin fabric of his shirt, emerged broad and beautiful. His shirt was a little way open, showing her a triangle of chest that was very inviting.

'I'm lucky,' she said, gallantly. 'You rescued me.'

'Don't think me noble,' he said. 'I don't deserve it.'

She didn't understand him. She thought perhaps his

self-esteem was dented because Nora had abandoned him. She didn't pry.

But neither did he talk about it. They sat, close, throwing stones.

Above them, in the trees, a figure moved. A tall blond man, throwing no shadow, stopped and raised binoculars to his steely-blue eyes. The glasses, round and black, reflecting nothing, found Cia and Rudy below and held still.

Petra looked down at her husband's face. She was sitting up against the pillows on their bed, naked. Her body was beautiful, her belly showing signs. Not much, but she could tell. He could tell.

When she was much younger, at least two years ago, she had dreamed of times like this – a lazy Sunday, skipping lunch to make love. She had bought the pillows with their first bit of spare money. Not his money, her money. She had saved it from her earnings at the bakery. She loved the pillows; big, white, frilly, cotton, handmade luxury pillows just like film stars had. But she had the strongest urge to throw the wine she was holding in his face and ruin them.

'How long is it since Angelina hatched her plan?' she asked.

'Not long,' said Gianni, non-committally. He was treading carefully as if along a high wire, balancing two women. He loved women. He loved the way they were unpredictable. He was scared too, but mostly he loved women, especially between their legs.

Petra put her wine down on the bedside table.

'Well?' said Gianni.

'Well what?'

'What do you think about the vineyard?'

'I'll think about it,' she said, and she began to get dressed.

'Why are you getting dressed?'

'Just going for a little walk,' said Petra, calmly.

Gianni was amused. He watched her go. See! he said to himself when she was gone, women were unpredictable. He wanted sex very much again. He thought about nipping round to Angelina. But that wasn't the thing to do really. He was an intelligent man, he told himself. Easily distracted but intelligent. He had to keep his mind on Petra. He had to convince her. He would wait until she got back.

Petra had known what had to be done the minute Gianni had confided in her. The question of the money to buy this vineyard had led to him confiding what Angelina had done. Petra fought hard with herself not to despise him for colluding in the English girl's murder. She knew that he was under the influence of evil. But she also knew she wasn't having a murder on her conscience.

It was no good going to the police station. They were all corrupt and stupid. She pressed the bell of the grand official residence of the *podesta*. She would say Gianni had sent her.

The servant who answered the door took some convincing, but Petra persisted.

The *podesta* received her in his study. He had no difficulty believing her story. This could mean an international incident – not something to be ignored in this day and age. He picked up the telephone receiver and asked the operator to connect him to Scotland Yard.

Rudy walked Cia back to Finnemore that morning. As soon as they entered the house she felt the sexual tension grow between them and no matter how much more appealing it had been to wait, things were suddenly different.

But he stalled. He seemed on edge. She made breakfast for them both and afterwards he got up quite quickly, saying he had business to do. He left.

She wondered, then, about the roof.

She had just gone upstairs to work when she heard a footfall on the stairs.

'Cia!'

'In here!' she called.

Rudy went into the workroom. She closed the scissors along the curving line of tailor's chalk on a piece of pale orange silk. She opened the scissors again.

'Hold on,' she said.

She cut once more and severed the piece from the rest of the silk. The orange fabric slipped across the table and fell in soft folds to the floor. It suddenly reminded Cia of its red, Chinese sister.

'That colour is beautiful,' said Rudy.

She smiled at him.

He leaned against the big table as she folded the freshly cut pieces of the blouse.

'I must tell you something,' he said, at length. 'I have watched you . . .' At first she thought he meant just now. Had he gone back on the roof after all? She hadn't heard him. 'One night I watched you take off your clothes and wrap a length of red silk around your body. You let go of it and you stood naked, as if you had shed a skin. You were lovely beyond words. I felt as if I'd never seen a woman before you.'

He paused. Cia looked into his eyes and saw depths she didn't understand. She wanted very much for him to touch her. Now.

'I didn't think I would ever admit it to you. But I must make you understand how much you woke up the man in me, Cia. I watched you more than once.'

Cia's body was filled with an arc of tender, aching desire. She placed the fabric she was holding on the table and unbuttoned the front of her dress.

He reached out for her skin and stroked her lightly and tenderly.

His touch made her feel like beauty itself. He kissed her breasts, unclothing her shoulders with his hands as his lips met her flesh.

She wriggled her arms from her sleeves and pushed her breasts into his mouth. His red lips against her white flesh were scorching. He held her waist firmly as he licked and sucked at her, cajoling her deep, deep tenderness to life.

Her sex opened and yearned for him. She stroked his dark hair and the back of his neck, feeling the contours of his shoulders within his shirt with delighted fingers.

She wanted to see his skin. She tugged at his shirt, pulling it out of the waistband of his shorts. It made him stop. He unbuttoned his shirt.

Cia watched the loveliness of his well-formed, broad chest, with its sprinkling of dark hair, unfold. The hair was denser in the centre of his chest. It ran down in an irresistible line to his waistband. His shoulders were broad and his upper arms were rounded with just enough muscle to please the eye.

He pressed his bare torso against hers. Her breasts squashed against him as a woman's breasts are made to. But here was a surprise! The hair on his chest was so soft it was divine, as if her own breasts were softly coated. She reached around his back as he enclosed her in his arms and kissed her lips with more urgent passion. The skin on his back was as soft as her own and underneath there was the muscle of a young, passionate man. A man that was becoming hers.

She wore a pair of silk knickers, with the narrowest lace imaginable around the legs. As he undid the buttons of her dress all the way down and it fell away from her, he looked at her waist and her hips with his head on one side, as if studying every curve and loving each in turn.

'Come to bed,' he whispered.

She went down the stairs half-naked, with her lover at her heels. In the bedroom he stopped. He was looking at the floor under the bed. The red silk was still there where she had kicked it. He picked it up and looped it over the old curtain wire, blocking out the world. All that was left of it were the rekindled geraniums, their new shoots lapping up the sun.

The silk reddened the light in the room. Cia grabbed the waistband of Rudy's shorts. It was a lifetime's ambition and she smiled a secret smile as she unbuttoned the next and the next button until all the buttons were undone and his shorts slid to the floor. She reached into the waistband of his underwear with both hands and enclosed his sex. She looked up into his face. His eyelashes rested on the soft tender skin under his eyes. He was completely helpless. Cia savoured the moment.

He pushed on to her hands. His urgent, slippery sex slid between her wrists and she met it with her belly.

He clasped her arse and lifted her on to the bed.

He lay next to her, a curious mixture of passion and hesitancy. He stroked her body, loving it with his hands. Then he slipped his hand in the waistband of her knickers and slid them down her thighs. She lay bare and he looked at her.

'My Cia,' he whispered.

He tenderly coiled the hair of her sex in his fingers and pushed it away from her clitoris.

Cia watched his face as he stroked her, unwrapped her, and delicately massaged her sex. She watched until a stab of pure joy leapt through her body and then she closed her eyes and gave up.

Then his tongue was on her clitoris, seeking it out, opening her. His warm, wet tongue, sending lust into every pore of her skin. She needed him soon. His fingers slid into her sex and she pushed on to him, rotating her clitoris into the heel of his hand. She opened and opened and opened. She was nothing but a woman.

A thought of Giordano suddenly went flashing through her mind and she opened her eyes. But it was Rudy's head between her thighs and he was Rudy Wicked, wickedly intent on her pleasure. Her thoughts faded. Nothing could stop her body from responding to her love.

And his fingers insisted inside her, plunging against the neck of her womb. She could stand it no longer. She buried her head in his shoulder and let out a groan of passion that pleaded with him.

He slid his cock between her legs. His wetness streaked her thighs. And then he was inside. She enclosed him.

'Rudy,' she breathed.

He didn't thrust. He gyrated, pressing his bone where it mattered. It felt so perfect. *She* did the thrusting against him, sucking him sweetly with her cunt.

Their bodies slid against each other's in the heat; stretching, loving, fucking. They took more than their fair share. They had their cake and they ate it. They revelled in their sex. They made it better for each other than it had ever been before. On and on they fucked. And, as her orgasm flooded down, he finally thrust really hard, again and again, with his coming. He surprised her into such total surrender of body and mind that she was turned upside down.

She felt, for a few glorious, mad moments, like an orange full of juice.

Chapter Seventeen

Cia and Rudy spent much of the day in bed, naked, making love and talking. It was only with reluctance that, at about 4.30 he got dressed to go to a meeting at the Royal Yacht Squadron that Edna had pressed him into.

Cia made herself a cup of tea and took it back up to the workroom where she picked up the orange silk and began to pin it. But she didn't last long. She was pleasantly tired; a cloak of love seemed to envelop her. She was in the mood to listen to music and dream. After about twenty minutes she picked up her half-drunk cup and went downstairs.

What made her look into the butler's mirror she never knew. Perhaps it was the spirit of Grandma, she thought afterwards, protecting her. She stopped in her tracks and looked at the distorted, tiny figure standing by the understairs cupboard. It was a fair-haired man, hiding where he thought she couldn't see him, and it wasn't anyone she knew.

She slowly turned round and went back up the stairs. But as she turned the corner on the first landing, she heard a noise behind her and she looked back. The first thing she saw was the knife. She flew.

'It's no good,' called Ninnolo. 'You won't escape me, Cia.'

He knew her name! It startled her. He knew her name! She ran so fast to the top of the house that she was panting for breath by the time she ran into the back attic and grabbed at the top bolt. The bolt was ancient, a relic from the days when Lord Finnemore, Great-Grandmother's husband, used to visit the house and the servants had to protect themselves. It was stiff, but it worked. She threw it. She bent down to throw the bottom one. As the thunder of the man's footsteps reached the door, the bolt hit home.

Cia was shaking so badly her teeth chattered.

'Now what are you going to do?' called Ninnolo. 'You've trapped yourself. I shall wait here until you come out.'

Cia suddenly felt more confident. Did he think she was a complete fool?

'What do you want?' she called.

She didn't hear his answer completely; she was too busy sliding up the long sash window. He wouldn't have heard it hopefully, over the sound of his own voice.

Outside the window was a ledge that ran past three attic windows. At the other end was the top of Rudy's ladder. She looked at Rudy's turret. He wasn't there. He wasn't watching her now.

She faced the room again. 'I'm not coming out,' she said. 'My friends will be here soon and I'm not coming out.'

'Putana,' spat the deadly, Italian voice.

Cia climbed out of the window and hurried as much as she dared along the ledge. Down below the ground was a long, long way away and her stomach lurched. She reached the top of the ladder and, knowing she only had a minute before he realised she was gone, she grasped it firmly. She detested ladders. She had trouble going down them even when her legs weren't jelly.

'God help me,' she muttered, and she stepped over the top rung.

She hurried as fast as she could but it seemed to take forever before she was down far enough to jump to the ground. Immediately she hit it, she ran towards the back door.

She heard the sound of running footsteps inside the house. She wouldn't be able to get to the door in time. But her bedroom window was open. She hoisted herself over the window sill, flung open her bedside cabinet drawer and grasped the pearl-handled gun and bullets.

She had only a vague idea of how to use it! Only from films! The back door banged. She loaded it with shaking hands just before the man appeared in front of her. She raised the gun with both hands, pointing it at his head.

'Drop that knife,' she said.

'I admit, you surprise me,' he said, as he dropped it by his feet. He took a step closer to her.

'Don't you fucking dare!' she growled. Her voice surprised her. She sounded lethal.

A flicker of something went across the man's face. He opened his mouth to speak.

'What do you want?' she demanded.

'To kill you,' he said.

'Why?'

'I am a professional.'

'Who is paying you to do this?'

'Are you going to use the gun?'

She glared at him. 'Answer my question.'

'What will you pay for an answer?'

'Nothing,' she replied. 'You're not in a position to bargain.'

He shook his head. 'You're not going to use it, are you?'

'Answer my question and I might not.'

He laughed.

'OK,' she shouted. She was so angry that hatred filled

her. 'OK. Answer me a different question. Are you a Fascist?'

'Of course I'm a Fascist,' he said, and he lifted the lapel of his jacket to show her his squad insignia.

As he looked up she shot the bastard, in the middle of the forehead.

Cia knew what she had done. When the police came pounding into the garden within minutes of the shot, she had the presence of mind to tell them everything except her final question and his answer.

There were two policemen, an older and a younger man, both familiar faces to her. Both of them were prepared to believe her because of the call from Scotland Yard. Both of them did believe her. There seemed to be no problem. When she came to relate the actual shooting itself, she broke down in tears. There was no triumph. Only shock.

The younger policeman went off to get Rudy and arrange for the body to be taken away. The older one, Sergeant Reder, stayed with Cia. He made tea and listened to her story again for the purposes of taking a proper statement. It was on the second telling that something seemed a bit odd to him. He couldn't put his finger on it.

Then her friends arrived and the first thing Rudy asked was: 'Who on earth would want to hire someone to kill Miss Finnemore?'

And it was at that point Sergeant Reder knew what was odd. She hadn't asked. Did she know? Did she know him? She said she thought he was going for a gun, but she had disarmed him.

Sergeant Reder was mystified. He discussed his doubts with his chief later on. There was difference between self-defence and murder and he had a hunch.

The chief would have preferred that the question hadn't arisen. But, as it had, he called Scotland Yard. The super dealing with it there decided to call Italy.

Thus it was settled. This was no time for a messy incident. Ninnolo Minaccia was disposable. Therefore it was self-defence. And Sergeant Reder and his hunches could go to the devil.

In Florence, the *podesta* put down the telephone and breathed a sigh of relief. Now for the other little problem. What to do with her?

One by one over the next two days The Big Class sailed into Cowes under spinnaker. Their masts soared almost 200 feet in the air and their sails billowed in curves of unbleached silk against the sky.

The sight of them gladdened Cia's heart, just because they were so beautiful. No matter how long she thought about it she came back to a tenuous certainty that she'd done what she had to. He would have killed her, would he not? But the parallel certainty that she had avenged Giordano was more difficult to live with.

Visitors arrived, out of concern – among them Plomer, as soon as he heard. Cia glossed over the truth, accepted sympathy and changed the subject. He had met a truly lovely girl in Scotland, he told her.

Then there was Hector, and Cia couldn't be bothered with him. She tried to be polite but grew terser and terser until Rudy came down the ladder looking for some more nails, and Hector bolted.

Rudy watched Hector go. 'I told Edna about us,' he said.

'Was she pleased?' Cia asked.

'You bet,' he said, grinning.

'She has a lover, doesn't she?'

'Yes,' said Rudy.

'Who is he?'

'You'd better ask her.'

Cia liked the fact he didn't tell her. It meant she could trust him with secrets.

'I'll be the envy of every man in Cowes soon,' he said.

Cia smiled and pushed him playfully.

'I like to see you smile,' he said. 'How are you feeling?'

'Fine,' she lied, quickly.

He took her in his arms for a lustful, long and lovely kiss. In his arms she forgot everything else. She came alive.

'Will you marry me?' he asked, holding her at arm's length.

Oh, God! she thought. She didn't answer immediately.

'Think about it. Maybe it's too soon,' he said doubtfully.

'I will,' she said.

She thought about it a lot. Being a Mrs was synonymous, in her mind, with putting on weight and becoming unhappy. Wives in Cowes took refuge from their broken dreams in social back-biting and devouring.

But Grandma had married Grandfather, eventually; she had loved him passionately and he her, by all accounts. Perhaps there was a lucky streak somewhere in the family that she had inherited.

She didn't need to get married, she thought – not anymore. She had an inheritance coming. Soon, she could do anything she wanted. She could open a fashion house and put her ideas into action. She could renovate Finnemore.

She found herself going up to speak to Great Grandmama's portrait more than once over the next few days. It was a way of wrestling with the decision.

The pale young face of a girl with shining dark eyes looked at her. Her dress was early Victorian, the neckline barely cut away, the sleeves puffing at her shoulders. The portrait had been painted by a little known artist. He was, perhaps, Great Grandfather but Great Grandmama had been discreet on that subject. There was no signature. Cia looked back along one hundred years of female life: she had never wanted to get married. She had had the daydreams but when her mother had married Mr Render and sent her away, the girlish dreams had stopped.

But to be loved and cherished for ever – now, by Rudy? This was the stuff dreams were made of. And her womb somersaulted with thought of his sex.

'I've killed a man,' she said to the portrait one day. 'Nothing can change that.'

There was silence. The silence of the dead.

The following Saturday morning Cia delivered Belle's clothes to her apartment at the Caryatids. The town was buzzing with activity. Cowes Week had begun that morning with the thunderclap of cannon and a puff of brown smoke that drifted over the turquoise sea and dispersed as the first yachts raced off. *Brittania* had hoisted her racing flag – the Prince of Wales' feathers upon a field of blue and red – and the Prince of Wales himself had surprised everyone by flying in for the week, in an aeroplane with his latest American friend. It was the aeroplane that was a surprise, not the woman friend.

Rudy, Plomer, Hector, Lord Walcarp-Etting, Sven, and half the wealth and crowned heads of Europe, were out on the sea, getting ready to race.

Belle was lying on her new leather couch reading a magazine when her houseboy, Jimmy, showed Cia in.

'Look at this. Lacey Valentine is here,' said Belle.

Cia took the magazine offered to her. The famous face looked at her from the cover like famous faces do – impersonally, with a smile that says nothing. On the former star's arm was a younger man, something like Clark Gable.

Cia gave the parcel of clothes to Belle. The trousers were linen, and the blouse in orange silk went with an olive green silk jacket.

'You're brilliant,' Belle kept saying as she held the clothes up to her body in the mirror. 'Wait till people see these. I'm dying to say, "Oh but darling, she's awfully exclusive. I'll put your proposition to her but I don't know ..." God, and you don't even need the money now either! Will you carry on?'

'I expect so. It's an obsession. It doesn't have anything much to do with money,' said Cia.

'Let's get out and join the party. Shall I change? No. I'll save these for King's Cup Day. Won't be a minute ...' said Belle and she went off to the bathroom.

Cia looked out of the vast windows on to the sea. What are your obsessions, Cia? She heard Giordano's voice in her mind. She felt disconnected, somehow, from everything and everybody.

They went down to the town quay and sat on the dock dangling their legs over the side. They watched as the Red Funnel ferry steamed through the huge fleet of yachts of all different sizes, carrying a full load of passengers. It seemed, from their perspective on the jetty, that there must be a collision. But there wasn't, miraculously. The ferry docked, disgorging the rich, the famous and the ordinary, all mixed up together but separated by invisible suits of social armour.

Launches were ferrying passengers back and forth from the smart yachts. One in particular caught the eye of the crowds, and especially that of the women.

'Good for her,' said Belle, focusing her binoculars on *Hobbema*. She gave a low whistle.

Cia asked for the binoculars. The crew of the *Hobbema* were all male and distinguished by the muscle it carried. Lacey Valentine was at the helm in a white ensemble that looked a bit like camiknickers. It was, in essence. She looked a treat. She also wore a skipper's cap and white deck shoes. She had the figure for it, thought Cia. The crew were dressed in dark blue. It was their jerseys that caught the eye, stretched across big torsos.

'Well, she should have an advantage in weight,' said Belle.

Cia took a deep breath and said, 'Rudy Wycke has asked me to marry him.'

Belle's head swivelled in Cia's direction. It was the first time Cia had seen her lost for words.

'You secretive devil! When? Oh God, I'm thrilled. I'm absolutely . . . Oh! Cia!' She flung her arms round Cia with such force they both tottered.

The tried to keep their balance but the momentum overtook them. It seemed to happen in slow motion. They landed in the water.

A group of yachting widows on the private jetty of the Royal Spartan Yacht Club tutted and shook their heads as Cia and Belle flapped about like honking geese.

The great Cowes Week party rolled on with sailing by day and dancing by night. There was a ball on Sunday, a ball on Monday and there would be balls on Tuesday, Wednesday and Thursday. The high street was awash with glamour. The press was out in force and Belle was photographed by both the dailies and the magazines wearing Cia's clothes on the deck of *Philae*, Sven's yacht.

As well as the big balls, there were other, private parties, on yachts and on land. Lacey Valentine was rumoured to have entertained the Dartmouth cadets on board their training ship. In fact, the press rumours were wrong. *They* entertained *her*. She found the sixteen to nineteen year olds particularly entertaining.

And there was one party that wasn't reported anywhere. It did see the light of day in print, but not for thirty years.

Dianna arrived at Belle's at seven wearing a white hat with a veil that covered her eyes and nose. Their launch pulled alongside the gently rocking, magnificent, white, 120 foot hull of *Philae* about twenty minutes later.

The accommodation below deck was stunning, with teak panelling everywhere. About half the length was given over to crew quarters and the galley. Further aft there were two huge staterooms. The party was assembling in one.

The big galley was a hive of activity. The chef, a French man called Alexandre, greeted Dianna warmly.

'I've already had a bath,' she said.

'With respect, Madame, I have to make sure the dish comes up to my standards,' he said, smiling. He showed her into a crew cabin. 'You can prepare yourself in here.'

Dianna took off her clothes. Her disguise for the evening was more elaborate than the veiled hat. Cia had made her a white velvet mask. It fitted comfortably over the top half of her face, leaving her red lips and her chin naked. She tied it in place with its ribbons and pulled up her hair into a bun that she fixed with a hair net. Only the night before she had been at a ball, a respectable matron accompanying her son. It amused her to ponder how tonight she was crossing into a different realm. Sex was like that, slippery. Wearing the mask, she was somebody else.

'Are you ready?' called Alexandre, knocking.

'Yes,' said Dianna. She opened the door.

There were two other men with Alexandre.

'This is Napoleon,' said Alexandre, introducing her to the patissier.

Dianna suppressed a giggle.

'I want her scrubbed,' said Napoleon to the sous-chef.

The man started on her feet, which was pleasant enough. He used a soft nail brush. Dianna closed her eyes. The gentle, circulating motion of the soft brush gradually crept up her legs, making her skin tingle. Higher and higher it went till it got to her thighs. He parted her legs and proceeded to wash her sex. This time he used a cloth, not the brush. She peeked. The young man's attention seemed perfectly professional, as if she were a duckling or a chicken and he was cleaning her. She kept silent, closed her eyes again and enjoyed the firm strokes. He washed her belly and her breasts, his hands still professional but gentle.

He dried her skin with infinite care and then massaged her with oil which smelled faintly of roses and soaked into her skin giving it a lustre. He probed every crevice with gentle, oil-soft fingers. By the time it was over, Dianna felt ready to be eaten. It felt like a long time since she had been loved by her Wilhelm, back in Florence. She daydreamed about his cock in the shoe ... But there was more to come. The sous-chef took her by the hand and led her out of the little room, naked and glowing, into the galley.

The mask obscured her vision just a little but she could see enough to take in the admiration on the faces of the staff. The business of preparing food for the dinner came to a halt, briefly. The boat rocked gently on the waves. Dianna was glad she'd lost a bit of weight. She felt beautiful.

Napoleon was quite a handsome man, she thought. He was Wilhelm's age, with playful brown eyes.

He helped her up on to a body-length salver on a big table at one end of the narrow, hot galley. She climbed up carefully, conscious of the fact that her bum was in Napoleon's face. She settled in the middle of a number of pale pink icing nests. Bunches of succulent black and white grapes filled five of the nests. The others were empty.

She felt so relaxed she could almost have slept like a baby but there was an atmosphere in the galley. No-one who was there, from the head chef to the washer up and all the staff in between, could avoid the preparation of the Napoleonic dessert – the naked, rosy body of a woman, oiled and breathing.

'*Alors*,' said Napoleon. 'Bring me the sugar paste.' He smiled at Dianna. 'I am not used to being able to converse with my desserts.'

His smile was very nice.

The general kitchen hubbub suddenly increased as a summer soup was ladled into Royal Doulton tureens. The pair of tureens were cream coloured, their lids dome shaped, with pale blue straight handles. They looked like breasts from another planet.

In the middle of the waiters' exit with the soup, a maid dropped some peelings and the chef swore under his breath as the door opened on to the corridor.

Dianna heard the deep voices of men talking in the dining room.

Napoleon took the sugar paste from his sous-chef and made a flat circle around Dianna's navel. The paste was like clay. In his oiled hands it was supple and malleable. On her skin it began to set. He worked quickly. The sous-chef stood next to the master. He covered the paste with a damp towel until it was needed.

Napoleon covered one of her nipples. It was cool. She swelled under his fingers. He piped the same cool covering on her other nipple, working with intense concentration.

One or two of the kitchen staff watched the proceedings in the momentary lull before the fish course. Dianna felt aroused under their eyes; excited behind her mask. She grew thirsty. The paste on her nipples started to dry.

For the decoration of her sex, Napoleon used his hands, slapping the paste on liberally and using a fine palette knife to smooth and shape it at the edges. He put a piece of rice paper over her clitoris and spread it down her thighs. He fixed it in place with paste, using slight pressure of his skilled fingers. The sugary softness on his fingers mingled with her pubic hair. Her sex swelled and opened.

He completed the effect of a sweet loincloth with tiny little nipples of paste around her hips like strings of beads. They draped over her thighs and sprinkled up towards her waist.

She was intoxicated by him. She was his creation. He smiled at her again.

'Water!' she whispered.

He clicked his fingers and it was done; the maid appeared with a glass and a straw.

The head chef yelled 'Fish!' and a sous slapped fourteen fillets of lemon sole on to the griddle. They were on and off the heat in a trice and the delicious smell of fresh fish perfumed the air as the used soup bowls clattered towards the sink. Still sizzling, the fish was put on to cream, oval servers.

Napoleon smoothed her shins with a sweep of his hands. He pulled her toes very gently straight.

Dianna sighed with contentment.

He began sculpting her a pair of soft white spats. He smoothed the paste up her shins, finishing with the palette knife where her legs began to curve.

He smiled at her.

'They look wonderful,' he whispered.

He touched her hair gently and she closed her eyes and dreamed about his hands taking liberties.

At her head he sculpted her a wig, snaking the paste to make locks of hair. And then he finished her off with a pair of oval earrings that stuck to her ears.

'The paste will set outside so it's crunchy and next to your skin it will remain soft and sticky,' he said, grinning. 'It should feel nice for you as well as the diners.'

The sous returned with the first of a series of trays covered in marzipan shapes and sculptures ranging in size from the smallest leaf to a three-inch replica of *Philae,* with white marzipan sails.

Napoleon began to apply the little shapes to her body as a flurry and fuss surrounded the meat course. He popped two small strawberries on her nipples, pressing them gently into the paste.

A huge side of beef, potatoes cooked to crisp, golden perfection and steaming vegetables floated out of the galley aromatically.

As the door opened and swung, Dianna heard the voices of the men again. They had grown louder with wine.

Napoleon placed little pink marzipan roses on her hips, green leaves around the strawberries on her breasts, orange curlicues in her wig, and red laces on her boots. The sugar paste set slowly as he worked.

On her sex he had placed an orchid that he clipped from its stem and around that dozens of tiny silver and chocolate drops. He stuck raspberries in one of the strings of paste beads around her hips.

To refresh her, he asked a galley hand to cut up some tiny pieces of succulent beef and feed them to her. She chewed away as Napoleon tweaked her skin with finishing touches. He found her a glass of delicious claret and a cocktail straw.

He filled the valleys of her sides with fresh flowers and ladled a dozen different fruits into the nests around her on the iced salver.

There were a few moments' calm while the sorbet was being eaten. Alexandre appeared and examined Napoleon's handiwork. The staff gathered round her.

'They've finished,' hissed a waiter. There was a flurry as the waiters disappeared.

Down in the stateroom the men were still talking about sailing, their faces flushed with the wine, the sea air and the good dinner.

Sven sat at the head of the table, conversing with the exiled King of Trnava, a heavy lidded, almost Turkish-looking man with a long nose. On the other side of Sven was a blond Swedish businessman, affectionately known as 'the king of biscuits' – because that's what he made. He was long limbed and easy in his clothes. None of the men were in mess dress, this being an informal party, but they wore dinner jackets and they wore them well. The king of biscuits had undone his bow-tie. It hung like two ears on his shirt front.

The Crown Prince of Botal was on the Swede's right; a small, dark man with a fidgety disposition who twirled a napkin around his fingers as he spoke. On his right the elder son of the Duke of Firth, Earl Bedrichton, the youngest of the men at 29, raised his weak chin and howled with laughter at an appallingly bad joke. Next to him Sir Cecil Critchley-Rawnipton, looking as if he was enjoying being out without Lady Sapphire immensely, twinkled.

Along the other side of the table two eminent bankers, worth millions, relaxed after an absorbing day in battle with the elements on the Solent. With them sat an assortment of English admirals, a commodore, three skippers, knighted, and a French count.

At the end of the table, opposite Sven, sat Belle, looking absolutely beautiful in a shimmering cream satin gown that fitted her like a second skin and left her shoulders, arms and the swell of her breasts exposed.

The staff cleared the table of salt cellars, crumbs, and glasses, and laid a cloth of the palest rose, with fine embroidery around the edges. When they had finished, the head waiter whispered something in Belle's ear.

Belle stood up and, immediately, the men fell quiet.

'I'd like to present you, Sven, and your crew here, with your other prize. Today you won the Prince's Cup and there it sits on the sideboard. Congratulations. But I wanted to give you something myself.'

Sven inclined his head quizzically. The men looked at her expectantly, with indulgent smiles on their faces. Earl Bedrichton went pink in the face of that much woman. Belle's dress bumped and curved so deliciously over her figure that she looked like a cream dream. She filled up their senses to overflowing.

All the galley staff gathered around Dianna and took up their positions to carry her in. Just before they lifted her, Napoleon put the model of *Philae,* with a small metal anchor, on her navel. Then he wished her luck.

The paste had set rock hard on the outside and was beginning to pull slightly on her skin as it set inside as well. They lifted her into the air.

The room went silent as she was carried in. The men around the table gasped as their dessert was laid before them in all her glorious flesh. The king of biscuits was the first to make eye contact.

'She's real!' he laughed.

'My darling Belle!' cried Sven. He swooped her close to him by the waist. 'How imaginative!'

Belle kissed him briefly on the lips and moved away. 'This is for you gentlemen alone,' she said.

Then she was gone. The staff were gone. The door closed and Dianna was alone with the men.

They were all so well bred they commented politely on the decoration in detail and waited for someone else to start.

Sven was at her head. 'Are you comfortable, my dear?' he asked her.

'Yes,' she whispered.

The King of Trnava stared at her intently.

'The first thing to do is kiss the lady's hand,' said Sven. 'Botal! You are ideally placed to begin, I believe.'

The king raised Dianna's hand and kissed it. Then he plucked a grape from its mooring on her middle finger. 'Mmm,' he said. 'This seems to be paste. It's sweet.'

'I thought it was plaster,' said one of the admirals. 'I wonder what this delightful little model of *Philae* is made out of?' he continued, gazing at Dianna's navel.

'Tuck in!' cried Sven, picking a raspberry from the end of her sculpted hair.

In an instant, Dianna's body was assaulted gently by fingertips as the fourteen men reached and plucked fruits. She closed her eyes. Every pluck was delightful. The fingers were gentle and stayed in safe waters. No-one had touched her sex yet – or her nipples. She longed for someone to. She opened her eyes and met those of the King of Trnava.

He looked ravenous. Very slowly he bent over her and put his mouth to one of the strawberries balancing on her nipples. A low rumble of male camaraderie went around the table as they realised what he was going to do. Fingers stopped picking. All eyes were on his mouth at her breast. Dianna closed her eyes again as he pulled the strawberry from its sugary mooring. Some paste clung to the strawberry and came away, exposing the tip of her nipple, pink and hard in its bed of white paste and green leaves. There was complete hush. Dianna's heart raced. She concentrated on breathing steadily. She opened her eyes and took a peek.

The king winked at her. He nibbled at the hard paste around her nipple, biting little pieces at a time. He sucked. He bit. He licked.

At her other breast the commodore plucked off the strawberry and giggled. Down at her feet, an admiral stripped one of her boots clean off and peeled off the red laces with his teeth. He stroked her shin with his other hand.

'I say,' said Sir Cecil, and he picked up the little anchor and chipped at her loins with the sharp end. He broke off a piece and handed the tool on. Earl Bedrichton, of the disappearing chin, took it and gingerly tapped her with it, breaking off another piece. A pubic hair came away and Dianna squeaked. The little anchor went round the table and each man got up from where he was sitting and did his bit to excavate her sex. They were gentle; the sugary paste crumbled.

The King of Trnava refused the pick. 'I prefer to use my teeth,' he said.

Dianna felt his teeth bite into the paste just above the rice paper. His chin touched her clitoris and her sex raged. He placed his hand on her thigh and said, 'I think the only way rice paper comes off is if you make it wet.'

Dianna opened her eyes as he began.

Lick. Lick. Lick. She lay as still as a mouse. Only a hand brushing her hip, as it reached for a peach by her side, entered her consciousness but it was nothing in comparison with the king's tongue. Another mouth started nibbling at one of her earrings and another at her right toe. And still the licking tongue at the rice paper licked rhythmically.

She felt a frosted cup of brandied cherries fall by her side. The liquid ran in a rivulet down under her ribcage and stopped at her buttocks.

Still the lick, lick, lick.

He was right. The rice paper disintegrated. His next lick was on the bare red swell of her clitoris. She was so aroused, she moved involuntarily and the cherry brandy found a conduit between her buttocks. Slowly but surely it seeped, finding her arsehole, her sex. It seeped slowly down one thigh, stickily.

It was a moment that everyone in the room seemed to share in, as if her licked sex, her feelings, aroused everyone else. There was no excuse now to touch her breasts – they were devoid of decoration. But there was cream and Sven poured it over them in a long white stream. Somebody licked it off and everyone cheered him on. Dianna began to tremble as she lost control.

And the King of Trnava was still licking. She knew he knew she was at the point of no return. He licked, and he licked bringing her to that point quickly. Her body shuddered. Then he stopped.

Someone broke a series of beads from her hip as her orgasm subsided.

Then all was still. They had had enough.

The staff appeared as the last napkin wiped the last mouth and the men sat back. As they lifted her up she opened her eyes and the King of Trnava was staring intently at her face. He knew.

'Three cheers for our dessert!' called Sven.

'Hip hip!' they called.

She raised one swan-like arm and waved goodbye.

The King of Trnava clapped with everyone else.

Back in the galley the staff gave her a glass of brandy and a round of applause. A waiter bustled in and handed her a note.

Will you come with me, just as you are? it read.

'Who is it from?' she asked the waiter.

She was so aroused that she would probably have agreed to go to bed with him even if he hadn't been a king, but when she heard it was him, Dianna threw back her arms, pushed out her breasts and breathed, 'Yes!'

She scribbled a note and stuffed her clothes into a bag. She broke the wig away from her hair and took off the hairnet. But she put her mask back on tightly.

Within minutes, she was wrapped up in the rose-coloured cloth and bundled down to a launch in the dark. She waited barely a minute before the king jumped down beside her. He kissed her hand and steered the launch himself towards the private jetty at Osborne House.

Dianna creamed with pleasure. Osborne House! The goddam King of England and the Prince of Wales were in residence!

'I need to take this lady into the house the back way,' said the king to the uniformed marine at the jetty.

The young man didn't bat an eyelid at the masked woman, wrapped in a tablecloth. He led them softly through the woods, to the house, and unlocked a door.

They climbed a narrow staircase.

In the big, dark bedroom, her lover unwrapped her, peeling back the cloth until he had her breast exposed. With a moan, he sucked at it, murmuring endearments in a language she didn't understand. He played with it, then played with both her breasts, rolling her nipples in his fingers.

She gave herself to him wantonly. She was masked, anonymous. Underneath, she could be herself.

He uncovered her body totally, so she lay on the bed with her wrapping spread around her like an opened gift. And then he stroked his fingers lightly across her masked face.

'When I was a child,' he said in heavily accented English, 'there was a woman in a mask at a ball . . ..'

He stopped and undid his clothes.

Dianna writhed, making herself comfortable, ready to

receive him. Her movements stopped him in his tracks. Only his shirt was undone. He fell on her breasts once more. He pushed them together and buried his face in her spectacular cleavage.

She pushed her sex against his bare waist. She ached for him inside her. She wrapped her legs around him and smeared his belly with her juices.

He opened her legs and licked the last of the sticky-sweet cherry brandy from her thighs.

'Tell me about the woman in the mask,' she whispered.

'She caught me,' he said. 'I was supposed to be in bed. But I wanted to see so I hid behind a tall plant in the ante-room. She came in, and thinking no-one else was in the room, she bent over and adjusted the bodice of her dress. She wiggled her shoulders and, of course, her breasts. I got an erection and I couldn't help but touch it. As I did so, she spotted me. She asked me who I was. I told her. She asked me what I was doing. I told her. I was incapable of telling her lies. She said, "Well my little prince, I'm going to take you back to your room."

'When we got to my room she told me to get into bed. I obeyed her. She sat down on my bed, very close, and she pushed her gown off her shoulder, exposing her breast. Then she took my hand and placed it on her breast. She moved it around and around and her nipple grew hard under my palm.'

As he spoke Dianna took his hand, as the woman in the story had done, and copied the formative experience.

He was mesmerised. He groaned. But he was no child now. He tore off his clothes and in the split second before he penetrated her sex, Dianna marvelled at the length of his body. Her eye had such a long way to travel down to the darkness of his pubic hair, and to his cock. He had well-formed legs and big, pale feet. The mask allowed her to take in every detail; to scrutinise without being coy.

She felt him push inside her and she wrapped her legs around him in pleasure.

No! He didn't like that. He reached down and took her legs away from his, pushing them gently out. He would have his way only.

Dianna rammed her hips at him in defiance. He might be a king but she was an American. A web of sensation weaved across her belly.

He thrust inside her, his body, sweating now, aqua-planing on hers, covering it in sweat. His hands reached to her neck and behind her ears to the ribbons that held the mask in place. His fingers touched the white velvet of her face and he groaned. He came.

She willed herself an orgasm, she broke through the web. She felt its strands burst. One by one they wriggled under her skin, the pieces flying off all around her body.

A while later Dianna turned on the taps in the bathroom adjoining his bedroom. He closed her in there and rang the servant's bell. She heard him order champagne.

She sat on a wooden stool and crumbled off the last of the sugar paste. Then, still masked, she slid into the bath and submerged herself, remembering his sex. She felt wistful.

He joined her, carrying the champagne. They clinked their glasses together. He washed her and when they got out, dripping, he dried her and found her crumpled clothes for her. He kissed her body as each bit of it disappeared.

He dressed in a casual pair of trousers and a sweater and then he took his wallet from his other trousers and held out some notes to her.

'I don't need your money,' she said lightly. 'I didn't do this for the money.'

'But you must . . . a token . . .' he said.

'No,' she laughed. She almost told him she probably had more wealth at her disposal than an exiled king, but she held her tongue.

Still mystified, he took her back through the forest to

the launch and they headed for the lights of the town across the dark sea.

As they neared the shore he slowed the engine to a purr.

'Take off your mask?' he asked.

She shook her head. 'No.'

He didn't press it any further, and drove the launch alongside the town quay. There was no-one about. He jumped on to the steps and helped her out, encircling her waist with one arm while holding the boat's rope with the other. And he kissed her lips.

She savoured the kiss and then turned her back on him and took off her mask. She pressed it into his hands and ran up the steps and away.

Chapter Eighteen

The manager of the Stellato bakery pulled down the sun blinds and Petra took off her apron. She was wearing a particularly fetching cream dress. It was a little tight anyway and her body was beginning to get rounder in all the right places. The manager's eyes followed her arse out of the shop.

She walked, as usual, the couple of hundred yards to Gianni's booth. He didn't always close for siesta because the tourist trade was continuous. Today however, he wasn't busy. He opened the back flap of the stall and let her in.

Gianni had been depressed since Angelina had disappeared. He had been to see the contessa who gave him some story about her daughter having been sent on a trade mission to South America. But Gianni was convinced Angelina had another lover and she was hiding from him. He missed her. However, he still had half his life. It didn't excite him as much but Petra was sweet and adorable and as the days went on he thought he could adjust and perhaps even get Petra to be a bit more daring in their sex.

She handed him his lunch. She always took him a fresh roll and salami. He opened it but he wasn't hungry.

He was thinking of the day Angelina had come up behind him . . . He was hard just with thinking about it. He put the roll down on the boxes underneath the counter and pulled Petra close and kissed her.

She laughed and drew away, looking out into the street.

'Come here,' said Gianni. 'Don't worry, no-one can see us.'

Petra allowed herself to be pulled closer but she felt his sex hardening and she pulled away. 'No!'

He insisted. He wouldn't let her go. He slid his hand up her skirt.

Over his shoulder Petra saw two men walking down the steps of the Uffizi. She saw them stop and one of them nudged the other. They were looking in their direction, amused at the little love scene going on in the booth.

'Stop!' she hissed. 'There are people watching!'

But Gianni was unstoppable. He was so aroused he would have his way. 'You are my wife,' he said. 'Don't push me away.'

'I'm your wife,' she said. 'Exactly. I'm not your whore. I don't – '

Gianni slid his fingers into her knickers and touched her sex.

Petra pushed him hard, putting him off momentarily, but he grabbed her again. She pummelled him with her fists. She hit him on the head. She showered him with a tirade of ripe street-Italian abuse, which shocked him enough for him to let her go.

She ran out of the back of the booth, straightening her skirt and still swearing. The two men on the steps were laughing. Furious, she swore at them too and marched off.

Gianni followed her out of the booth and called after her. She ignored him.

And then one of the two men started after her. He

caught up with her at the corner and, watched by a furious Gianni, he stopped her.

'Signorina,' he said, 'd'ya speak English?'

'No!' shouted Petra.

'You sure are beautiful!' he said.

Petra raised an eyebrow at him. Her eyes flashed dangerously. 'I am not a whore,' she said.

'No ma'am, you certainly aren't. But did you ever act?' he asked, in rudimentary Italian.

She didn't answer him. She had been very interested in drama at school. But life, love and making a living had changed all that.

'We're making a film up at Fiesole,' he said. 'We need a local actress to fill a part like the one you just played in that booth there with your boyfriend.'

'That man is my husband!' she fumed.

'Perfect! Could you get that mad with a man acting the part of your husband?'

Petra looked at him suspiciously. There *was* a film being made up at Fiesole. The single girls in the bakery could talk of nothing else. She was flattered.

'I *can* act,' she said. 'I used to be good at it.'

'Well, let's do it. Let's get you a screen test. This afternoon?'

'I'll have to ask my husband,' she said. 'Do you have a card?'

He handed her one. It read: 'David B Ceswicz, Universal Studios.'

Gianni was not pleased. In fact, he was ready to punch both Americans on their noses. Petra showed him the business card and hissed at him to think of the money.

'How much will she make?' Gianni asked.

'Well,' said Mr Ceswicz, 'it's hard for me to say. She has to discuss that with the boys in accounts. But she'll do OK, I promise you.'

'I'd like to do it,' said Petra, gingerly.

'But she is pregnant!' cried Gianni in desperation.

'Perfect!' said Mr Ceswicz.

Petra made up her mind. 'I'm going with him,' she announced. 'Eat your lunch.'

She turned away from Gianni's distress and went.

First she went to the Hotel Berchielli with them to talk to the accountant and from there she went on take her screen test. She was beautiful on celluloid. She made the film.

It wouldn't be true to say it was the last Gianni ever saw of her. But it was the last he saw of the Petra he thought he knew.

Chapter Nineteen

Cia stepped out of her bath and wrapped a towel around her. Her mind was not really on the ball she was getting ready to go to. She was thinking about the hair and figure of a friend of Belle's, and the kind of fabric that would suit a coat for her. This wasn't the only customer who had come her way over the past two days.

She also thought about her inheritance and how she would spend it, although it had a feeling of unreality about it. She had spent so long without money that it would take some time to get used to. The only concession to it she had made was to buy a bottle of champagne which it was keeping cold in a bucket of sea water in the scullery. Meanwhile, her creative imaginings were far more absorbing.

Rudy was due to arrive at eight. It was seven. She set to work, and by ten to eight she looked magnificent. Her hair shone, framing her face in dark waves, and her skin was flawless now. She wore a light dusting of blue on her eyelids and a coat of black on her long lashes. To her lips she added just a touch of Romantic Mist, her favourite lipstick.

Her dress was midnight blue. It had a high neck and a wide panel in the front, to which batwing sleeves were sewn. The seams of this detail ran down from her collarbones to her waist, flowing exactly over her two nipples. The effect was to turn her flat-chestedness into slender sensuality. The waist was detailed with a tiny diamanté buckle that rested on her navel. The heavy crepe fitted over her hips perfectly and fell more fully to the floor.

If she stood like a mannequin, with her hips slightly forward, her bones jutted fashionably. She laughed at herself in the mirror. Most pretentious, she thought, and she straightened up.

But it was a handy stance to have in reserve. The number of times she had felt in awe of beautiful, fashionable women had taught her that if you could tap into what you had yourself, you could produce awe if necessary. And the Squadron dames could be a menace to the self-esteem.

There were two things that gnawed at her: her continuing guilt about the shooting was one. But, as she knew there was nothing she could do except wait for the memory and doubt to fade, she put it firmly to the back of her mind. A more pressing concern was that she had no necklace to complete the dress. She could have sorely done with one and a voice inside her head kept telling her that it was her own fault she didn't have one – she had the money to buy or hire one and she could have done it easily the day before. If she was a more efficient woman she would have one. She was an idiot sometimes, she thought. She was passionately angry with herself.

There was a knock at the door. Cia turned away from the mirror and her reflection showed her back, fleetingly, as she moved. The *pièce de résistance* of the dress was that it had no back panel, only the edges of the sleeves, crossing loosely where her back curved into her waist.

'You look gorgeous!' gasped Rudy.

She could have returned the compliment. He wore his dinner jacket as easily as he wore any other clothes. He was one of those rare men who, when dressed formally, just make a woman more eager to get at what's underneath. The only stuffing in his shirt was in the imaginative eye of the beholder.

She poured him a glass of the champagne, and they clinked their glasses together.

She couldn't help it. She blurted it out. 'I wish I had a necklace!' she wailed.

Rudy grinned from ear to ear.

His reaction only made her more disgruntled. What on earth was he grinning at?

He reached into his inner pocket. 'I brought you something,' he said, taking out a necklace case. He gave it to her. 'I'm hoping I can give it to you as an engagement present.'

Cia had half-opened the case. Inside, the diamonds glinted against a background of black velvet. She snapped the case shut.

'I can't marry you,' she said. 'I can't.'

His face dropped and his body flinched as if she had dealt him a blow.

She handed back the case.

'No,' he said stiffly. 'Borrow it for the evening.'

Cia sat still, holding the case in front of her. She was in an agony of indecision. Should she tell him why?

He solved the question for her. 'May I ask why not?' he said.

Cia stood up and walked to the back door for no particular reason. Then she turned back and faced him.

'I shot that man deliberately,' she said. 'I knew he was disarmed and posed no threat. I asked him if he was a Fascist and when he said he was I murdered him. All it took was a little movement of my finger. I didn't even think about it. I just murdered him.'

Rudy stood up and encircled her with his arms. 'Is that the only reason you can't marry me?' he asked.

She looked up at his dear face. She knew she was going to cry and ruin her mascara. She nodded.

'I love you, Rudy,' she croaked. 'I've always loved you.'

He took the necklace case from her hands, opened it and put it around her neck. 'In that case,' he said, 'I consider us engaged.'

'But Rudy! God knows what I'm capable of! How can you dismiss this so lightly?'

'Cia,' he said solemnly. 'If the man who drove Nora to suicide ever steps foot in England again, I will kill him and he knows it. I can dismiss this because I know I would have done the same thing to avenge the death of someone I loved. I don't judge you for it.'

'But you *wouldn't* do the same thing. You didn't! You threatened him and gave him the chance to leave. I actually did it!'

'You've got that wrong,' said Rudy. 'I got so close to killing him that he had to spend his last few weeks in this country in hospital. His friends stopped me, our friends, actually, and they made sure the police were never involved.'

'I bet you're glad though, that you didn't kill him?'

'Yes. But Cia, the man you killed was not a marriage wrecker, he was a killer and a Fascist.' Rudy stroked her hair. 'He would have killed you and he would have gone on to kill many more people. The Fascist creed is built on hate. They'll kill and kill and kill until . . . I think it will probably take another war to stop them.'

She was still thinking about that when there was another knock at the door and Edna popped her head round.

'Wait,' said Rudy. 'Give us a moment.' He shut the door in his little sister's face. 'Can you put me out of my misery? Is your answer still no?' he begged.

'No,' she said quietly.

He gritted his teeth and a pulse started in his jaw.

'No my answer is not no,' she said.

His face twisted itself into a smile.

'It's yes. Yes please,' she said, still very quietly.

He took her in his arms and kissed her.

'Erhem!' coughed Edna. 'Sorry to break this up but – '

Rudy, complete with Romantic Mist smears over his cheek, said, 'Cia has agreed to be my wife.'

When Edna smiled, her eyes shone. 'You'd better wash your face.' she said, and she hugged Cia tight.

'What's the story then?' asked Hector, entering through the porchway.

'Cia and Rudy are engaged!' Edna beamed as she spoke.

Hector took Rudy's hand and pumped it vigorously. 'Jolly good show!' he said.

He planted a kiss on Cia's cheek.

Then Dianna was at the door, followed by Plomer, Lady Walcarp-Etting, Lord Walcarp-Etting and LJ. They all congratulated the happy couple and Cia poured a little bit of champagne into an assortment of mismatched drinking vessels.

Lady Walcarp-Etting was the only one who didn't look very happy. Cia felt for her.

The Squadron ballroom was dressed up and twinkling like a fairy tale. There were hundreds of people. King George did not dance, but sat with his wife, Queen Mary, benevolently watching. The Prince of Wales made up for it. He was as dashing and handsome as ever, and at one point Edna danced with him, which gave their party plenty of mileage to tease her with. She took it good-naturedly but Cia thought she looked a little wistful.

'What's a prince when the man you love is somewhere else?' whispered Cia.

'He's here,' said Edna. 'In Cowes, I mean. We decided he would come but it was too late – all the tickets were gone. I'm . . . don't tell anyone but I'm going to slip away later.'

'Watch your glass slipper!' giggled Cia. 'Don't want to end up with the wrong one!'

Edna smiled. 'I won't.'

When Cia danced with Rudy, it occurred to her that she had dreamed this dance every night for a year when she was fifteen. To have it now, as a mature woman, with both a past *and* a future, was breathtaking. He danced better than any man she had ever danced with. Their bodies seemed made for each other.

She also danced one dance with Hector, out of politeness. They spoke little and when the dance ended he led her off the floor. When they reached their table all the others were up on the floor. They sat down and a waiter poured them coffee. Cia wanted to talk to him but it was difficult to know where to begin. She watched his eyes following LJ round the dancefloor.

'You love that man, don't you?' she asked, putting her cup down on the saucer with a clatter.

'Yes, of course. He's my friend,' Hector replied, without hesitation. Then he looked at her in fear.

'Then you should follow your nature,' she said. 'I was extremely angry for a while that you and your mother had plotted to trap me in a marriage that would be no marriage.' There was pure panic on his face. 'I'm no longer angry,' she continued. 'I want to be your friend. Please stand up to your mother and soon. Men live together under the guise of bachelor companionship. They have friends around them. If you continue trying to follow your mother's wishes you'll end up isolated because any woman would hate you if you did that to her. You mustn't do it.'

Hector sat silently, looking very uncomfortable. Then turned to her.

'I've never spoken to anyone . . .' he paused. 'It's the title. Most chaps aren't the Earl of Eachester.'

'What the hell does that have to do with anything?' asked Cia.

'I was brought up to be an earl. I have certain restrictions and responsibilities that I can't deny. I don't like it. But it's a fact.'

'You have responsibilities to yourself too.'

He looked as if she had twisted a knife in his gut.

'If I wanted to live . . . happily,' he said, 'I would have to disappear entirely from public life. I could do that if . . . if my lover was the kind of person who could do it too. But he isn't. He craves attention and social life. I risk prison every time we go out in public. At the moment the family . . . people think it's a phase and they're tolerant. But they won't be if I flout the rules. They'll throw me to the dogs. My mother would be the first.'

Cia knew he was right. She felt immensely sorry for him – and angry. They sat in silence for a moment. Then an idea occurred to her.

'You could marry a lesbian,' she said. He looked at her in astonishment. 'Then the arrangement could be explicit between you. And no-one would be hurt.'

'That's an awfully good idea,' he mused slowly. 'You mean, someone in the same position as myself?'

'And don't tell your mother,' said Cia.

'It's a terrific idea, in fact!' he laughed. 'But I don't know any!'

'Well, I'm sure you could find one if you looked, couldn't you?' suggested Cia.

He took her hand and kissed it. 'What do you want for a wedding present?'

'Ha!' she laughed. 'I want you to bring a lesbian to my party.'

'Ssshh,' he whispered. The music had stopped.

Rudy asked her to take a turn out on the balcony with him. It was getting late but the ball would go on all night and the guests would be served breakfast. Down below them the sea lapped gently on the shore.

'Shall we go?' he asked. 'I want to be alone with you.'

Cia smiled at him. 'Yes.'

Along the balcony, Cia noticed, Dianna was talking to a handsome, dark-haired man.

'Who's that?' Cia asked Rudy.

'The ex-king of Trnava,' said Rudy.

* * *

Dianna saw Cia and Rudy leaving out of the corner of her eye.

'If it takes me all night I am going to get you to admit it,' said the ex-king. His name was Vaclav, he had told her.

'I don't know what you are talking about,' Dianna said smiling, for the umpteenth time.

'I know all about you. It wasn't hard to find out that your husband is a cad,' he said.

'Is it really common knowledge?' asked Dianna.

'Why don't you divorce him?' asked Vaclav.

'Why should I?'

'Then you could run away with me!'

'Why should I do that? I don't know you!' Dianna laughed.

'You should have worn a dress that covered your exquisite arms or had your pretty jaw broken and reset to make you ugly. Come, my dear Dianna. Won't you feel sorry for me then? I have no home. I'm condemned to wander the globe. I need a woman to make my life bearable. And you made me happier last night than any woman I have ever known, even the first.' He brushed her ear with his lips.

Dianna moved away from him. This was not at all what she had planned.

'You are such a spirited woman. I thought I had lost you but the minute I saw you tonight, I knew. No mask could hide your beauty.'

'Look,' said Dianna, 'I am a middle-aged, married woman. This is absurd.'

'Dance with me,' he whispered.

She went on to the floor with him, where he whirled her around. He was a great dancer. And little by little she began to soften. It was hard not to, when such a man was that close and aching for your body.

'Don't go home,' he murmured. 'Never go home.'

Dianna clucked at him, trying to be sensible. But she wasn't born to be sensible. . .

* * *

Somewhere in Italy, Angelina woke up face down with a terrible headache and a bilious stomach. A foul smell hit her nose: stale urine and sweat. She turned her head sideways and opened her eyes. She was in a dormitory full of women in various stages of mental decline. The sight and the closeness of the lunatics chilled her to the bone. This was not the first hole she had been in over the last couple of weeks. She had been in a cell, in a train (handcuffed to the bunk), and now here.

For a moment she almost despaired. But as she turned on her back and got her nose away from the stinking bed, she felt a little better. Her iron will reasserted itself. If there *was* a way out of this, she was determined to find it.

She looked at the other women. They were mostly completely mad but there were one or two who looked less bedraggled and rather quieter.

Angelina sat up. Her head felt weird, as if she'd been drugged, which she assumed she must have been. She got slowly to her feet. Her dress was creased and crumpled but at least it was hers. There didn't seem to be an institutional uniform.

She walked over to a woman in a red dress sitting on the edge of her bed. From a distance she looked quite normal but as Angelina drew up closer she realised she'd made a mistake. It was the eyes. They were unfocused. The woman opened her mouth as Angelina approached, in the manner of someone in a dentist's chair.

Angelina quickly turned away and walked down the aisle, past several raving lunatics to another woman. This one wore a black cardigan and skirt. She sat on the edge of her bed, writing something. She looked perfectly sane. On seeing Angelina though, she quickly put the notebook she was writing in away.

'*Ciao*, said Angelina.

The woman shook her head wildly and squeaked like a mouse. She lay face down on the bed and muttered.

If she hadn't seen her writing, Angelina would have

been convinced. But that and some instinct told her that the woman was acting. She let her be. She would return later and work on her. If she had something to hide, she had something to lose. That might prove useful.

Angelina saved her best shot for the male guard – a Blackshirt – who stood motionless by the door. She ambled over to him and breathed a '*Ciao*' into his face.

He stared into the middle distance.

She sighed, exaggerating the motion of her breasts. She made her way to what looked like a toilet. She looked in the cracked mirror. She looked awful. Her hair was all over the place. She tidied herself up as best she could and sashayed back to the guard. She opened her big eyes as wide as they would go.

'Please help me,' she purred. Her voice had gone up an octave and sounded like an eight-year-old girl's. 'I haven't got anything! I shouldn't be here. It's a mistake, I'm sure. How can I keep myself sane if I don't even have a hairbrush?'

The guard looked at her and there was a flicker of interest in his eyes that encouraged her.

'I'm not mad,' she begged. 'At least can I have some clean sheets?'

'I'll see what I can do,' he said, and then he looked away from her again, purposefully.

As Angelina walked away from him, she looked back and saw him talking to someone at the door. She watched as, after a few minutes, a pair of clean sheets and a cover appeared through the hatch.

He beckoned her over.

She took the sheets and gave him a dazzling smile. 'Thank you,' she mouthed.

When she had changed the bed she lay down on it, on her side, so that her hips formed a spectacular curve, and she stole a look at the guard. She was just in time to see him turn quickly away. He had been studying her.

Angelina concentrated on her sex. She closed her eyes and imagined it was throbbing, the most delicious sex any man could imagine. Her hips moved as she used her imagination. They talked, those hips.

The guard could no longer take his eyes off her . . .

Cia and Rudy walked hand in hand back towards Finnemore. In his other hand Rudy carried an open bottle of champagne. The night was ending. A pre-dawn light was gradually bringing the road, the trees and the houses into view.

'Let's go up on the roof of the turret,' he said. 'I want to see the sun come up.'

So they climbed the hill to Tennyson House. They found two champagne flutes in the dining room then they climbed the stairs to the turret. Rudy unhooked the narrow metal ladder from the ceiling and unlatched the hatch, then Cia hitched up her ball gown and climbed up on to the circular roof with Rudy following her.

Cia leaned against the shoulder-high battlements as he closed the hatch, watching the grace of his body and the handsomeness of his face. She knew she would never stop loving that face.

He joined her and poured the champagne. 'To you,' he said.

'And you,' she replied.

They both drank as they looked out to sea and chatted about the ball, and their friends.

Suddenly Rudy said, 'Look!', and pointed over the brickwork towards the east.

The first rays of the sun were visible over the rooves of the town. As they watched, it gradually sprinkled gold over the landscape, over Finnemore, over the calm sea.

And then the surface of the road down below by the beach changed from grey to brown to a dazzling sun-gold.

'The road,' she whispered. 'It's gold!'

He put his arm around her waist and gently pulled her close.

'Do you believe in omens?' she asked him.

'Of course I do,' he said quietly.

She turned to him and he kissed her gently. His lips grew more passionate very quickly and she responded.

He held her tight and kissed her neck. He slipped her sleeve forward and kissed her shoulder and the morning air caressed her skin.

He slid the dress down and uncovered her breasts and kissed them. She arched her back, giving herself to him in the privacy of the encircling walls. Above her head, the blue dawn sky seemed so close she could touch it.

He pulled her hips close into his own and whispered her name as he ground into her sex. She held his head in her hands and caressed his soft hair, then kissed his face, his lips, his eyelids.

He bent down and lifted the hem of her ball gown. He slid his hands up her thighs and he groaned with the touch of her soft skin. And then he knelt and she took her hem from him as he parted her thighs and ate her sex.

She leaned heavily, her head resting on the battlement, her breasts caressed by the new day, and her man's head between her legs until the strength of her arousal was too much.

She grabbed his shoulders, urging him wordlessly to stand, and when he did, she broke open the buttons on his fly and caressed him.

He found her sex with his own and penetrated her, and they fucked each other senseless under the sky.

LOOK OUT FOR THE ALL-NEW BLACK LACE BOOKS – AVAILABLE NOW!

All books priced £7.99 in the UK. Please note publication dates apply to the UK only. For other territories, please contact your retailer.

PEEP SHOW

Mathilde Madden

ISBN 0 352 33924 1

Naughty Imogen likes to watch. When her boyfriend Christian is out at work she spends her evenings spying on the neighbours through binoculars and viewing her secret porn collection. Most of all, though, she likes to go online and pretend to be Christian while she chats up men on a Manchester gay dating site. But when her latest virtual beau and borderline obsession Dark Knight asks for a photograph, her voyeuristic games become complicated. Suddenly Christian is being drawn in to her sleazy thrills without his knowledge. Imogen's getting more eye candy than she ever dreamed of, but at what price? **A potent and dark modern erotic novel that explores sexual anonymity in the heart of the urban landscape.**

RISKY BUSINESS

Lisette Allen

ISBN 0 352 33280 8

They come from different worlds, but their paths are destined to cross. Liam is a working-class journalist fighting a passionate battle against environmental injustice; Rebecca is a spoilt rich girl used to having whatever, and whoever, she wants. They are thrown into a dangerous intimacy with each other when Liam – on the run from an irate enemy – is forced to hijack Rebecca's car. Using his rugged charm, he manages to access her true sexuality – something no man has ever done. The usually cool Rebecca is forced to make a choice between her sophisticated but bland lifestyle and the exciting but unpredictable world offered by her charismatic captor. **A freewheeling story of what happens when posh meets rough!**

UNDRESSING THE DEVIL

Angel Strand

ISBN 0 352 33938 1

It's the 1930s. Hitler and Mussolini are building their war machine and Europe is a hotbed of political tension. Cia, a young, Anglo-Italian woman, escapes the mayhem, returning to England only to become embroiled in a web of sexual adventures. Her Italian lover has disappeared along with her clothes, lost somewhere between Florence and the Isle of Wight. Her British friends are carrying on in the manner to which they are accustomed: sailing their yachts and partying. However, this serene façade hides rivalries and forbidden pleasures. It's only a matter of time before Cia's two worlds collide. **Literary erotica at its best, in this story of bright young things on the edge.**

Also available

THE BLACK LACE SEXY QUIZ BOOK
Maddie Saxon
ISBN 0 352 33884 9

- What sexual personality type are you?
- Have you ever faked it because that was easier than explaining what you wanted?
- What kind of fantasy figures turn you on – and does your partner know?
- What sexual signals are you giving out right now?

Today's image-conscious dating scene is a tough call. Our sexual expectations are cranked up to the max, and the sexes seem to have become highly critical of each other in terms of appearance and performance in the bedroom. But even though guys have ditched their nasty Y-fronts and girls are more babe-licious than ever, a huge number of us are still being let down sexually. Sex therapist Maddie Saxon thinks this is because we are finding it harder to relax and let our true sexual selves shine through.

The Black Lace Sexy Quiz Book will help you negotiate the minefield of modern relationships. Through a series of fun, revealing quizzes, you will be able to rate your sexual needs honestly and get what you really want from your partner. The quizzes will get you thinking about and discussing your desires in ways you haven't previously considered. Unlock the mysteries of your sexual psyche in this fun, revealing quiz book designed with today's sex-savvy woman in mind.

Black Lace Booklist

Information is correct at time of printing. To avoid disappointment check availability before ordering. Go to www.blacklace-books.co.uk. All books are priced £6.99 unless another price is given.

BLACK LACE BOOKS WITH A CONTEMPORARY SETTING

- ❑ SHAMELESS Stella Black — ISBN 0 352 33485 1 £5.99
- ❑ INTENSE BLUE Lyn Wood — ISBN 0 352 33496 7 £5.99
- ❑ A SPORTING CHANCE Susie Raymond — ISBN 0 352 33501 7 £5.99
- ❑ TAKING LIBERTIES Susie Raymond — ISBN 0 352 33357 X £5.99
- ❑ ON THE EDGE Laura Hamilton — ISBN 0 352 33534 3 £5.99
- ❑ LURED BY LUST Tania Picarda — ISBN 0 352 33533 5 £5.99
- ❑ THE NINETY DAYS OF GENEVIEVE Lucinda Carrington — ISBN 0 352 33070 8 £5.99
- ❑ DREAMING SPIRES Juliet Hastings — ISBN 0 352 33584 X
- ❑ THE TRANSFORMATION Natasha Rostova — ISBN 0 352 33311 1
- ❑ SIN.NET Helena Ravenscroft — ISBN 0 352 33598 X
- ❑ TWO WEEKS IN TANGIER Annabel Lee — ISBN 0 352 33599 8
- ❑ PLAYING HARD Tina Troy — ISBN 0 352 33617 X
- ❑ SYMPHONY X Jasmine Stone — ISBN 0 352 33629 3
- ❑ SUMMER FEVER Anna Ricci — ISBN 0 352 33625 0
- ❑ CONTINUUM Portia Da Costa — ISBN 0 352 33120 8
- ❑ FULL STEAM AHEAD Tabitha Flyte — ISBN 0 352 33637 4
- ❑ A SECRET PLACE Ella Broussard — ISBN 0 352 33307 3
- ❑ GAME FOR ANYTHING Lyn Wood — ISBN 0 352 33639 0
- ❑ CHEAP TRICK Astrid Fox — ISBN 0 352 33640 4
- ❑ THE GIFT OF SHAME Sara Hope-Walker — ISBN 0 352 32935 1
- ❑ COMING UP ROSES Crystalle Valentino — ISBN 0 352 33658 7
- ❑ GOING TOO FAR Laura Hamilton — ISBN 0 352 33657 9
- ❑ THE STALLION Georgina Brown — ISBN 0 352 33005 8
- ❑ DOWN UNDER Juliet Hastings — ISBN 0 352 33663 3
- ❑ ODALISQUE Fleur Reynolds — ISBN 0 352 32887 8
- ❑ SWEET THING Alison Tyler — ISBN 0 352 33682 X
- ❑ TIGER LILY Kimberly Dean — ISBN 0 352 33685 4

❑ COOKING UP A STORM Emma Holly ISBN 0 352 33686 2
❑ RELEASE ME Suki Cunningham ISBN 0 352 33671 4
❑ KING'S PAWN Ruth Fox ISBN 0 352 33684 6
❑ FULL EXPOSURE Robyn Russell ISBN 0 352 33688 9
❑ SLAVE TO SUCCESS Kimberley Raines ISBN 0 352 33687 0
❑ STRIPPED TO THE BONE Jasmine Stone ISBN 0 352 33463 0
❑ SHADOWPLAY Portia Da Costa ISBN 0 352 33313 8
❑ I KNOW YOU, JOANNA Ruth Fox ISBN 0 352 33727 3
❑ THE HOUSE IN NEW ORLEANS Fleur Reynolds ISBN 0 352 32951 3
❑ HEAT OF THE MOMENT Tesni Morgan ISBN 0 352 33742 7
❑ THE WICKED STEPDAUGHTER Wendy Harris ISBN 0 352 33777 x
❑ DRAWN TOGETHER Robyn Russell ISBN 0 352 33269 7
❑ LEARNING THE HARD WAY Jasmine Archer ISBN 0 352 33782 6
❑ VELVET GLOVE Emma Holly ISBN 0 352 33448 7
❑ UNKNOWN TERRITORY Annie O'Neill ISBN 0 352 33794 X
❑ VIRTUOSO Katrina Vincenzi-Thyre ISBN 0 352 32907 6
❑ FIGHTING OVER YOU Laura Hamilton ISBN 0 352 33795 8
❑ ARIA APPASSIONATA Juliet Hastings ISBN 0 352 33056 2
❑ THE RELUCTANT PRINCESS Patty Glenn ISBN 0 352 33809 1
❑ HARD BLUE MIDNIGHT Alaine Hood ISBN0 352 33851 2
❑ ALWAYS THE BRIDEGROOM Tesni Morgan ISBN0 352 33855 5
❑ COMING ROUND THE MOUNTAIN Tabitha Flyte ISBN0 352 33873 3
❑ FEMININE WILES Karina Moore ISBN0 352 33235 2
❑ MIXED SIGNALS Anna Clare ISBN0 352 33889 X
❑ BLACK LIPSTICK KISSES Monica Belle ISBN0 352 33885 7
❑ HOT GOSSIP Savannah Smythe ISBN0 352 33880 6
❑ GOING DEEP Kimberly Dean ISBN0 352 33876 8
❑ PACKING HEAT Karina Moore ISBN0 352 33356 1
❑ MIXED DOUBLES Zoe le Verdier ISBN0 352 33312 X
❑ WILD BY NATURE Monica Belle ISBN0 352 33915 2
❑ UP TO NO GOOD Karen S. Smith ISBN0 352 33589 0
❑ CLUB CRÈME Primula Bond ISBN0 352 33907 1
❑ BONDED Fleur Reynolds ISBN0 352 33192 5
❑ SWITCHING HANDS Alaine Hood ISBN0 352 33896 2
❑ BEDDING THE BURGLAR Gabrielle Marcola ISBN0 352 33911 X
❑ MIXED DOUBLES Zoe le Verdier ISBN0 352 33312 X

❑ EDEN'S FLESH Robyn Russell ISBNO 352 33923 3

❑ PEEP SHOW Mathilde Madden ISBNO 352 33924 1

❑ RISKY BUSINESS Lisette Allen ISBNO 352 33280 8

BLACK LACE BOOKS WITH AN HISTORICAL SETTING

❑ PRIMAL SKIN Leona Benkt Rhys ISBN 0 352 33500 9 £5.99

❑ DARKER THAN LOVE Kristina Lloyd ISBN 0 352 33279 4

❑ THE CAPTIVATION Natasha Rostova ISBN 0 352 33234 4

❑ MINX Megan Blythe ISBN 0 352 33638 2

❑ DIVINE TORMENT Janine Ashbless ISBN 0 352 33719 2

❑ SATAN'S ANGEL Melissa MacNeal ISBN 0 352 33726 5

❑ THE INTIMATE EYE Georgia Angelis ISBN 0 352 33004 X

❑ SILKEN CHAINS Jodi Nicol ISBN 0 352 33143 7

❑ THE LION LOVER Mercedes Kelly ISBN 0 352 33162 3

❑ THE AMULET Lisette Allen ISBN 0 352 33019 8

❑ WHITE ROSE ENSNARED Juliet Hastings ISBN 0 352 33052 X

❑ UNHALLOWED RITES Martine Marquand ISBN 0 352 33222 0

❑ LA BASQUAISE Angel Strand ISBN 0 352 32988 2

❑ THE HAND OF AMUN Juliet Hastings ISBN 0 352 33144 5

❑ THE SENSES BEJEWELLED Cleo Cordell ISBN 0 352 32904 1

❑ UNDRESSING THE DEVIL Angel Strand ISBN 0 352 33938 1

BLACK LACE ANTHOLOGIES

❑ WICKED WORDS Various ISBN 0 352 33363 4

❑ MORE WICKED WORDS Various ISBN 0 352 33487 8

❑ WICKED WORDS 3 Various ISBN 0 352 33522 X

❑ WICKED WORDS 4 Various ISBN 0 352 33603 X

❑ WICKED WORDS 5 Various ISBN 0 352 33642 0

❑ WICKED WORDS 6 Various ISBN 0 352 33690 0

❑ WICKED WORDS 7 Various ISBN 0 352 33743 5

❑ WICKED WORDS 8 Various ISBN 0 352 33787 7

❑ WICKED WORDS 9 Various ISBN 0 352 33860 1

❑ WICKED WORDS 10 Various ISBN 0 352 33893 8

❑ THE BEST OF BLACK LACE 2 Various ISBN 0 352 33718 4

BLACK LACE NON-FICTION

❑ THE BLACK LACE BOOK OF WOMEN'S SEXUAL FANTASIES Ed. Kerri Sharp ISBN 0 352 33793 1 £6.99

❑ THE BLACK LACE SEXY QUIZ BOOK Maddie Saxon ISBN 0 352 33884 9 £6.99

To find out the latest information about Black Lace titles, check out the website: www.blacklace-books.co.uk or send for a booklist with complete synopses by writing to:

Black Lace Booklist, Virgin Books Ltd
Thames Wharf Studios
Rainville Road
London W6 9HA

Please include an SAE of decent size. Please note only British stamps are valid.

Our privacy policy
We will not disclose information you supply us to any other parties. We will not disclose any information which identifies you personally to any person without your express consent.

From time to time we may send out information about Black Lace books and special offers. Please tick here if you do not wish to receive Black Lace information. ❑

Please send me the books I have ticked above.

Name ....

Address ....

....

....

....

Post Code ....

Send to: Virgin Books Cash Sales, Thames Wharf Studios, Rainville Road, London W6 9HA.

US customers: for prices and details of how to order books for delivery by mail, call 1-800-343-4499.

Please enclose a cheque or postal order, made payable to Virgin Books Ltd, to the value of the books you have ordered plus postage and packing costs as follows:

UK and BFPO – £1.00 for the first book, 50p for each subsequent book.

Overseas (including Republic of Ireland) – £2.00 for the first book, £1.00 for each subsequent book.

If you would prefer to pay by VISA, ACCESS/MASTERCARD, DINERS CLUB, AMEX or SWITCH, please write your card number and expiry date here:

....

Signature ....

Please allow up to 28 days for delivery.